T0146685

THE ASTEROID MINERS

C. W. HALLETT

authorHOUSE®

AuthorHouse™ LLC
1663 Liberty Drive
Bloomington, IN 47403
www.authorhouse.com
Phone: 1-800-839-8640

© 2014 C. W. Hallett. All rights reserved.

No part of this book may be reproduced, stored in
a retrieval system, or transmitted by any means
without the written permission of the author.

This is a work of fiction. All of the characters, names, incidents,
organizations, and dialogue in this novel are either the products
of the author's imagination or are used fictitiously.

Published by AuthorHouse   09/24/2014

ISBN: 978-1-4969-3949-4 (sc)
ISBN: 978-1-4969-3950-0 (e)

Library of Congress Control Number: 2014916644

Any people depicted in stock imagery provided by Thinkstock are models,
and such images are being used for illustrative purposes only.
Certain stock imagery © Thinkstock.

This book is printed on acid-free paper.

Because of the dynamic nature of the Internet, any web addresses or
links contained in this book may have changed since publication and
may no longer be valid. The views expressed in this work are solely those
of the author and do not necessarily reflect the views of the publisher,
and the publisher hereby disclaims any responsibility for them.

Introduction

The Wheel Spacecraft had long been recognized as the preferred model for space travel. The single or multi-wheeled design is ideal for long duration flights in space because the human body will still function normally inside it. People living on the inside of the outer rim feel perfectly normal when the wheel is rotating at the proper speed. The engineering necessary to control its rotational speed and prevent imbalance when people and cargo are moved around inside it was however too complicated to be feasible. In the beginning there was no choice but to try to combat the physical effects of long-term exposure to low gravity.

The physical problems associated with long-term exposure to very low gravity and the very serious consequences of running out of fuel are the major limitations to working in deep space. It is true that necessity is the mother of invention and without a doubt it will take some major innovations to solve these problems. The impossible is often overcome by innovators who are willing to explore what seems like a good idea regardless of the possibility of failure. Innovation after all is the driving force behind the advancement of the human condition. Nobody knows where the future is taking us but it will be the innovators who take us there.

Inventions like the Reaction Drive, Fusion Power and Artificial Gravity will revolutionize the design of Space

Habitants. The Reaction Drive allows the forces of reaction and action to be converged via an integrated electric motor and gear set so that electricity can be used to control the rotational speed of the space station. This removes the obstacle to using electric motors because the reaction forces are contained within the drive unit and actually help to do the work. As long as you have a source of electricity you can effectively control the rotational speed and the balancing system of any space station without using up your precious supply of rocket fuel.

The same type of a breakthrough will give us Fusion Power and Artificial Gravity.

The cover background pictures were courtesy of NASA/ JPL-CALTECH

I would like to thank my great niece, Megan Ebbett for bring my words to life when she created the cover pictures.

Foreword

Solar panels or small nuclear power plants were used to provide dependable and inexhaustible electricity for extended periods so rotating Space Habitants soon replaced the low gravity stations. It was now possible to stay in space for very extended periods with almost no physical side effects.

In the beginning water-balls were the most sought after asteroids but mineral rocks became more valuable as the reservoirs filled up and the factories started to be built. Iron-nickel rocks were the most plentiful but the most sought after were the PGM (Platinum Group Metals) asteroids. They usually contained some combination of Platinum, Osmium, Iridium, Ruthenium, Rhodium, and Palladium.

Mining in general and Asteroid Mining in particular consists of hours, days and even weeks of drudgery peppered with a few Eureka moments.

Chapter 1

I have been asked to record this so that the true story will be known long after I am gone. It all started when I was a lowly miner working in the Asteroid Belt trying to make a living and an impression on Dad.

Ok, I've almost got it! Just a small burst to the left and fire!

I could see the flame from the small rocket in the flagging probe as it tracked straight and true to the rock that was coasting past us on the right.

We were drifting along just a bit slower that the rocks orbiting in our ring so they were catching up to and passing us. This gave us lots of time to analyse them without burning up any of our fuel. We had a continuous stream of rocks floating slowly past us that we could pick from. Every now and then we had to reposition ourselves in the ring to get close enough to flag one but that took a lot less fuel than racing around trying to find a treasure rock. If you're patient, they will come to you.

So far we have four small water/iron rocks and one waterball flagged. That's a pretty poor showing if we expect to make any real money this term. We're talking about leaving them here and moving to a new sector because they are in a stable orbit and we can always come back for them. Normally we would gather them all together but we didn't want to use up our rocket fuel in case we lucked into a big one. We have to decide this week if we are going to move so we will have time to reposition and search for a better payload.

Our claim is in Claim Ring 10 located in the Asteroid Belt about three quarters of the way between Mars and Jupiter. We have lots of uncharted territory to check and the chance of finding some better rocks was pretty good. Our claim is far enough out so that we are also in a good position to catch a looper. The bigger rocks tend to be in the outer orbits and are almost always in an elliptical orbit. When they loop around at the outer end of their orbits they often cross through several spherical claim boundaries.

Even a big iron core one has enough ore to make it worthwhile to snare and they usually carry a lot of water ice with them as well. The steel factories on Mars love them because they are almost completely useable. They use the iron to make steel after they smelt the other minerals out of it. They also distil the water for the settlement reservoirs or to make rocket fuel. The problem is that they are quite common in the inner asteroid rings so are not worth our trouble unless they are over 100 metres in diameter.

Space rocks in tow are permitted to enter another claims boundaries without loss of ownership but loopers are fair game. They are ours to claim from the time it entered our outer boundary until it crosses into the next claim so if we had our act together we could snare one.

Nothing on that one. Reset the orientation and go again.

The United Nations and the Interplanetary Council have agreed on a format to clarify the ownership and access to space rocks.

Space rocks are defined as any object that is not in orbit around any of the planets. Any object that is large enough to have a gravity of 10 gravitons or more is considered to be a dwarf planet and is thus an independent solar object and may not be claimed by any single entity. We don't have to worry about that because a rock with that much gravity would be at least 100 kilometres across and far too big for us to handle.

Solar objects including all the planets and their orbiting moons (other than Earth) are governed by the Interplanetary Council and subject to the laws of ownership as laid out in the Treaty of Space of 2045. Any mining activity of these objects must be approved by both the Interplanetary Council and, if applicable, the resident Planetary Committee. All other objects are unclaimed and this has led to several severe and sometimes brutal fights over ownership.

Even the contentious issue of loopers and rocks that stray into two or more claims are usually peacefully settled after the present system of claim ownership was adopted. Any object that travels outside the solar system such as a comet is free for the taking if it remains outside the orbit of Jupiter. If it does pass through an established claim then it's the same as any other rock and it belongs to that claim owner as long as they can capture it within their boundaries.

Registered individuals or a corporate entity have the right to claim any objects within a specific spherical solar orbit. The miner must be the registered owner of that ring (claim) or under contract to the registered owner. The claim owner must have at least one ongoing mining operation in the ring within 5 years from the filing date of ownership with the Interplanetary Council and then maintain a human presence for at least one month out of each year. You can obtain ownership by simply paying the filing fee to the Interplanetary Council if the ring in unclaimed or by purchasing the claim from its registered owner. The filing fee is usually much cheaper than purchasing the claim but there are usually no rings left unclaimed. If one is forfeited because the owner failed to meet the work commitments it is usually grabbed up in a matter of minutes. They are talking about extending the ring system out into the Kuiper Belt beyond Pluto. There is an almost unlimited supply of minerals out there but they are extremely expensive to mine.

The claims are concentric spherical bands with the sun as the center point. They are 100,000 kilometres wide radiating outward through the Asteroid Belt between Mars and Jupiter. The claim boundaries are determined by accessing the Space Positioning Beacon Network that consists of 10 beacons equally spaced around the sun close to the orbit of Mercury for this purpose. This was necessary because the orbits of a lot of the space rocks are elliptical and the claims are spherical. It was crucial to be able to determine your exact claim boundary because any given rock might cross three or four different claims during its orbit.

The further out from Mars, the larger the number of potential mineral bearing rocks but the greater the cost of accessing and mining the claims. There are also a greater number of claims to cross to reach the markets with the expensive possibility of knocking a valuable rock onto a different claim.

Several hotly contested lawsuits have resulted from a rock being knocked onto another claim because of an impact with a rogue rock or a towed load. The most famous started out as a simple complaint of a dislodged minor rock but ended up in multiple claims of ownership and counter suits because the "minor rock" turned out to be a PGM asteroid. It was even more valuable than normal because it was so close to major markets and it contained more than the usual trace amounts of Iridium.

Thomas O'Grady owned Ring 8 where the alleged collision had occurred and he claimed that the rock belonged to him because it had been illegally knocked off course and was therefore not a stray rock. He maintained he had been robbed and filed a claim for the commercial value of the rock with his insurance company. They in turn filed a lawsuit against Astro Mining and their contractor Jake Perkins to recover their losses. Jake was a crusty seasoned miner who was under contract to the Astro Mining Corporation and he claimed that the rock was part of his load that had broken loose and had strayed off course. He maintained that the rock in fact belonged to him and was not a stray rock as Terry Loganski claimed.

Terry Loganski was the owner of Ring 5 and he had captured the rock as it traversed his claim. He claimed the rock as his because it was a stray and he sold the rock to the Stellar Steel Company before any of the lawsuits were filed. All the other insurance companies sued both him and the young Stellar Steel Company to recover the money from the sale of the rock. Nobody would dare do that today because they would be up to their eyeballs in lawyers from Stellar Steel before the papers hit the desk at the filing office.

The Astro Mining Corporation owned several of the outer rings and usually contracted one of the small miners to mine them. This fulfilled their commitment to maintain a presence on their claims and was much cheaper than actually mining the rings themselves. They usually received 25% of the selling price of the rocks without actually doing any of the work or taking any risks. They very wisely carried a liability insurance policy to protect them from this type of incident.

The good news is that Jake also carried a liability policy and it was with a different insurance company so they went to bat for him. He could never have survived if he was forced to defend himself against the other insurance companies because he didn't have deep enough pockets for that kind of a fight.

It turned out that Jake had the most believable case because the trajectory of the "stray" rock was very similar to the flight path on his inbound journey. O'Grady couldn't prove that the rock had actually been orbiting in his ring space so Jake's story about losing a rock in tow was the most plausible. The court did not recognize a lost rock as a "stray" rock so Terry Loganski could not claim ownership. The courts were leaning heavily toward awarding ownership of the rock to Jake until Terry Loganski's lawyer asked for a review of Jakes computer records.

The review of his ships cockpit monitor showed that Jake was asleep when the impact happened and that the ship had received a hard jolt as he was traversing O'Grady's ring.

O'Grady's lawyers then challenged Terry Loganski's claim to the rock and sued him for legal expenses and the value of the rock. Loganski's lawyers took the fight all the way to the Interplanetary Judicial Court.

In the end the court found that the rock was not legally a stray rock because it had been knocked out of its orbit by an act of man. It further found that Loganski had acted legally when he captured and sold it because he believed it to be a stray rock. The court ordered O'Grady and Loganski to split the proceeds from the rock because Loganski had incurred a lot of expense in capturing and transporting the rock to market. Neither of them were happy about that decision because there was nothing left after the lawyers were paid. They both sued Astro mining and Jake to recover their legal expenses.

After the dust settled, Jake's insurance company had to pay all the legal expenses of all the parties involved. Several law firms (except Jakes') had a very good year because Jake chose the wrong time to have a nap. Jake is no longer mining in the belt because nobody would contract to him unless he had liability insurance and no insurance company would accept him as a client. It's almost impossible to get insurance if you are the cause of a major disruption such as the one Jake caused and no insurance - no mining.

All rocks in tow now have to be tagged as a direct result of this case and most miners do the same as we do. They tag any rock they have captured as soon as it is brought to the holding area. A tag is legal proof of ownership so a rock can't be tagged until it has been physically captured. Most miners flag any rock that is in a stable orbit and doesn't cross into another ring. A flag isn't proof of ownership but it has come to be recognized as a proof of origin.

Miners towing their loads inbound now also have to broadcast four hours in advance the time they will enter and their flight path through each ring. The only good thing that came out of this mess for the miners was that the definition of a "stray rock" was made more specific. Any rock that is knocked out of its orbit by an impact with another rock or comet (an act of god) becomes a stray rock as soon as it crosses into another ring. Even a flagged rock can become a stray rock if it was dislodged by an act of god. Any rock that has been dislodged as a result of an act of man such as an impact with or being pulled by the gravity of a towed load remains the property of the ring owner. This was a necessary compromise of the lawmakers because the rocks in the rings are continually being knocked around by impacts with other rocks.

That is why we flag any rock that looks like it might be valuable. A flag is usually just a shaft shot into the rock with the company identity code on it. A tag is a band that encircles it and is secured with spikes to the rock with the company identity code on it. The band is to prove that you were actually in physical possession of the rock.

A miner is well advised to immediately capture and control any rock he has dislodged from another claim because he is libel for any damage it may cause. It is far cheaper to capture and transport the rock to the market than pay the damages it may cause. The claim owner must be notified that his rock is in tow because the rock still belongs to him. The claim owner is listed as the owner of the rock when they reach the market holding area on the Moon or Mars and is credited with the value of the rock after it is sold.

The requirement that each claim be visited for at least one month each earth year led to the deployment of the long term mining habitants to the rings. If you have to go to the expense of traveling out to your claim, then you might as well make it pay. This proved to be much more profitable than trying to luck into a good rock with a single flyby. It is far better to sit and wait for the rocks to come to you and to bring back a load of rocks rather than one at a time.

We used a high-resolution scanner to probe the spherical space around us out to a 20,000 kilometre limit. We also did a spectrographic analysis of anything inside our claim boundaries that looked interesting to tell us what kind of a rock it was. In addition we had an early warning scanner that did a roaming scan continuously out to 40,000 kilometers and beeped us if anything bigger than a pebble was coming our way. It also tracked their extended orbits to check for a future collusion risk or to see if it is going to loop into another ring.

Most of the rocks in the Belt are in a stable orbit and traveling roughly in the same direction. Most of is definitely not all of. There are always rocks flying across the usual flow and they are very capable of striking a rock in a stable orbit and sending it careening off in a new direction and orbit. For this reason we had to scan continuously because a stray rock can come at you at any time from any direction.

Nothing on that one. Reset the orientation and go again.

Wow, look at that. I'm almost through my shift and I haven't thought of Kelly once. Damm, I broke the spell. Kelly is hard not to think about. She's got a body that just doesn't quit and she's a top notch rock herder as well. I'm sure I would go stir crazy out here without her. We don't get a lot of time together because of the swing shifts but the time we do get is amazing. One of us is always either waking up or tired after a shift so it works best if I stay awake until she gets off shift.

We have a quick snack together and then she puts me to bed. I can assure you that she is really good at putting a guy to bed and it makes for a deep restful sleep. Thinking of our time together sure helps to get through these long shifts not to mention the vision of her coming in from the bathroom. I swear that she looks better in a negligee than she does naked and she's not a bit hard to look at naked.

She's a little tall at 5 ft 10 in. but nobody would call her lanky. She has an almost innocent face that is framed by her shoulder length auburn hair. Her slightly small nose resting between two bright green eyes that actually sparkle in the right light adds to the illusion.

She keeps to a rigorous workout schedule and that has resulted in firm smooth legs with muscles that ripple under her skin as she walks. Her movements are smooth and fluid and are complimented with a straight authorative posture.

It doesn't matter what angle of view you have of her. Her perfect hips, slim waist and trim upper body topped with that innocent face will almost take your breath away the first time you see her. Her side view is almost as good with the firm butt, flat stomach and nicely protruding breasts. Her breasts aren't large but they are big enough to create beautifully formed mounds in her negligee as it molds itself around and then falls off of them to her toned stomach. And those nipples! They seem to be permanently hard. Muum!! I can just feel her soft silky skin as I cup one of them in my hands and lick her bouncy nipples Muum!! I swear they actually tickle your palms when you rub across them.

Enough of that! I'd better go back to looking for rocks before I lose complete track of what I'm supposed to be doing.

Chapter 2

An Iridium rock would sure fill the bill. Even small Iridium rocks can be worth a year's income. Iridium is very rare on earth but not so in space. There are even rocks of almost pure Iridium floating around in the belt. They are remnants of supernova explosions that have remained intact for billions of years.

Iridium rocks were valuable even before the steel factories were built on Mars but then the Stellar Steel Company made the discovery that Iridium could be added to stainless steel to produce an extremely dense steel that is almost indestructible. It is not only super strong but also a perfect radiation shield for space vehicles and habitants. It reflects the radiation without becoming radioactive itself even on the outer surfaces.

Nothing again. Not even a bogie to dodge. One more scan and Kelly will be here.

In a brilliant advertising move, they named their discovery "Steller Steel" so the company and the product are forever linked. This didn't mean much while their patents were valid because they were the only source of the steel. Now that other steel companies are also making a Steller Steel product, they are still recognized as "the" source for Steller Steel because of the name recognition. The price skyrocketed when the patients expired because of the increased demand for Iridium so the competition for raw materials is ferocious. In another brilliant move, The Stellar Steel Company have offered a 20% bonus over the best price received at the most recent rock auction on Mars.

Most miners take them up on their offer because it's a guaranteed and immediate return. There are a few who prefer to take their chances at the auction because the prices fluctuate so much that it's possible to get twice the previous price. This works well for everybody because it keeps the price very high and the miners get a windfall whichever way they sell it. We have always sold our Iridium to Stellar Steel and they have just offered their steady suppliers an additional 10% because they don't want to lose any Iridium to the other steel companies should a miner decide to take his chances at the auctions.

Ah, here comes Kelly. Perfect timing, the scan is just about done.

Good morning Kelly. Umm, a hug and a kiss. That's the way to end a shift.

Good morning yourself. Did anything interesting show up overnight?

Yea, I flagged another small iron rock but that's it unless something shows up on this scan. I've been thinking about moving back to the outer end of our orbit to see if we can catch a looper. What do you think?

"Yea that could be good, answered Kelly. It looks like we'll be hard pressed here to make any bonus at all this term. We're half way through and we still haven't even found a good PGM rock. I was hoping to retire after this term but if things don't get better I'll be back out for another 6 months."

"Yea, I know what you mean, I said. I was hoping to get married and settle in at headquarters for a while. It's time I got more involved with running the company rather than grubbing around out here in the belt. Virginia is really pushing me to stay home and start a family. Do you think Dwaine is still up? Maybe we should talk about this now before we run out of time to move.

My scan finished so I checked it for blips that would have highlighted anything coming our way.

Nope, nothing promising on this one either.

That's sounds good to me. Dwaine and I had breakfast together and he should be still up, Kelly answered.

Ok, start your scan and I'll get him to come over.

Kelly watched Wade retrace her path through the sealed door of the airlock to the living quarters common area that is really an oversized air lock with four exits, one for each bedroom and the operations room.

To most people Wade looked quite ordinary. He is almost exactly 6 feet tall with a kind face that doesn't stand out. He wears his brown hair short and combs it with a part on the right side. His husky build is starting to show the effects of the time he has been spending in the exercise room. The muscles on his arms, chest and shoulders are hard but not big. He's neither barrel-chested nor heavy boned and his arms and legs seem perfectly proportioned to the rest of his body. What stands out is his stature. He carries himself with a sure and confidence stride and his mannerism toward other people projects a degree of competence that puts most people at ease around him.

The common area is a combination kitchen and dining room with a food island for a table. The stove and sink are built into the island with the fridge and cupboards on the wall. Like everything else the two stools in front of the island are bolted down so they wouldn't move around in the case of a zero gravity event or a jolting impact from a space rock. It could easily be mistaken for a kitchen on earth except for the size.

Two people fit in quite comfortably but it's a bit crowded with three and there are only two places to sit but there is provision for a third chair in the event there are four people on board. It was designed that way because someone is supposed to be in the operations center at all times so there is always one less chair than there are people on board. The operations center is a bit bigger and there are four chairs instead of an island taking up the center of the room so our meetings are held there.

You have to go through an airlock to move between rooms because all the compartments on this end are pressurized. A blue light over the door flashes if the pressure in the adjacent room is more than 2 P.S.I. different from the room you're in. There is also a pressure gauge above the door to give an accurate readout of the pressure in the next room. The door will not open without an override code if the compartment has depressurized. Every compartment is connected via an airlock and the doors must be sealed at all times. If a door is left open longer than 30 seconds or does not seal when closed then an alarm sounds in every compartment and a red light flashes above the unsealed door. Every compartment also has its own carbon dioxide filter canister with at least two spare canisters stored in each compartment to ensure a supply of fresh air in the event we all get trapped in one compartment for an extended period.

This was crucial when they were using thin-skinned titanium shells on the space stations because of the fear of a puncture from a stray space rock or high-speed pebble. The change to Steller Steel has made that almost impossible but the design has been retained to cover all bases. It is conceivable that the station can be hit hard enough to breach the skin but not very likely. A rock that big would knock us around a bit but it would take a direct head-on hit to even come close to cracking our shell.

Dwaine must be getting ready for bed.

Hello Dwaine, are you in there.

What do you want, came from the bathroom off the dining room.

The bathroom like the kitchen looks and works the same as it would on earth thanks to the artificial gravity supplied by the rotational speed of the space habitant. Our exercise equipment is also housed in the bathroom next to the shower.

All mining stations of our design are called simply "Spokes" because they are just one shaft with an enlarged pod on each end. A single shaft that has several pods in an arc on each end is called an "Arc" to separate them from the full wheel design of the larger stations. The wheel stations are usually named whereas the rest are given call signs. Our call sign is "Sigme 3." The Sigme Corporation owns three Spokes and one is always out in the rings.

Chapter 3

Space habitants may be as large as multiple wheels connected at the hubs or just one spoke out of a wheel as is the case for the mining habitants. The Spoke consists of a hub in the center that houses the docking station and rocket chamber. A storage module and power station pod are on one end of the Spoke and the living quarters and operations compartment on the opposite end. The operations and storage compartments are stacked inward from the living quarters and the power pod compartments respectively. From the outside they looks like one big compartment at each end of the station but it reality they are separate pods.

The docking station, platform, elevators and the elevator shafts are all open to space so protection must be worn when you enter these areas. Both elevators connect the respective pods to the unloading platform and they are used to transport the people and supplies back and forth from the platform.

The storage and power plant pods can be pressurized but are usually left closed and depressurized. There is a pressurized dressing room at each outer end of the elevator shafts that is used to suit up or undress and to store the space suits. This room is depressurized before the outside door is opened to minimize the air loss and it must be pressurized again after you enter the air lock before you remove any of your protection. There are spare suits stored in each dressing room as a safety precaution in the event you damage the one you are wearing. The dressing room at the reactor end of the spoke is usually left depressurized because it is used so little. Most of the time it isn't necessary to remove your space protection because you are just storing or picking up supplies. The only reason for staying longer would be if there were a problem with the power plant and they are bullet proof so we almost never have go in there.

The configuration of the stations is the same regardless of their size. The center housing with the docking station and rocket chamber is stationary because it is much easier to dock to a stationary object than a rotating one and the added mass of a docked transport vehicle does not affect the momentum of the habitant. The passengers and cargo enter the docking station through the docking ports and proceed into the station access chamber. The circular access chamber is split into two parts. The stationary platform is part of the docking station and the moving platform is part of the hub structure encasing the docking station. The hub or center housing and the docking station are connected via two large electro-magnetic bearings. The rotating loading dock platform is actually the upper race of one of these two frictionless bearings. There is a bearing at both the docking station and the rocket chamber end housings. They transmit the thrust from the rockets to the rest of the station as well as hold the docking station in place while allowing it to remain stationary.

The use of the wheel or rotating spoke design added an engineering problem that wasn't relevant to the stationary low-gravity units. If one side of the wheel or arm became out of balance with the other then the station could shake violently enough to knock people off their feet. It was very similar to an earthquake on earth and could be just as destructive. The unbalance also created an axis wobble and when the two were combined it rendered the habitant unliveable and unsafe. The control module for the two Reaction Drive units is also used to control a moveable weight network that automatically balances the station when people or cargo is moved about. The elevators that move along the spoke have a counterweight on the opposite arm so the balancing weights only have to compensate for the weight being transported. The balancing weights are independent of the elevator counterweights and are mounted around the outside of the elevator shafts so they can be used for the smaller adjustments. This makes for a smooth ride at the outer ends because the speed control module senses the added weight as soon as it is transferred to the rotating section of the loading dock. The Reaction Drive Unit automatically increases its power setting to compensate for the tendency of the arm to slow down as the added weight moves outward in the elevator. Conversely the station would speed up if people or cargo is moved inward toward the hub so that excess energy must be absorbed.

The Reaction Drive power module supplies the torque or dynamic brakes as needed to maintain the rotational speed within the comfort zone. The sense of gravity is directly relative to the speed of the station and your location inside it so gravity appears to increase as the elevator moves you outward from the hub. A second Reaction Drive unit powers the balancing system and between them they keep the ride nice and smooth regardless of what is happening on the station.

Chapter 4

Are you going to be long in there Dwaine? We want to have a meeting before you go back to bed.

Ok, I'll meet you there in about 5 minutes.

I grabbed a cup of coffee and headed back to operations.

Kelly was busy setting up her scan schedule when I came through the airlock. She knew that the meeting would take our attention away from the monitors so she was setting the system for an automatic double scan. We don't usually do an automatic search scan because we might not have enough time to react if something good is coming our way and we can't afford to miss a good rock. The long-range scanner will pick up and warn us of any dangerous rocks so we only have to focus on rocks close enough for us to grab. We scan it for size and if it looks big enough to be worth towing back we then hit it with a short laser burst to see what it's made of. In this case we set the short-range scanner to warn us of an approaching rock as well and trust that we will be quick enough to react when we hear the buzzer.

Dwaine came through right behind me. He is the stockiest of the three of us. He is of Welsh heritage but he was born on Mars. He is 5 ft 8 in. and built like a brick outhouse. He is big boned and perfectly proportioned. His legs and upper body are almost the same length and his arms are heavy boned and well muscled. On Earth he could easily have been a wrestler or a boxer. He has a rugged look about him because his jaw and brow are also heavy boned with his eyes set slightly back under heavy eyebrows. His pitch black eyes shine with a brightness that foretells the intelligence behind them. His face is complimented with a nose that is perfectly proportioned to his features as well. His bushy black hair finishes the image of a rugged capable man ready to face the world and win.

We sat facing each other in the center of the room and as the commander; I spoke first.

I think we have to make a decision today if we plan to stay here and built a load from what we have locally or we can move to one of the crossover sectors to see if we can snag a PGM looper. It will also give us fresh territory in our ring to scan as we travel back so we won't miss any good rocks.

Kelly joined in, I'm with you on this Wade. I think we should go for it. I for one could really use a big score on this trip.

What do you think Dwaine, I asked? We're all in this together so we win or lose together.

Dwaine rubbed his chin as he said, I'm not too sure this is the right move. I'm worried that we could burn enough of our fuel in the move that we couldn't come back to get our flagged rocks. We already have half a load flagged and we could just as easily luck into a treasure rock right here. If we move and don't find anything really good we will be left with almost nothing to take back. If we don't make our costs, all we get is our base wages. I think we could be better off in the long run taking our chances here.

Kelly jumped in, come on Dwaine, we should listen to Wade! We've talked about this! If you don't go for it you will never score big.

Ok you two. Calm down, I said. I have to admit that I like the idea of catching a big treasure rock but I also have to weigh the cost of the gamble because I'm the one that has to answer to Sigme.

Yea right Wade! Kelly said! You're the boss's son so you should be able to handle any flak that the Procurement Manager might dish out. Hell, you probably know him by his first name.

Yes Kelly, I do know him but I also know that my father told him not to give me any slack. If I'm going to run this company someday, I'll have to prove I have what it takes to get the job done and a big part of that is making the right decisions at the right time. Coming home empty handed just can't happen. I'd rather bring in half a load than no load. Having said that all it would take is a couple of good PGM rocks to more than make up for what we leave here.

Ok Kelly, Dwaine added, I know we talked about this and I may be a little over cautious but Wade has a point. A bird in hand is worth two in the bush and we could just as easily luck into a good rock here.

Well yes we could, I said, but Kelly has a point as well. We will be moving against the flow of rocks on our way back along the ring so we might luck into a PGM rock during our repositioning. We aren't going to miss anything that would have come to us and we would end up in a better position.

There's also the fact that we have this sector pretty well mapped now and we can get credit for that as well as the rocks we've flagged so we wouldn't really be going back empty handed. If we move out to the end sectors we can map there as well and we just might be able to snag a looper off one of the other rings. We have enough fuel and all our nets so all we would need is a little luck.

Ok Wade, Dwaine said, I need the money just as bad as you guys, maybe more. I'm a lifer out here so I guess one bad trip won't be the end of the world but I hate to pass up a sure thing even if it's less than we had hoped for. How about we give this one more day?

Like I said Dwaine. We're all in this together so if we don't all agree on the move then I guess we stay here and hope for the best. How about this? If by the end of my shift tomorrow there isn't anything good on the horizon we take a vote. That will give us all time to think it over and if it's not unanimous, then we stay.

Kelly?

That sounds good to me. One more day won't make or break us.

Dwaine?

Yeaa, good by me.

Ok, great. I think I'll get something to eat and watch a movie before I hit the sack.

Dwaine winked at Kelly and said, yea right Wade, I've heard that before. What movie did you have in mind?

With that we said good-bye to Kelly and went back to the common area. Dwaine and I talked for an hour or so while I was cooking supper. He wasn't really dead set against us moving, he just needed time to adapt to the change in plans. He went back to bed and I watched some old western reruns while I was waiting for Kelly to get off shift.

I was about ready to start another movie when I saw the light come on in the kitchen through the porthole in the door. I didn't bother to get up because I knew Dwaine was having something to eat and making his lunch so that meant Kelly would be here soon. I have to admit I was especially looking forward to seeing her tonight even if it did mean losing a little sleep.

My alarm went off 5 short hours after I went to sleep and I woke up thinking of Kelly. I'm going to have to be careful. That girl is starting to get under my skin and if I call Virginia "Kelly" while we're in bed I'll be a dead man.

Chapter 5

I think I'll have an old fashioned breakfast this morning. Bacon, eggs and pancakes with maple syrup

I arrived just as Dwaine was finishing his last scan and nothing interesting had shown up overnight. He left to have supper and I started my scans the same as usual. Even the long-range scanner didn't show any big rocks out there. Usually there is one or two a shift going by in the other rings.

I guess we will have to swing the Spoke around so the rockets can sent us back along our ring to the end sectors. There are four retro rockets on the outside of each pod that are used to change or make fine adjustments to our orientation. The four propulsion rockets on the opposite end of the docking stations just push us in the direction we are pointed. We can use the main rockets for steering as well by varying the power output from the individual rockets. We don't use them unless we have to because it is hard to be accurate with them and the ride this far out on the arm can to be quite rough and jerky.

We don't usually lose our artificial gravity during a reorientation but things tend to move around so we will have to make sure that everything is put away or fastened down. We always fire at least two Retro's in unison; one on each pod so the station swings around smoothly. We feel a jolt as the station swings around in answer to the push from them and again as we stop the rotation. The Spoke never stops rotating but the docking station and the rockets are stationary in relation to them. If we have time we can time the bursts so that the arm is at the midpoint of our change in orientation. That makes it a lot smoother and uses less fuel but it takes longer because we have to wait for the arm to swing into the right position. The momentum of the spoke adds mass to the station and that makes it harder to turn than a stationary station so we have to use fairly strong bursts. A strong burst creates the jolt that moves stuff around and it will actually knock you off your feet if we try to swing in a hurry and you aren't ready for it.

In this case we will have to do a short rocket burn to speed us up after the station is swung around. That will increase our speed so that we move along our ring toward the outer sectors. Then we will have to do another short burn to slow us down which means that we will have to swing the station back around again so the rockets are facing backward instead of forward. The retro rockets will keep us on track once we swing around. We can burn two or more of them at once for minor course corrections.

It's always a trade-off between getting there faster with a long burn on each end or saving fuel by a shorter burn and a longer flight. In this case I think a short burn is best because that will give us time to scan as we go. If something really good comes up on our scope we can grab it with the netships and still go back for the flagged rocks.

Nope, nothing promising on this one either.

The netships are securely docked to the docking station and are loaded with their nets so they won't need any special attention. The center housing has four docking ports. Three are for the netships and one to receive visitors. We use the fourth port a lot when we are in orbit around Mars but almost never out here.

The netships used to capture the target asteroid are patterned after the first crafts designed to change the course of a rogue asteroid that was barreling toward an impact with Earth. In the beginning they were intended to be launched from Earth on very short notice but later they were placed in orbit for even quicker deployment.

A netship is actually two individual rocket powered crafts joined together via a cargo bay. The cargo bay contains a net made of a high strength carbon fiber rope. The net is connected to each half of the cargo bay so it looks like a tennis court net when it is deployed.

The netship was deployed to a point directly in the path of the incoming asteroid but it was traveling at a speed just slightly less than the speed of the asteroid. After it was in position, the crafts would separate and pay out the net between them so the asteroid would literally fall into the net. The impact of the asteroid striking the net is not great enough to break through because of the slight speed difference between them. The asteroid would instead cause the net to fold around it like a rock in a slingshot pocket and this would cause the two crafts to trail behind it. After the asteroid was firmly in the net the rockets were fired and this would slow the asteroid enough to change its arrival time in Earth's orbit and thus avoid a collision.

The first netships used for mining were an exact copy of the earlier crafts and were remote controlled but the miners wanted a craft that they could control manually so a pilots compartment and a docking port were added to one of the cargo compartments. This made for a much more versatile vessel because it could either be manually or remotely controlled.

This was a perfect craft for the asteroid miners because of its low construction costs and the fact that most of its components are reusable. Even a tumbling rock can be brought to bay with this system with precise timing of the rocket bursts. The miners leave the asteroid in the net until it has been delivered to the client. After it is captured the net makes it easy to tow the asteroid and deposit it in orbit around one of the other planets or even the moon where it can be easily mined of its water and minerals. The nets can be released from the net ship and attached to the main tow-line of a Spoke. This frees the netships up so they can be refueled and reloaded with a fresh net and they're ready to go again.

Whoa, what the hell is that?

Holly shit!! I'd better go get them both up. We're going to need all hands for this.

I actually ran across the common area and burst into Dwaine's room. Kelly was so startled that she jumped out of the bed naked. God she looks good.

Wow Kelly, I'm glad you're here. Get some clothes on, we've got a lot of work to do.

I shook Dwaine to wake him up and I started talking as soon as he started rubbing his eyes. You guys aren't going to believe this. There's been a collision out in the outer belt and rocks are bouncing around like balls on a pool table.

That got Kelly's attention.

What!! How far out? How many? Are they coming our way? Are there any good ones?

Whoa, slow down Kelly. One question at a time! I haven't done any accurate tracking or analysis yet. There's no question there's at least one coming our way because the long-range scanner marked it as potentially dangerous. You guys get yourselves together and meet me in the operations room.

I sprinted back to operations and started to sort out the good from the bad.

I think Kelly was a little embarrassed with me seeing them in bed together. We don't usually see the other one with her because of the shifts. She must have fallen asleep in Dwaine's arms. She usually gets up later and returns to her room when that happens with me.

Kelly is not only a good rock herder, she is also a great comfort woman.

When we first started to mine the asteroid belt the mental health of the miners proved to be a much bigger problem than any physical side effects they might suffer. The miners were cooped up together for months at a time and there were several examples of miners gone wild. Depression and paranoia were their biggest foes. A person would either become unresponsive or aggressive and could suffer mood swings from one to the other. It was called Cabin Fever in the gold fields of the Klondike in the 1850's. The addition of a comfort woman solved most of these problems and created one more, "jealousy". A good comfort woman was capable of keeping jealousy in check while providing enough intrigue to keep boredom from taking its toll. Now, almost all the miners contract a comfort woman for the term out in the rings. Married couples are not allowed on the same station unless they both agree that she can function as a comfort woman. Her job is to be sexually active for all of the men on the station. Comfort woman get the same base pay as the herders and an equal share of any bonuses as well. In Kelly's case she gets double pay and double bonuses because she performs both functions. Neither Dwaine nor I resent this because someone would have gotten the pay anyway and she certainly does both her jobs well.

Most comfort woman retire after two or three terms because they have made their nest egg and want to start a new life. In Kelly's case she wants to start her own business so she took double duty and this will be her 3rd term so it's easy to see why she wants to score big this time.

Chapter 6

Kelly and Dwaine came through together. I had already made sure that there was nothing dangerous in our immediate area. We each picked one of the bigger rocks on the long-range scanner and started to plot its track.

It looked like the collision had been quite a way behind us and in the outer ring. The rocks out there still orbited the sun because Jupiter's gravity was not yet strong enough to pull them in. We were just seeing the leading edge of the impact zone but it was obvious that there had been a lot of rearranging as a result of it. My rock was still too far away to get a good picture of it but I could tell that it was on a slow track inward through the rings. It would be easy to capture if it were worth the effort. It was either a PGM or iron core rock because it hadn't broken up in the collision. I marked it for the computer to track and moved on to another one. This one was about 250 yards across and twice as long. It was coming at a much sharper angle than the first one so it would pass through our ring fairly fast. We could handle a rock that size if we used all three ships. All we had to do was plot the point where it crossed into our ring and meet it there.

What have you got Dwaine?

I got a track on 50,000 ton block of ice that looks like it was chipped off something really big. It's quite a ways out but

I think it will eventually cross over to us as long as someone else doesn't get to it first.

Kelly added, I've got one coming really close to us that looks like it might be an icy rock also but I can't tell what it is made of.

Well, I said, you guys might think I'm crazy but I've marked what could be about a 1 million ton iron rock coming in quite fast. If we're going to snag it we'll have to move right away. Do you guys think we can handle a rock that big?

Dwaine answered first, there's still stuff coming out of the zone but nothing to match that. That's at the upper limit for us to handle. Theoretically we should be able to capture it but there won't be any room for error. That would sure give us a nice bonus along with the rocks we've already flagged.

Kelly?

Yes! Let's go for it.

Ok, I said, I've put the track up on the big screen. We'll have to do a burn so we get to the penetration point before it does. Kelly and I will suit up and put the auxiliary tanks on the ships in case we need them. It's no time to run out of fuel when you're tied to a rock that size. We're going to have to move fairly fast Kelly if we want to put tanks on all three ships.

Great, she said. Let's get started. We have to wear our suits in the netships anyway so we'll be killing two birds with one stone. Our suits have enough battery, oxygen and fluid to last for a full day so we should have lots of oxygen to do both with some to spare. The built in extra life support capacity will still give us enough of a safety margin to be rescued in the event one of us does end up stranded with an empty netship.

We try not to use the main rockets on the netships for manoeuvring because we have an auxiliary retro-rocket system for final positioning but we do need the main rockets to get us there and to control the rock after it's in the net. The extra tanks could well be needed for a rock this size. We really should use all three ships on something this big. One ship acts as a safety and stays back in reserve so it can easily deploy the net and help if it's needed but if it's not, then it returns to the Spoke. In our case, because there are only three of us, the Spoke would be left unmanned with all three ships deployed so we don't commit the third ship unless it's absolutely necessary. That isn't usually a problem since we know everything in our vicinity because of our scans but in this case that could be a problem.

On second thought guys, I said, I think we had better cover out butts on this one. We don't know what will come out of the zone while we are busy in the ships. I don't think we should leave the ship unmanned this time. Any Suggestions?

Dwaine said; I've been thinking the same thing. With the extra tanks you two should be able to get the job done. I can always get suited up and be ready to come help on short notice.

There may be another way added Kelly. We can bring the Spoke in really close so if we get in trouble or run out of fuel then the other one can release the net and shoot back to the station for the other ship. If we both run out of fuel then Dwaine can come and get us. The worst that can happen is that we have to release the rock so it doesn't drag us out of range and the ship is still safe.

I like that Kelly I said, but let's add a little more safety margin. I'll be the primary ship and deploy my net first. You come in at 90 degrees to me with the short net the same as usual so we both have the rock in our nets. We both have to fire our rockets but you only use ½ power. If it looks like we're not going to be able to stop its descent then I'll shut down and release my net while I still have enough fuel to get back to the station. I'll grab the other ship and come back to help. Everything should be ok as long as you shut your rockets down in time to leave you with enough fuel to get back to the station if things go wrong. Dwaine can be suited up so he can be our back-up. If need be he can leave operations and come refuel my ship with the extra tank we will leave on the platform and come pick us both up if we have to release the rock. That should cover all our bases.

Everybody agreed? Great, let's get going we're running out of time.

We all three suited up and Kelly and I took the elevators down to the docking platform and them out to the storage pods to get the auxiliary tanks. We also brought down an extra spare tank and a spare net as well.

Dwaine had turned the ship around and finished his calculations and was ready to fire the rockets by the time we had finished.

Dwaine burned the rockets for 30 seconds to bring us back along our ring to the penetration point.

Ok Dwaine, we can launch anytime. How does the track look?

Not very good, I think we may have a problem here.

What's happening? Do you need us back there?

No, I think I can handle it. It looks like we are going to arrive at the penetration point just after the rock and I think that's cutting it a little close. I don't have time to turn us around and slow us down so I'll have to give us another little boost. That could mean that we're a long way from the penetration point by the time I get us stopped and the rock will be moving away from us as well.

Ok Dwaine, we'll stand by. Don't take any chances. If anything happens to the station we're too far from home to get back without it. Do you think you could swing us around as soon as you finish the burn? That should save you some stopping distance without endangering the station.

Ok Wade. I think that will work. If you guys launched before we pass the penetration point that should put you in front of it. That will give you some extra time to get in position and deploy your nets. You will be moving away from me so I think I should chase after you as soon as the rock gets in front of me. That'll cut your return time to the station as much as possible.

That sounds good Dwaine. Kelly, we'll have to time this right and be ready to launch as soon as Dwaine gives us the word. This is the biggest rock we have ever tackled but I've got a good feeling about this, we're going to snag this thing.

Dwaine's timing was perfect and we launched just before the rock entered our ring. We were only a couple of miles in front of it and we had to keep the power on to get enough speed to stay in front. It took more fuel than we wanted to spend but we were both in position 5 miles ahead of it when we deployed the nets.

It was gaining on us a bit fast but the nets held and we had it. More truthfully, it had us. It really gave us a snap when it hit the net. Thank god for head restraints. I fired my rocket as soon as Kelly had it firmly in her net. Everything was going as planned but it was obvious that we were not going to be able to stop it with just the two ships. I shut down with just 1/8 of a tank left in the auxiliary and released my net. Dwaine had stopped the ship and was now bringing it up to us. He wasn't coming very fast because he didn't want to overshoot us and that meant I had further to go to get to the ship than I had planned. Thank god for a separate retro rockets system. I wouldn't have been able to dock without them because my tanks were spent.

I switched ships and immediately launched to go help Kelly. Dwaine left operations after a final check for danger in the area and refuelled my ship. He didn't want to stay away from operations any longer than necessary so he didn't load the net. I had winched the two compartments together while on route to the station so they would have had to be separated again, the net is stowed with each end secured to one of the compartments and then the compartments rejoined. That was too much time away from the scanners with all those rocks moving around out there.

Kelly had shut down by the time I got back and things didn't look really promising. We had definitely slowed the rock down but it was still descending through our ring. We would have to release it and lose our nets if it reached the next ring.

I'm back Kelly. How are you doing?

Not very good! This thing is heavier than we thought. I was hardly affecting it with half power. How about if you try to swing it rather than stop it? If we can change its course rather than slow it down it will still have enough speed to stay in our ring. That will give us enough time to go get your ship again and the both of us can tackle it.

I like that. We've spend too much time and fuel to lose it now. That will also give Dwaine time to close in on us a bit.

Kelly released her net and I deployed in front the same as usual but this time I maneuvered off to the outward side before I fired my rockets. Kelly was right, this sucker was heavy. I used half my fuel before it swung around to where we wanted it.

Now that we had it securely within our ring, we recovered our nets before we went back to the ship. The station was still gaining on the rock slowly so we developed a new plan. We loaded the spare net into my ship and recaptured it. All we had to do was wait until the station was within range and then we could attach the net to the stations tow-line. That will give us lots of power to handle our Iron Maiden.

We had refuelled all the ships and reloaded them with their nets while we were waiting to catch up to it. Kelly grabbed the net on the first try with the tow-line and I tagged our rock to tell the rest of the world that it belonged to us. We were in a celebrating mood when we had finished. It had been a very profitable days work for us. We met in the operations room for a drink to commemorate the capture of our prize. This one rock alone would ensure a trip to bonusland for all of us. I broke out our one and only bottle of champagne and we finished it.

Chapter 7

We were all tired but someone had to stay with the scanners and I was elected for the first four hour shift because I had interrupted their sleep. Kelly and Dwaine both went to their separate compartments and crashed. Kelly and then Dwaine were going to do a 4 hour shift each before we were back on our regular eight hrs. rotation beginning with my next shift.

We've been lucky so far. Nothing else has come out of the zone to threaten us. We now have our prize firmly in tow and are slowly moving back to our old sector. We'll probably collect the other rocks we have flagged and go home early since we are so low on fuel. It took twice as much fuel as we normally use to capture this one but it was worth it. The long-range scanner still shows some juggling going on out in the outer rings but so far nothing seems to be headed for us. There were a couple of small rocks that streaked through behind us but they were no loss. I hope we don't run across another big one like this, I don't think we have enough fuel to grab it and it would really pain me to have to let it go.

Humm! Kelly is a little late. That's not like her. Oh! Here she comes.

Sorry I'm a bit late Wade. It seemed like I just got to sleep and the damm alarm went off.

That's ok Kelly. We all had a hard day today. There's nothing interesting on either scanners so try not to fall asleep and run into a stray rock. I think I'll just crash and eat when I get up. Goodnight.

No problem Wade, I've got it. I just hope Dwaine gets up on time. He was really beat and I'm not sure I could do a full shift. Goodnight, sleep tight. I'll probably still be sound asleep when you get up.

I went straight to my room and flopped on the bed. The next thing I remember was my alarm going off. I was still in my clothes but I had slept well so I had a shower and changed before I cooked breakfast. I was really hungry since I hadn't eaten anything last night so I cooked three eggs, two ham steaks and two pancakes.

Dwaine was ready to leave as soon as I got there. All he said was, Nothing's happening, see you later.

He was right. Both scanners were clear and our flight path was right on the money. We would be back where we started from by the middle of my shift so I swung the station around to be ready to slow it down and pick up the two flagged rocks. It was slow coming around and of course took more fuel that usual because of our heavy load.

It would be nice to be home early. Virginia will be pleased because with the credit for bringing back this load I will be able to transfer to head office and start training to manage the Procurement Department. That would mean I could stay home and we could get married and start the family we had been talking about. The only problem I can see is reassuring Virginia that she is still the only girl for me because she was a little testy about Kelly being out here with us. She accepts the fact that Kelly serves a crucial purpose but she doesn't like it. I'm sure she'll get over it soon just as long as I don't call her Kelly at the wrong time.

Ok there they are. The long-range scanner had just picked up the first of our flagged rocks and it would have the other one soon. I had better start slowing down now so we don't overshoot. Ok, there's the other one. I think I'll stop between them so it'll save some fuel to get to them. Maybe I'll wait a couple of hrs. so that Dwaine gets his much needed rest and Kelly will be just about ready to get up. Capturing even tame rocks like these two needs an alert crew. Mistakes out here can kill us all or almost as bad, we could lose the rock and it would go careening down through the rings. The last thing we need is to be responsible for a rogue rock banging around in the rings.

Good good, we're stopped. Well we weren't really stopped. We had just stopped moving in relation to them. We were all still circling the sun at 50,000 miles per hour as we travelled in our orbit. Movement is a relative thing, especially out here.

Chapter 8

Ok, that's it I'm going to get them up. Oh oh, what's that? That's the rock I marked before we started out after the Iron Maiden. It has just crossed over into our ring but my projections showed that it would take another half of an orbit before that happened. It shouldn't be changing its track that much.

I should be able to reach it with a laser shot and get a picture of it. Good, I got it. It's not the best vapor cloud I've seen but we should be able to get a read on it. That's odd. There's the usual water and iron but something else as well. I'm going to give it a double burst this time and see if I get a better picture.

Kelly came in just as I fired my second burst.

What's happening? I was just finishing my breakfast when I heard the laser bursts. Are we in trouble?

No no, I think we've got ourselves another gem. Have a look at this readout.

I put the readout up on the big screen and we both stood there with our mouths open.

I spoke first: You had better go get Dwaine up. We're going to need him.

Kelly slammed the door on her way out and ran to get Dwaine. They were both back in 5 minutes. I did another double burst to double check the readings.

Dwaine just gaped at the screen when he saw it.

I don't believe it, he said. Half of that vapor cloud is Iridium.

I didn't believe it either, I said. That was either a lucky shot or that rock is laced with Iridium. The first shots showed a strong trace as well. I know that it's hard to believe but we are looking at a major find here. The question is, what do we do about it?

Kelly jumped in, there's no question, we grab it.

I tend to agree with you, I said but there are some serious problems with that. First we already have a very valuable rock in tow and it's so heavy that we can't do much playing around. It takes a lot of fuel to even swing us around not to mention change our speed.

How much extra fuel do we have left Dwaine?

Not a lot. There are only three auxiliary tanks full and if we drain any more out of the stations tanks we might not be able to control our descent to Mars. The good news is we have all three ships fuelled and fitted with auxiliary tanks. We also have all our nets available except the one around our beauty out there.

That's cutting it pretty close, I said. Unfortunately I swung us around and slowed down to position us to capture our two flagged friends out there. We would have to turn back around and speed up just to get close to this one. Then we have to swing around again and slow down to capture it. That's going to use a lot of fuel out of the main tanks. Let's look at our options.

Option one. We let it go and take the two flagged rocks with us. We've got lots of fuel to do that and a little to spare.

I don't even want to think about that Kelly spurted out. That rock could well be worth more than all three of these. If we leave these two where they are we have a good shot of taking both our Iron Maiden here and that Gem out there back with us. Think of the bonus that would get us.

That's definitely an option Kelly, I said, but not the only one. We could leave our iron friend here in a stable orbit and go get our Gem. As you said it's probably worth more than all of these put together so we would still get a nice bonus. What do you think Dwaine, you've been awful quiet.

I think I may have an idea, he said, what if we released the Iron Maiden here and then swing the station back around to go after the Gem? That would take a lot less fuel because we wouldn't have to manhandle that heavy rock.

Guys, Kelly shouted, I really don't want to leave the Iron Maiden out here!! Don't you see, this is the chance of a lifetime! We're not just talking about a good bonus here, we're talking about a windfall that could change all our lives!

Relax Kelly, Dwaine said, listen to the rest of the plan before you panic. Now as I was saying, first we release the Iron Maiden and go get our treasure rock. After we have it in tow we slow down and let the maiden catch up to us. We'll already be pointed in the right direction to slow down and start our descent after we recapture it and we will have done it with half the fuel.

I like that Dwaine, I said, but there are a couple of tricky parts to it. We're going to have to do a strong burn to get enough speed to jump out ahead and close on the Gem. That means we will also have to use fuel to slow us down so we can grab it. Then we have to slow everything down so the others can catch up to us. Then we have to reacquire the Iron Maiden and again slow everything down to descent to Mars. With all that messing around we are going to be almost out of fuel. There won't be any safety margin left if anything goes wrong.

Everything was quiet for almost a minute so I called for the vote.

I'm for it, I said

Kelly? Yes definitely.

Dwaine? Yes, let's go for it.

Great, let's get started. Let's leave the tow-line connected to the maiden and release it from the ship. We can use our spare tow-line for the Gem and that will give us more to snag when we want to capture the maiden again. We're going to need to suit up again, who's turn is it to stay onboard?

It's still your shift Wade so it's your turn, Kelly said.

Yea. I thought so. I'll swing around as soon as we are clear of the tow-line. Kelly you be primary this time with Dwaine on the short net. Let me know when you've cast the tow-line off Dwaine.

Chapter 9

The short net is used so that the two ships don't collide when they fire their rockets to capture the rock. The rockets on each half of the net ships are angled in toward each other at a 15 degree angle. If the rockets were not pivoted inward and they were fired with a rock in the net they would slam into each other as the net tightened. The rock looks like a marble in the pocket of a slingshot while it is being slowed or towed. After we've got the rock where we want it we can slack off and release the nets from the ships. They are then connected together so the net can be secured to the tow-line. The two ship halves are then reconnected using the retro rockets and a winch on the cockpit half and then secured to their docking ports.

Ok Wade, the line is clear, Dwaine said. Kelly and I are going out to get the spare tow-line from the storage pod now. Do you want it connected right away?

No, we've got lots of time so let's wait until after we've got the Gem under control. Just leave it on the platform with the spare tanks. I'm ready to swing around now so it will be about 5 minutes when I fire the rockets.

Roger, we'll be ready, answered Dwaine, just give us a heads up before you start.

I used the retro rockets to swing us back around for the push out to catch the Gem. This is where one of the new stations would be handy. They use a Reaction Drive fitted between the rocket and docking compartments to swing the stations around. This saves a lot of fuel and that would be a really good thing right now.

Ok, you two hang on, I'm firing on the count of 3. 1, 2, 3.

I gave a strong 30 second burst and shut down to see how I had done. Whoa, that may have been a little too much. We're really closing on the Gem fast.

Are you guys ok out there? The station moves a lot easier when it's not tied to a rock.

We're good here Wade, Kelly answered. Do you want us to man the net ships yet?

No, you better stay inside until I swing back around and slow us down again. This may be a little jerky, I've got to come around fairly quick.

I brought the ship around and slowed it so that we were going the same speed as our gem. I freely admit that I have done a smoother job but I got it done on time and that was more important than a smooth ride.

Ok, Kelly we're in position about ten miles behind the rock and going the same speed. It's up to you two now.

Thanks Wade. We could feel it. We're just boarding our ships and will let you know when we're ready to launch.

They both launched about 5 minutes later and zoomed out to deploy the nets. When they got closer to the rock Kelly radioed back.

Hello Wade, you had better turn on your Orientation Beacon. This thing has more wobble to it than we thought so I think we're going to need it.

Ok Kelly, it's on. Are you going to be able to handle it?

Yes there shouldn't be any problem but I think we had better change our plan of attack.

Whatever you think Kelly, it's your show.

Right, I'm thinking that we should link Dwaine's computer to mine after we deploy so that everything happens together. We're going to have to snub it pretty hard to take the momentum out of it and I don't want to tear one of the nets. Also I think we should deploy really close to each other so my net doesn't get wound up before we get to Dwaine's. Are you ok with that Dwaine? You'll just be along for the ride and it could be a little rough.

Yea, I'm ok with that Kelly. How close do you want my net to be to yours?

As close as you can without touching it. Ten to twenty feet would be great. Try to get as close as you can to a 90 degrees offset from mine as well.

Ok, here it comes. Let's go about 10 miles ahead before we slow to its speed. That should give us time to get ready. Ok, slowing and deploying now.

I'm with you Kelly, give me a minute to get everything ready here. Ok, linking to your computer now. Be gentle with me Kelly.

Yea, right, like I'm not always. Stand by Dwaine. Let me know when you feel it start to pull you and I'll fire a strong

15 second burst from both ships and then have a look at what we have. It might be a good idea if you backed off a bit more Wade in case we slow too much. I'm going to leave it to you to match our speed and stay out of the way so I can concentrate on taming this thing.

We're on the same page Kelly. I'm backing off another ten miles now.

It was a good move to back off. Kelly's first burn slowed the rock down so much I had to do a power burn to keep from catching up to them. It did knock the fight out of it though. Most of the wobble was gone but it was still rotating at about 2 rpm's. Kelly honed in on my beacon and used 10 bursts of Dwaine's Retros to stall it. All she needed them was a couple of short bursts on hers and it was dead in the water.

My beacon was their lighthouse so to speak. My beacon was a stable point in space so they could tell where they were and how they were moving in relation to me and that told them what they needed to do to bring it under control. With the ships offset by 90 degrees they could counteract any wobble or rotation within its spherical displacement by co-ordinating the bursts from their ships.

It was a classic capture and within an hour they had the Gem in their nets and under control.

Congratulations Kelly, that was pretty to watch. Now comes the tricky part. Dwaine why don't you recover your net and come back here so you can pay out the tow-line? Kelly can tie her net to it and then tag our Gem before she comes back to fuel up.

We've got a little time before the Iron Maiden catches up to us so we should get ready. We're going to need both ships to slow that iron baby down so lets pump what's left in your auxiliary tanks into your main tanks and replace them with the spares on the platform. How do you want to do this Kelly?

I've been thinking about that. I don't want to risk ripping the net by both of us pulling on it so I think Dwaine should hook the end of the tow-line and I will recapture it in my net so we will have two nets to pull with.

I like that, I said, because we can then connect both tow-lines to the mainline and we wouldn't have all our eggs in one basket. I mean it's possible that if we have both rocks on the one tow-line it could break under the load when we decelerate for the flight in.

Here's something else to think about. When you slow it down to match our speed that heavy iron devil is going to start to descent on its own. If we don't have a good hold on it and get it connected to the station before you guys run out of fuel then we're going to lose it. Then we would have a rogue rock on our hands with our tag on it. If it raises havoc in the other rings then we're responsible for it. I can pretty well guarantee that that will eat up any bonuses we are thinking of. As a matter of fact, I doubt we would even be able to find work out here in the rings so let's do this right.

There's one more thing, Dwaine added, we are starting to degrade our orbit because we slowed down so much for the Gem. We're ok until the maiden catches up to us but the station will be in the lower region of our ring. We will be higher up when we first contact the maiden so that might give us a little extra time to work with especially if we go out to meet it.

Yes, I said, but I think we may have another problem as well. The tow cable end has to be physically attached to the mainline ring. That means we will have to have some slack in the line so we can disconnect from the net ship and then connect to the mainline. That's going to be hard to do if our rock is degrading too fast.

The tow-line is actually attached to a winch in the center on the central housing. The winch is anchored to the bulkhead between the docking stations and the rocket mounts. The mainline pays out the center between the four rockets and there is a heavy ring on the end of the cable that the tow cables attach to. The mainline is stronger than the two tow-lines combined and there is lots of room for two tow-lines to be connected to the ring so that should eliminate any problem we might have by towing both rocks. The mainline is normally trailing out from the ship by about 50 feet so the fairlead in the center of the rocket mounts can keep the cable away from the station even when we are swinging around.

Good point Dwaine, I said, this could get out of hand really fast. Is there anything we can do to improve our odds?

Well, Dwaine said, maybe we should change our approach. Kelly is the primary so maybe she should take the tow-line so she can see what's happening and I'll net the rock. Do you have a long or a short net in your ship Wade?

It's got a long one. What have you got in mind Dwaine?

Well, I was just thinking. I've got a short one so we could net it with both ships. We could link your ship to my computer and launch both ships. With Kelly on the tow-line and both ships on the nets we can pretty well do as we want.

Now you're talking Dwaine, Kelly said. I like that idea a lot.

Me too, I said. I'll pay out the straw line with the grapple hook so I can pull the tow-line in when Kelly brings it to me. I'll winch the mainline in as far as the fairlead so I won't have to leave the station but I will be out of operations for a bit. You're going to have to be careful not to get tangled in the tow-line for our Gem Kelly.

Yes, I was thinking about that. Are we ready to do this?

I'm a go, I said.

Ready when you are Kelly, added Dwaine.

Everything went like clockwork. Kelly and Dwaine went back to meet the maiden and they had it firmly in hand by the time they caught up to me. It took two 15 second burns from all three ships to slow it down. Kelly dropped the end of the tow-line into the grapple like it was childs play. Once the tow-line was in the grapple I left operations and winched the line in to the ring on the mainline. We had a little trouble there because it was too tight for me to release it from the straw line grapple and hook it to the mainline.

Dwaine did a 30 second burn with his two ships and I slipped the clevis over the ring.

Dwaine disengaged both ships and recovered the two nets with them. It wasn't long before the maiden tightened the line again since it was degrading faster than before because we had slowed it down so much.

As a matter of fact it was pulling us down with it. That created another problem. We were all back in operations before we saw what was happening and it became abundantly clear that we had to do something fast. Kelly was the first to notice it.

Do you guys see what's happening out there?

What's up Kelly, asked Dwaine.

Kelly's voice raised an octave as she pointed to the big screen. Look at what's happening with the tow-lines, she said.

Chapter 10

The maiden was pulling us down but the Gem was still holding fast in its orbit. Our tow-lines were spread into a giant "Y" and there was a real danger that the Gem might swing back into the rotating spoke of the station as the Y stretched out into a straight line with us suspended in the center.

Did anybody refuel their ship, I asked?

Nope, I didn't, blurted Dwaine, how about you Kelly?

No, me neither but I do still have half a tank left.

Not me, said Dwaine, I'm down to 1/4 tank. That last burn was at full power.

Ok, I jumped in. We need to do something fast or we could be in serious trouble. We've still got the auxiliary tanks on the platform so you two get suited up quick while I try to come up with a plan. All hell will break loose if we swing into our tow cables.

Right, we're on our way, Kelly yelled over her shoulder. We can use the spare suits Dwaine so we have lots of air. My life support system was down to half as well.

Let me know as soon as you're on the air, I said. I'm hatching a plan as we speak.

Kelly and Dwaine were suited up in record time and were on the air in 5 minutes.

Kelly was first, ok Wade we're on our way to the platform. What's your plan?

Well obviously, I said, we need a little extra time because you guys have to fuel up and then reload one ship with a net.

My ship is already loaded interrupted Kelly.

I forgot about that Kelly. That could be the break we needed. Here's what I had in mind.

We've got to get this under control before we leave our ring. We are taking up far too much area and there's no way we can navigate through the rings strung out like this even if we could manage to keep the spokes from getting tangled in our tow-line. We will most certainly hit other rocks on our way through and then we'll be liable for any damage it might cause. We just can't allow that to happen.

I can help bring them back together by a short burst from the stations rockets. The problem with that is that will slow us down even more so we will just get strung our again faster than before. What I'm thinking is that we can capture the Gem and tow it down to the maiden and attach it to the tow-line from the maiden. That way they can't spread apart again.

I think I see what you're driving at, interrupted Dwaine, but how do we attach to the tow-line without overloading it with the weight of both rocks?

I haven't worked that out yet, I said, I was thinking of somehow wrapping a net around both lines with the ends tied together so it was a big loop.

I don't think that will work very well Wade, added Kelly.

What do you see that I don't Kelly?

I don't think that will hold the lines together. We need some way to keep the net in place otherwise it will just slip along the towline.

I was thinking the same thing, injected Dwaine, and I think I have an idea. What if we connected one end of a net to the outer ring at the end of each towline. That net would be like a tie strap between them so they couldn't spread further apart and still allow each towline to carry its own load.

Great idea Dwaine, I said, I'm going to have to do a burn in the next five minutes. How soon can you guys be ready?

We're just finishing with the fuel tanks, said Kelly, We can launch now because I don't think we should load Dwaine's net. I like Dwaine's idea about the tie strap but I think we should change our plan a bit. I can launch with my ship and net and Dwaine can attach only one end of his net to his ship and launch with his net dragging behind him. That way it will be already stretched and ready for one end to be attached to the tow-line ring for the maiden.

The maiden, I said, I thought it would be easier to tow the Gem down to it because it's so much lighter.

That was my first thought too, said Kelly, but I have another idea. If we hook onto the maiden first and them tow it up to the Gem that will give us more time in our ring to get everything under control. As a matter of fact, Dwaine might be able to give it a pull and increase our speed a bit so we aren't degrading so fast. That would save you a little fuel on the station because you wouldn't need to do a burn.

I don't know Kelly, I said, the Gems tow-line is getting really close to the station. How about if you go after the Gem at the same time? You could capture it and pull it down to meet Dwaine. That will pull the Gem away from the station and if we do this quick then I won't have to slow us down. I think it's worth the risk to save our fuel but I'll be ready in case you don't get there in time Kelly

I'm launching now Wade. Is that the final plan?

Yes, as soon as either of you get hooked up pull your rocks away from the station but don't release them until they are connected together.

Kelly was hooked on first because she didn't have to go out to hook onto the ring. Dwaine had to jet pack out to the end of his net to put the clevis into the ring on the maidens line. Kelly was almost to the mid-point between them when Dwaine got back into his ship.

Wait there for me Kelly, Dwaine said. I'll be there soon.

Dwaine took up the slack with his retro rockets and then did a thirty second burn to pull it up to meet Kelly. I could feel his pull on the station but the maiden didn't want to move.

Kelly, Dwaine said, I think I'm going to need some help down here. Why don't you bring your line down to me and I'll hook us together?

I'm on my way, Kelly said. Do you dare leave your ship while you're tied to that rock?

I don't think I have any choice, I'm in the best position to do it.

Ok, Dwaine, Kelly continued, but I think you'll have to release your net so I can get in close enough without hitting your ship.

Yea, I never thought of that, answered Dwaine. You can always pick me up and bring me back to my ship if it drifts too far.

You can count on that Dwaine! I'll come in slow and give you some slack to work with.

You guys are making me nervous, I said, don't take any unnecessary chances out there.

No worries, Dwaine said, we've got this under control. Bring it in a little more Kelly. Good, good I've got it, he shouted, the pin is in!

Great work you two, I said, now all you have to do is pull them both out in front and we're home free.

I had used the Retros to swing the station enough to keep the maidens line away from the Spoke as soon as Kelly had pulled the Gem away. Dwaine got back in his ship and moved it down to the ring on the maidens tow-line. He hooked into the ring with his towing clasp and they both fired a full one minute burn. The tie strap worked like a charm and they pulled both rocks out ahead of us as well as giving the station a little more speed. We now had enough speed to stay in our ring until we came up with a decent plan for a controlled descent to get us onto the Mars Orbital Plain.

Kelly recovered her net and both she and Dwaine had everything secured and were back in operations within an hour.

Chapter 11

Kelly and Dwaine came in together and the celebration started immediately. We hugged and danced around and then Kelly kissed Dwaine with so much passion that I felt the heat from it two feet away. I have to say that I was starting to feel like a third wheel when she turned around and did it to me. I was out of breath and my heart sounded like a drum in my chest when she let me go. She wrapped an arm around each of us and said with the most sultry voice I have ever heard.

Boys, I think we should celebrate. Your place or mine?

I hated myself for saying it but I said it anyway. I absolutely hate to be a wet blanket but someone has to stay and watch the scanners and it's still Kelly's shift.

That settles it, Kelly said. It'll have to be my place. Those two rocks out there are definitely going to make this my last term out in the rings and I have really enjoyed being with both of you. To be truthful, I have dreamed about the three of us together. If either of you object to this please stop me now before I make a bigger fool of myself.

I'd be lying if I said I hadn't thought about it a time or two, admitted Dwaine.

I admit that I'm already warmed up to the idea, I said, but someone still has to stay with the scanners.

Good, Kelly said, I told you I had dreamed about this and here's how I made it happen. We had a double bed right here in the middle of the floor and we were having the time of our lives. I can hardly wait to feel both of you inside me at the same time. I hope you boys aren't tired because I've got big plans for tonight.

Well Kelly, I said, I'm literally up for this if you know what I mean. How about you Dwaine?

I'm way past warmed up. You're the primary on this Kelly, what do you need us to do?

I'll set the scanners on automatic and the alarms at maximum and then I'm going to go freshen up a bit as soon as you guys get back with your mattresses. By the time you get the beds made up I'll be out of the shower so why don't you take turns doing the same. I promise we won't start without either of you but please don't be too long. I'll tell you what; I'll wait in my room and you give me a call when you're both back here. I love to make an entrance and I want you both together when you see me in my new outfit. This is going to be so much fuun!!

I don't need to tell you that we didn't waste any time taking our showers. I decided that there was no need to dress for the occasion so all I wore was my housecoat tied loose so there was a slit showing up the front. Dwaine was a little more formal. He wore his best polka dot boxer shorts. Dwaine knocked on Kelly's door on the way past and there we were standing at the head of the bed as eager as any stud ever has been when the door started to open.

Our jaws dropped when she came into the room. We had both seen her body before but not looking like this. She was wearing a two-piece black leather outfit made from thin leather straps loosely woven together. The straps were about ½ inch wide and gave the look of an animal harness rather than a covering. The bottom piece was highlighted by two black straps that curled up over her gleaming thighs and then merged into a heart in the front that encased her pubic mound. The top was a halter affair but it wasn't designed for support, she didn't need any. It was the contrast between those thin black straps and her firm smooth skin that made it almost impossible to take your eyes away from her. She stopped at the bottom of the bed with her legs spread slightly apart to give us the full effect of those black straps against her glistening skin. And those nipples!! I thought they were enticing before. I swear they were screaming "kiss me" as she very slowly and deliberately walked toward us. We never moved a muscle until she stopped between us. She didn't say a word. She just reached out and gently wrapped her fingers around our rigid love handles and pulled us down onto the bed with her.

I'm sorry to admit that I played out first. I had worked my full shift and half of Kelly's so even though my mind was willing my body just wanted to sleep. It wasn't that I didn't thoroughly enjoy myself, I did, it's just that I was completely satisfied and I couldn't help myself. I just went to sleep.

Kelly woke me up before she and Dwaine crashed and we did the short shift cycles again. Kelly relieved me after four hrs. and Dwaine relieved her with a full eight hrs. sleep under his belt. I didn't see Kelly again until she came to relieve me from my first full shift. We hadn't talked when she came in after only four hrs. sleep. We just hugged and I gave her a quick kiss goodnight.

We were both rested now and things were a bit awkward at first. After a brief hug, Kelly backed away a step and studied my face as she said.

I hope I didn't push you into doing something you weren't comfortable with the other day. I'm afraid I just got caught up in the excitement and I let my hair down. I hope I didn't go too far. I would hate to lose you as a friend.

First, I said, let me assure you that I thoroughly enjoyed myself and you definitely haven't lost me as a friend. Here's how I've sorted it out in my mind. It was neither an orgy nor a "ménage a trios" in the normal sense. It was an act of love from one woman to two men and from two men to one woman where love was the driving force rather than raw passion. It is a memory I will cherish for the rest of my life.

Oh, I'm so pleased, whispered Kelly in my ear as she gave me a bear hug. I wouldn't have been able to put it into such beautiful words but that's exactly the way I feel. I was afraid you would either resent me for being so forward or expect a repeat performance. You realize that was a onetime event don't you.

Yes, I said, I don't see how we could function as a crew again if we don't go back to our normal routine. But don't think that will keep me from thinking about our next time together. That's one of the things that gets me through the boring shifts.

On that though, Kelly said in her new sultry voice, I'm hope you'll be there when I get off shift. You left the party a little early the other day and I was hoping to make it up to you.

I can't think of anything I would like better, I said as I planted a juicy one firmly on her lips and said goodnight.

I had a quick lunch and a short nap and I was up and showered with a steak in the pan when Kelly came in after her shift. Kelly showered while the steak was cooking and we had a good meal together. We sat and talked about nothing in particular for a while to let the meal settle and then Kelly took me by the hand and led me into her bedroom. Our lovemaking was very passionate with a lot of petting, cuddling and heartfelt sex and I was completely satisfied when we were finished.

Life is good.

Chapter 12

When I relieved Dwaine in the morning I asked him to come back with Kelly when she came to relieve me so we could plan our trip home.

One of the first things I did when I started my shift was to send a secure message to head office to tell them about our load and to ask for a supply ship to meet us as soon as we dropped down to intersect the Mars Plain. I emphasised that we were heavier than we had ever been and that we did not have enough fuel to transit into an orbit around Mars. I didn't tell them that I wasn't even sure how we were going to get down to the Mars Orbital Plain. There was a 25 minute delay to converse with head office from this far out and they are sometimes quite slow to respond. I received a request for a confirmation of the weight and composition of our rocks just before Dwaine and Kelly came in.

Hi guys, I said, head office doesn't believe me. They asked me to confirm our cargo again and that we're coming home early. That's never happened before.

I hope you used a secure channel, Kelly asked, I would hate to have the whole world know about our Gem. Not to worry Kelly. I used the private channel. What we really need to do is make a plan to get us down to the Mars Plain. I'm really worried about our fuel supply. This is the biggest load I have ever tried to handle and maybe the biggest to have ever been brought in with a Spoke. Even the Arcs would have trouble handling this load.

Maybe they should come out to meet us suggested Dwaine

I've asked for a supply ship to meet us when we get to the Plain but they won't have time to get to us before then. By my calculations we are degrading faster all the time because of our weight and like it or not we are on our way down now. The best we can do is control the fall and try to avoid hitting anything valuable. Any suggestions?

I'm worried, said Dwaine, I think there's a real danger that we could come in too fast and shoot right through the Mars Plain. If we get too close to Earth they'll confiscate our rocks and we'll be left with nothing.

That's what been gnawing at me too, I said, I've plotted our flight path through the rings and everything looks good except ring 2. It might give us some trouble. I don't know how fast we will be coming in exactly so we may have to do a burn to slow us down so we can get a clear track across it. The other thing to consider it that we will be looping through the end of our orbit soon and I'm not sure how many rings we will cross. With our weight we might swing out further than usual and then come back in with a fury. It could get really hairy because a lot of other rocks will be doing the same thing.

Kelly piped up, I just thought of something. When we start to loop, our load is actually going to be pulling us out with it. That means that we will be like a ball on a string. Because we are a lot lighter than the load, the sun's gravity will pull us around so we are in front of it and that will in effect swing us around without us having to use any of our fuel. If we do a burn right then, we can pull the rocks out of the long loop they were starting and at the same time add enough speed to keep us from crashing down through the rings. If we do it right we may never leave our ring.

That's an awesome idea Kelly, I said, but what do we do then?

Give me a minute, Kelly said, I'm thinking. Will we reach Mars before we swing back around the other end?

No, I don't think so, I said, If we stay in our ring we'll have to wait until we come back to this side before we line up.

Ok, this might work, said Kelly, It might take us a few days longer to get home but we can do it with the fuel we have on board. We'll have lots of time to set this up so we'll be in the right place at the right time. We may have to do a couple of short burns to hold us up here until we're ready but that shouldn't be a problem. It's still a lot less fuel than swinging us around or trying to control a free fall through the rings.

I'm not quite with you yet Kelly, said Dwaine, How is this going to work again?

Ok Dwaine, here it is in a nutshell. We let the sun's gravity swing us around so we can use our rockets to limit the loop at the end and increase our speed at the same time to stop our free fall through the other rings. Think of it like a race car powering out of a corner. After we power out of the loop we will still be out in front of the rocks so we can hold our speed with a couple of short burns to keep us in our ring. With the added time to position ourselves as we are coming down the backside we can swing around with our retro rockets so the rocks are pulling us again. This time we can use the rockets to slow us down enough so that we do a controlled fall down onto the Mars Plain just after the Suns Gravity has slowed us down but before we start to loop through the other rings. We can time it so we pass through them when there is a much clearer path because they won't have started to loop yet.

I've done the math Kelly, I said, we should have enough fuel but that's going to leave us almost empty and helpless with Mars barreling toward us.

Yea, answered Kelly, but didn't you say that we had a supply ship waiting for us.

Well not waiting exactly, I said, but they can be if you are right about this. This sounds like it might work. Any other comments?

It would sure be nice if they could bring us some fuel while we were coming down the flip side said Dwaine

That's a good idea Dwaine. I said, I'll ask them about it but you know how head office can be. If they think they can save a dollar then that's what they will do. Most of those guys have never been out here and have no idea what it takes to bring these babies in. All they see are numbers in a ledger. There's a major fuel saving between waiting patiently for us to come to them than powering off from Mars orbit and trying to catch up to us out here. I would rather drop in behind them and let them come back to us but that might not be an option.

Ok, I said, we have a plan, let's put it into action. This is your shift and your plan Kelly so I guess you're the primary on this. How do you want to handle it?

Well, I think timing is the most critical part so I would like some back-up. Dwaine is the freshest because he's had a nap while he was waiting for me to get up. To be honest I would be more comfortable if we were all here for this part.

Thanks Kelly, I said, I wouldn't want to miss out of this. How about if both Dwaine and I do the calculations and compare our findings before we do anything?

Awesome Wade, I love it. Ok you two, how much time do we have before we start the loop?

Chapter 13

Things couldn't have worked better. We were right to assume that we would loop out further than usual and that worked in our favor. The station swung around under the rocks almost as quick and a lot smoother than if we had used our retro rockets. It took a two minute burn to pull us out of the loop and up to speed so we didn't drop down into the next ring. We may have brushed Ring 11 for a minute or two but most of the time we were entirely in our own ring. We settled down to our usual routine while we traveled down the back side of our orbit around the sun.

We would be six weeks instead of four getting home this way but we had saved enough fuel to get us down onto the Mars Plain. There wasn't much to do but someone had to stay with the monitors just in case. It wasn't unknown for a rock to come out of nowhere out here and it was even more likely since the collisions in the outer rings. We passed the time by flagging and inventorying any rock that looked interesting but our main job was just avoiding a collision.

I filled my spare time by finishing my reading of the history of the renowned terraced Mars Habitant and its manufacturing facilities. Like everything else in life they didn't start out as impressive as they finished. They evolved over time from trial and error and the innovation of some very insightful people.

The first inhabitants on Mars were housed in inflatable domes placed on the floor of the Galle Crater. They were supposed to shield the astronauts from the solar radiation and give them shelter from the elements. They were very basic and better than nothing but just barely. There was a major investigation the first time an incoming asteroid punched through a dome during a Perseid meteor shower. A fist-sized rock ripped a hole too big to repair in the top of the dome and killed the four guys inside. The crash investigation panel determined that pitching a tent in the middle of a pock marked field from previous asteroid strikes may not have been the best approach. The habitant designers and the project manager came under harsh criticism because it was felt that they should have known that a tragic accident was inevitable.

The next plan was to bury the habitants under three feet of surface soil. This did harden them up some and protected against the small pebbles. After the next meteorite storm it was obvious that they wouldn't stand up to any kind of a real rock so the decision was made to use them only until they had tunneled into the side of the crater. The first tunnels had 200 feet of solid rock above them and would have been considered bomb proof on Earth. Tunneling was very expensive and time consuming but it was the only thing that would stand up to all but the biggest rocks and they were a one in a million year event. They didn't really have a choice because the crash panel passed a law that prohibited human occupation in the open after the fatal accident in the dome. They only had one Mars year (697 earth days) to move everybody inside the tunnels or off the planet into orbit.

They had a small tunnel finished in time and everybody was moved to safety inside. This was the beginning of the development of Mars. After the construction crews were housed in the safety of the tunnels, their first job was to build an airlock and seal the tunnel walls so it could be pressurized. They could now relax and socialize in comfort and safety so they immediately set about building more tunnels to house the expanding population.

Behind every habitant was a water reservoir that was required to hold at least a one month supply for that unit. Every unit also had its own water recycler, carbon dioxide filter and fuel cell. The main life support machinery normally performed these functions for the entire complex but each unit was required to have a back-up system that could take over in the event of a machine failure or loss of power from the fusion power plant. These rules still apply today even though they haven't had a serious incident in fifty years. Every unit is still self-contained and could survive for at least a month even if all outside help was cut off.

It wasn't long before they had a map of any rock in the vicinity that was even remotely likely to find its way to the Mars surface and these were the first to be captured and placed in a stable orbit even before the steel mills were built.

Living on Mars turned out to be easier than expected because there was enough gravity to keep the muscles and joints healthy. The first construction crews were rotated back to Earth every three months and after a week or so of physiotherapy they were able to readjust to Earth's gravity. It was the air quality on Earth that gave them the most problems. They were used to the oxygen rich filtered air from the life support systems and soon played out if they were doing anything physically stressful on Earth. Martians could never compete in the Olympics on Earth any more than Earthers could in the Mars Games. The lower gravity on Mars takes a lot of getting used and unless you were born there and grew up with it, your timing and balance instincts will be all wrong.

The first factories were built close to the habitants for convenience and ease of access. As the number of industrial compounds increased the human inhabitants found themselves sandwiched between noisy and dusty neighbours. It became obvious that they needed their own compound removed from the noise and dust coming from the factories. It also became obvious that they were going to need a lot more living quarters because the number of industries was steadily increasing and they all needed personnel to run them. Robots can only do so much and they have to be maintained.

The floor of the crater is 10 miles across with 200 foot walls that are at a 60 degree angle so they are stable. It was decided to divide the crater in thirds with two thirds of the wall designated as industrial space and the rest living quarters.

The factories needed more headroom than the habitants so a lot more rock had to be removed and piled off to the side. Unfortunately there were no useable minerals in this crust rock so it all had to be cast aside.

One day one of the steel company engineers had an idea. Their waste rock pile now reached half way to the surface and was taking up a lot of valuable floor space. He designed a support for a shallow arched roof that would allow them to use the floor space at the bottom of the pile.

The arch design had been used since the time of the Romans for building bridges and as supports over entrances and windows. It was just a matter of designing a single span bridge that was strong enough to carry the weight of the waste rock above it. The height and length of the pillars for the arch ends combined with the length of the arch determined the area of the working space under the arched roof. The pillars were resting on the undisturbed crust rock and were wide enough at the base so that they would carry an extreme weight. The strength of the roof was the biggest hurdle to overcome. They found an old design that had been used to build long span bridges over small streams on logging and construction roads that with very little modifications fitted the purpose perfectly.

Steller Steel hadn't been invented yet so they were still making carbon steel ingots at the factories. The red-hot ingots would be shaped into all manner of commercial products or rolled into plates of different thickness. The computer modeling revealed that several thicknesses of the thinner corrugated plates was stronger than one thick plate. It turned out that 4 plates of arched ¼ inch corrugated mild steel properly installed had the same strength as one flat 3 inch plate with 1/3 of the amount of steel used and they were 1/3 lighter as well. As an added bonus the arched design did not need any support posts so the entire area under the span was usable space.

What the hell is that? Oh, it's just another sandstorm. Sandstorms in space are really the dust trail left behind from a comet that has passed through our solar system. The heat of the sun melts the ice and that releases the sand it has collected on its travel through interstellar space. There are so many that a lot of them are not named. We don't chart them because we are so well protected that they don't pose a threat to us. It still gives you a bit of a scare when you come into one unexpectedly. They sound like heavy raindrops hitting a tin roof on a shed on earth. More of a clatter than a pitter patter.

Ok, where was I? The key to this turned out to be the design of the pillars as well as the precision cutting of the plates. The plates for each layer were cut at a different length because the plates were laid on top of each other and they were in an arch. That meant that each layer from the bottom up had to be a little longer than the one below it. The ends had to be flush when they were fitted into the pillar support bracket to preserve the strength of the arch.

The cost saving was twofold. The canopies provided thousands of cubic feet of protected work-space much cheaper than blasting it out the crust rock. It also provided a place to dispose of the rock that did have to be blasted out to create the extra space needed. Otherwise the waste rock would have had to be taken out of the crater and stored on the surface or piled up against the wall and that would have taken up some very valuable space on the crater floor. Piling it on top of the canopy provided a thick protective cover over the entranceway and was far cheaper than taking it up over the rim.

The best approach was to build the canopy up against the face of the wall. Most factories required at least a 50 foot ceiling so the support pillars were 50 feet high as well as 50 feet long. This made a great entranceway for the cavern that was to be built behind it. The cavern would then be built as far back as needed and could easily be extended off to the sides as well. The canopy was covered with the waste rock from excavating the carven. Any suitability waste rock was also used for making concrete for the pillars.

The pillars had to set back far enough into the rock face so that the roof plates could butt up against solid rock under a three foot overhang. They were made of steel reinforced concrete and were a minimum of three times wider at the bottom than the top. The leftover crushed rock from the metal processing plant was added to the crust rock to make concrete and they also used the water obtained from the water rich asteroids.

Water was also available from the polar ice caps but it was only used in an emergency. This is the planetary reserve in the event something happens to the water reservoirs at the settlement. Water is essential for the life support system so using it for construction was dangerous and short-sighted because of the very limited amount available. They used up over 10% of the southern ice cap before they became self-sufficient with the water and minerals captured from the water/iron rocks in the close vicinity of Mars. They brought the rocks into a synchronous orbit 300 miles out where they were kept until they had been processed. As soon as they had the distillation plants built on the surface the rocks were dissected into manageable pieces and special rocket powered sleds are used to bring the pieces down to the surface. They keep two small mountains of these chunks on the surface at all times. One pile of ore is being processed while the other is being replenished from orbit.

The days just seemed to roll by because nothing important was happening and one day was basically the same as the next.

Good morning, Kelly said, anything interesting happen while I was gone?

Not much, I answered, I flagged a couple of iceballs earlier but other than that I've been reading.

Am I going to see you tonight when I get off shift, she asked as she gave me a long hard hug.

That sounds good to me, I said, I've got a lot more energy now that we're not out chasing rocks. I'll see you in 8 hours, I said as I kissed her good-bye.

Both Dwaine and I had always left it to Kelly to initiate any sexual activity. That was especially important now because we were definitely feeling our oats so to speak because we were bored and well rested and it would have been really easy for Kelly to grow to resent us if we asked too much of her. I have to add that we have not suffered at all under this arrangement. Kelly has been very sensitive to our needs right from the start. Some of the other crews use a "my night-your night" type of arrangement but I have to say I much prefer this one. The down side to our version is that we have become very close because of our arrangement. I have to admit that I feel a lot of affection toward Kelly especially since our celebration. It would be awful easy to fall in love with her and that would cause no end of problems when I get home. Virginia is already a bit jealous of Kelly and if she gets even a hint that this has turned into more than a business arrangement then we would be through and I don't want that to happen. At least I don't think I do. Is it possible to love two women at the same time?

Kelly was as affectionate as ever and our lovemaking was quite intense last night. I always have a great sleep after an encounter with Kelly but I need to get my mind back to the business at hand.

Chapter 14

We are over half way home so it's time to start thinking of our drop down onto the Mars Plain. We will be starting to swing out into the loop by my shift tomorrow so I need to start mapping our route through the other rings down onto the Plain. Our ring looks clear and there hasn't been much activity in the other rings as far as we can see. The problem is that we are traveling progressively faster than the rocks in the other rings because of the speed we have to maintain to stay out this far. Other than that we would be in a free fall into the sun and god help anything that got in our way.

The good news is that the lower rings are already well mapped so all I have to do is calculate where we will be and then see if anything else is going to be there at the same time. Then I have to broadcast our intended course through the other rings so the owners will know we are coming. It sounds easy and the computer does most of the calculating but we still have to be on the lookout for a rogue rock. For an operation like this we have the scanners on full resolution and maximum range. We still don't have direct line of sight contact with head office because we haven't caught up to Mars yet as it is still on the opposite side of the sun from us. It would be nice to have an up to date map of the rocks in the lower rings.

I guess now is as good a time to start as any. Good, good, no warning bells or flashing icons. Humm!! What's that on the edge of the upper right quadrant? It must be a rock coming down from one of the outer rings. It's big but it doesn't act a rock. A rock that big should be falling but this one is holding its position. No wait, the computer has picked it up now and it looks like it's going to intersect our course in about an hour. I think it might be under power. It sure moves like it. I'm going to put out a general hail just in case.

Damm it looks like it speeded up again. It's going to be right on top of us in 30 minutes. I had better turn on our locating beacon and send out another hail.

What the hell was that? They just fired a laser blast at our Gem. Holy shit, these guys are after our rock. I sounded the general alarm just as they fired another laser blast but this time it was aimed at the towline rather than the Gem. That first shot must have been to confirm the compensation of the Gem.

Dwaine came barging in first with Kelly only a minute behind him. Dwaine had gotten up to go to the bathroom so he had a head start on Kelly who woke out of a sound sleep. Your adrenalin kicks in immediately when a general alarm sounds and they were both wide awake. I was just starting to explain when the phantom ship took another shot at the towline. Kelly was the first to understand what was happening and she just screamed.

They're pirates. Those bastards are trying to steal our Gem.

The next shot was at our mainline. I guess they decided the Gems towline was too hard to hit.

They can't do that, yelled Dwaine, we've got them tagged. What do they think they're doing?

Dwaine! Kelly said with great exasperation, pirates don't give a damm about tags. They'll just cut them out and put their own on in place of ours.

I had started to jog the Retros to keep the lines moving so they would be harder to hit. It suddenly occurred to me that if they didn't have any luck hitting the towlines, they might start shooting at us so I barked an order at the other two.

Get into your suits. If they start shooting at us and pierce our hull then someone has to be able to take over for me.

I was jogging the lines back and forth because I didn't want to get too far out of position for the burn down to the Mars Plain. If we could hold them off until then we would have a direct line to head office and we could call for help. This is probably why they had decided not to wait any longer to act. They had to at least cut the rocks free before we were scanned by the Mars Approach Monitors. Even if they weren't able to get the tags off before we were scanned they could always claim that we had lost our rocks on the descent and they had salvaged them. That might not stand up in a court of law but possession is nine tenths of the law and they would have a strong case for at least splitting the proceeds from the sale of the rocks. The closer we got to our burn window, the more desperate they would get. Dwaine was back first so I put him on our lasers in the chance he could get a shot at them. Our ships are pretty tough because of the Steller Steel but our rockets are our Achilles Heel. All they had to do was get a good shot at them and we would be dead in the water and they could do what they wanted with our load.

Kelly wasn't far behind Dwaine and she manned the radio. She was just starting to broadcast a mayday when we heard a laser beam bounce off the outside of the pod and the radio went dead.

Things were getting really serious now because it looked like they were going to take us out of the picture first and then deal with the rocks later. Kelly pointed at the screen and bellowed so loud it hurt my ears.

Holy crap, there's two of them. We're screwed!

She was right, there was another ship coming up on us really fast and they were dead on course to join the fight. All we could was watch the monitor. The first pirate ship had even stopped firing at us but I was still jogging the Retro's as hard as I could. The second ship did a power burn to slow to our speed and let loose with a long laser burst. I can't believe it, I said, he missed.

No, he didn't shouted Kelly, take a look.

There were a few fiery spurts coming from the first pirate ship where his rockets should have been. Our headphones crackled and a voice came over our ships communication system.

Are you guys all right over there?

Wow, I said, are we ever glad to see you. Who are you?

We're Sigme 2, he said, is anybody hurt?

No, we're fine Sigme 2, I said, what's going on here? You guys came out of nowhere with the laser blazing just in time.

Glad to hear nobody's hurt Wade, he said, we were a little late realizing what was happening otherwise we would have been here sooner.

Were you expecting trouble, I asked?

Yes, I'll tell you about it later, we have a few things to do here first.

I can't wait to hear, Sigme 2, we're in a bit of a hurry here as well. We have to get back into position. Our burn window is coming up fast. I guess we'll have to wait a bit longer for the story.

With that we started to get the ship in order for the burn. Kelly went out to check the antenna while Dwaine and I recalculated for the burn. Kelly came back with the antenna in her hand so we were all safely back in operations when we started our burn.

We had been watching Sigme 2 on the monitors. They launched a netship and it went out and attached a towline to the pirate ship. There wasn't anything they could do about it because even their Retros had been burned off by the laser blast from Sigme 2.

Thing went really well with our burn and we glided down onto the Mars Plain about two days in front of the planet. Sigme 2 slid in behind us about 4 hours later with the pirate ship firmly in tow.

We were already transferring fuel from the supply ship that was right where it was supposed to be. A good thing too because there's no way we could have made the transit to a Mars Orbit with the fuel we had left. They had brought 10 auxiliary tanks with them and we were half way through transferring the fuel into our tanks when Sigme 2 came down.

Chapter 15

Dwaine and I were suited up and Dwaine was pumping the fuel into our tanks while I ferried the tanks back and forth. We had left Kelly on duty in operations to watch the monitors so Juan was able to venture out of his ship to give us a hand. We were still using our internal communication system because the main antenna wasn't fixable. Juan had relayed our report to head office and we were focused on transferring the fuel when our headsets came alive.

It looks like you guys came through ok, is there anything we can do to help?

Well, if it isn't our knights in shining armor, I answered, we're good here now, how about you and who are you? What took you so long? I was starting to get worried.

I'm Wes Hammond and my crew and I didn't just happen to be in the area. We were send out to escort you in. I'm sorry we were so long coming down but we had to secure the pirates inside their ship so they couldn't go anywhere before we turn them over to the authorities.

I hadn't even thought about that, I said, I guess I was only thinking of our own worries. How did you manage to do that?

We used a net and wrapped it around the entire docking port. They're not launching any ships or even going out for a spacewalk until we get to port. Listen Wade, I've got to report to head office and radio the Mars Spaceport Authority.

I think they're going to want to have a long talk with our pirate friends. We'll talk as soon as that's done.

Ok guys, I'm back Wes announced in our ears. Do you need any help with that fuel?

No, I said, we're almost done but we are dying of curiosity. Why don't you tell what's going on while we finish up here?

Ok answered Wes but I don't know where to start.

We haven't heard a word since I verified our load to head office so tell us how you got involved I suggested.

Ok, Wes answered but maybe I had better explain the reason for the radio silence. Shortly after head office got your call and the spectrographic analysis of the Gem, head office loved that name by the way, they found a bug planted in the floor under Mr. Fredericks desk. They couldn't trace it but they knew that someone else knew what you had and where you were going to be. Your dad didn't want to tip his hand until he knew who was listening so head office played it the same as normal. They made a big time about the expense of sending a ship out to meet you with fuel for the benefit of our listeners and went ahead with the plan to meet you with a supply ship. They even sent the supply ship out a little ahead of time to make it look good.

In the meantime, they readied Sigme 2 for an early launch to take your place out in the ring. They also made a big time about the expense of the extra crew time because of your early arrival. What they didn't say anywhere close to the office was that Sigme 2 was loaded for bear instead of mining. There had already been reports of a pirate ship stealing rocks that had been tagged and changing the tags to their own. Some of the rocks at the auction had some suspicious marks on them but nothing could be proven. If these guys knew about your Gem them they would almost certainly try to steal it.

Sigme 2 launched while we were sling shooting out of the first loop and instead of taking a casual fuel saving path out to Ring 10, they did a power burn that not only took them out to a low tract in Ring 11 but it put them behind us as well. They had planned on bringing us the fuel we had asked for and escorting us in but then they spotted the pirate ship dogging us. Sigme 2 recently had the newest sensor package installed so they could hang back just out of the pirates sensor range and wait to see what would happen.

They were a little slow to realize that the pirates were making their move so they had to come in at full speed or it would have been too late. That laser blast that burned the rockets off the pirate ship came from the newest enhanced model that had been quietly installed in port. They had actually scrounged it off a Port Authority patrol ship. It could even penetrate the hull of a Steller Steel ship if it were focused in one spot more than 30 seconds.

Ok Wes, I butted in, I'm still having problems with the company sending both a supply ship and a guardian. Do you have any idea why they would spend that kind of money?

I really don't know where to start, said Wes incredulously, how much do you guys know about the metal markets in the last month?

We haven't heard a thing Wes, Kelly chimed in, what's happening? Did they crash or something?

No, they didn't crash, Wes said, the price of Iridium has tripled and iron has doubled as well.

What's going on, I blurted, how the hell did that happen?

All three of us listened in silence as Wes filled us in.

To start with, the Interplanetary Council has extended the ring system to include the Kuiper Belt all the way out to the end of the solar system. They have created a sector system that divides each ring out past Pluto into four sectors that are defined by the Solar Locating Beacons around the sun. The side boundaries of each claim is marked by a pie shaped wedge radiating out from any two Locating Beacons. The rings are now 200,000 miles wide out beyond the orbit of Pluto and any rock that moves into the next sector is fair game, flagged or not. The only exception is if they are being towed.

Holy shit, I said, that's going to change everything.

Right! And it already has, interrupted Wes. The change that's most important to you three is the price. The mining companies have had to rethink how they mine because the Kuiper Belt is so far out and they must now secure their rocks inside their own sector. They are now talking about robotic ships that tow the rocks in as soon as they are captured. Mining stations will still be necessary inside of Pluto but they have dropped the requirement to maintain a physical presence in the Kuiper Belt so robotic harvesters are by far the best way to go.

Alright, alright, we've got the picture, Kelly said as she joined in. We're a dying breed, but what's that got to do with the price increases?

Boy, you guys sure know how to ruin a good story, whined Wes. Ok, here it is.

Robotic spacecraft manufacturing plants sprang up almost overnight. The steel companies have more orders for Steller Steel that they can fill in five years so the bidding at the auctions has been ridiculous. The smaller steel companies had no choice. If they couldn't get a source of Iridium then they couldn't make Steller Steel and they wanted a piece of the action really bad. For the most part the bigger companies just kept bidding until the small guys ran out of money. In desperation the smaller companies have started buying directly from the miners based on the prices at the auctions. Now comes the good part. Because of our contract with Stellar Steel and the bonus for selling to them, the Gem as you call it is worth more than last years entire production of steel. That depends of course on the verifying of your spectrographic analysis that you sent in.

Holy shit, piped in Kelly, you're being straight with us aren't you Wes? This sounds too good to be true.

It's real Kelly and it gets even better if you can believe it. That iron rock has also doubled in value because they need the iron as well. You guys are going to have more money than you can spend in a lifetime.

There was dead silence for what seemed like an hour as we tried to absorb his news. Finally Wes said, are you guys still there?

Yea, we're here Wes, I said, that's a lot for us to digest all at once so we're going to need some time to get used to it. Wow, why didn't head office tell us about all that..

I don't know for sure, answered Wes, but I bet it had a lot to do with the fact that they thought our communication were being monitored. We've been on radio silence since we left the port.

Ok, I said, let's not count our chickens before they're hatched. We've got to get these babies in orbit first and then we can start planning how we are going to spend the money. Are you going to follow us in Wes?

Yes as far as the Port Authority Patrol Station. I've got to drop our friends off there for a long visit.

Ok, don't forget that you'll be our voice until we get there. They'll be able to talk to us directly once we're inside the Spaceports boundaries.

Dwaine and I had finished our refueling operation and were back in operations with Kelly by the time Wes finished his story.

We just stood in the middle of the room and hugged each other. We hugged and talked and hugged some more. It was the start of Dwaine's shift before we could even think about sleeping. Dwaine offered to cook us all a meal so Kelly and I stayed in operations while he cooked. I was glad for that because I wanted to talk to Kelly alone.

Chapter 16

I walked over to her and took her in my arms. She was a little surprised but them she melted into me and we just hugged for a full minute. She pulled away from me a little and opened her mouth to say something. I stopped her with a gentle kiss and then said.

I think we had better say good-bye now because it's going to be pretty hectic tomorrow. I'm sure Virginia will be there to meet me and I don't want her to see how close we've become. I wanted the chance to tell you that I have become very fond of you and I know that I'll miss you a lot. Shush: let me finish. I'm not just talking about our time together, which was fabulous, I'm going to miss having you around to talk to and I've really enjoyed working with you. I wanted to say that to you so you don't misunderstand what I have to say next. I'm going to have to shut you out of my life if there is any chance for Virginia and I to build a relationship that brings us as close together as we have become. I hope you understand.

Kelly spoke softly and looked me straight in the eye as she said, the last thing I want to do is to come between you and Virginia. I know that you were deeply in love with her when you left for this term. I also know that you've been apart for four months and that will take a toll on any relationship.

Dwaine came in while we were still in our loose embrace and immediately turned to leave. Kelly stopped him and asked him to come back in.

I want you both to hear this, she said as she reached out to Dwaine so that he could take one of her hands and said.

You both know that this is my third term and that I've done this so I can build a nest egg big enough to allow me to start my own company. I was hoping that this would be my last term but I was willing to do one more if need be. What you don't know was that my first two terms were not what I had expected. I don't know which was the hardest, the first or the second. On the first term the guys were very competitive and in the end quite demanding. They were actually keeping score to be sure that one didn't get more than the other. At one point they almost had a fight over whose turn it was. Don't get me wrong I was treated as an equal as far as work was concerned, but it was a very uncomfortable situation to be in. On the second, they treated me more like a love slave than a co-worker. They didn't abuse me or make obscene demands but whenever they felt the urge they expected me to accommodate them. It didn't matter if I was tired or what I felt like. When we were on the job they didn't ask for my input and always took the more responsible jobs on themselves. They obviously felt that I was just there to help with the work and that my primary job was to provide for their needs. I don't know which is worse, being appreciated too much or not being accepted as an equal.

I don't know what the future holds for me because I never imagined having this much money. What I do know is that by the time we were half way through this term, I knew it would be my last one. That's why I was so hot to grab both of these rocks. I knew that I couldn't go back to the way it was with them.

The two of you treated me like an equal right from the start. I admit that I was a little confused when neither of you made any advances toward me. I thought that I had done something to offend you so I was pleased when you each responded to my advances. I soon figured out that you both were going to leave it to me to be the initiator. I can't tell you how much I appreciated that. It made our time together much more meaningful and pleasurable for me.

Me too, I said.

Schuus! Kelly said while putting her finger over my mouth, it's my turn to speak.

I have become so close to both of you that I really don't know how I'm going to be able to stand being apart. You are different to be with but it is wonderful with each of you. In all honesty I don't think I would be able to choose between you.

No, let me finish, she said, as Dwaine started to speak.

I know that we all have our own lives to lead and that we have to move on but I want both of you to know that this term will always be a highlight of my life.

Can I talk now, interjected Dwaine?

Go ahead, Kelly said as she gave him a hug.

I have been toying with an idea and now might be the only time we get to talk together in private. As you know I am a dedicated rock herder and in the back of my mind I have always liked the idea of having my own company. This bonus money might make that possible. Would you guys be interested in a partnership?

Not me, I said, I'm already a major shareholder in Sigme and I think I have had enough of space flight for a while. I'm really tired of being cooped up in a small space. Dad wouldn't like me telling you this Dwaine but I think you would make an excellent miner in your own right.

I expected that answer from you Wade, said Dwaine, that was my subtle way of asking Kelly if she would be my partner.

Me, Kelly said, I hadn't even thought about something like that. If I were going to be a partner with anyone I would certainly consider you Dwaine. I'm not saying no, I just need time to think about it. I like the idea of owning my own company but I'm not sure I want to go back out into the rings even as a boss.

I know, Dwaine said, that was what was holding me back as well as the lack of money. This bonus will take care of that problem and when Wes mentioned that we were now allowed to robot mine in the Kuiper Belt, I swear a light came on in my head. I admit I haven't thought it all the way through yet but it's something I would love to do with you Kelly.

Wow, Dwaine, that's an awesome idea, Kelly said, I'll have to give that some serious thought. When do you need my answer?

I don't think there's any big rush, answered Dwaine, there'll probably be a couple of months delay before they process our rocks anyway. The only thing that's really time sensitive is the staking of our claim. If we wait too long all the closest sectors will be taken and we'll be left way out in the outer rings or they might be all taken.

Maybe I can help with that, I said, I'll ask Dad to advance you enough to buy your claim. I don't know what they have in mind but maybe you can get one close to ours so you can work together if you need help. That's a long way out to be by yourselves.

Thanks Wade, answered Dwaine, do you think he will still be willing to do that if he knows we will be competing with Sigme?

I don't think that'll be a problem, I answered, there's more than enough to go around and I'll point out that without your able help we wouldn't have those beauties out there. Just say the word and I'll see what he says.

Thanks again, Wade but I think I should talk to Kelly about it before I go any further.

No problem, I said, just say the word. I think we're all going to want to be awake tomorrow when we get to Mars so how about we switch to 4 hr. shifts again.

I was tired and went directly to my room after we ate. Kelly woke Dwaine up and they had just relieved me as we were approaching the Mars Spaceport. Wes had handled all the approach notifications and had given them our internal radio frequency so that they could talk to us directly now that we were inside the Mars Approach Zone.

To our surprise all the paperwork had already been submitted by a Sigme attorney and we were cleared to pass right through to the Stellar Steel stockpile zone. Wes stayed behind and handed his charges over to the Port Authority. Even more surprising, we were met by a factory shuttle and they took the Gem off our hands for immediate processing. Wes hadn't been kidding when he said they were desperate for Iridium. We dropped the Iron Maiden off at the steel stockpile and docked at the Sigme spaceport.

Chapter 17

I think the entire office staff of Sigme had come up to meet us. Dad was the first in line to meet us as we came out of the docking port.

James Frederick is the CEO and Chairman of the Board of the Sigme Corporation. He is one of the success stories of the space industry community.

He had been a cattle rancher just outside of Calgary Canada when his wife Irene was killed in a car accident (they hadn't finished the automated road network yet and she was broadsided by a drunk driver one morning while she was on her way to town). James took her death really hard and when he heard about the construction boom on Mars, he sold off the stock and leased the ranch out to a neighbour. I was only six at the time so he took me to live with my Aunt Irene in Calgary and went to Mars to make his fortune.

We were not very close as I grew up because I only saw him a couple of times a year but we did talk every month via video phone. He worked on the construction of the first Stellar Steel mill and after that was built he went into space as a crewman on a rock miner.

He was very frugal with his money and had built up a bit of a nest egg so when they auctioned off a used netship at a rock auction, he bought it. That was the turning point for him. He ventured out into the asteroid belt with his lone netship as a contractor for Stellar Steel. He was doing very well because his little ship was perfect for capturing iceballs and Mars at that time was desperate for water.

He had brought in a few iron rocks as well and one day he hit the jackpot. He lucked into a 500 ton PGM rock and that set him up. Always an opportunist (Dad has often said, things happen fast out here in the rings and if you want to get ahead, you had better be ready when the opportunity presents itself). Dad talked Stellar Steel into backing him for the purchase of a Spoke so he could venture further out into the rock fields. As part of the deal, Stellar Steel required Dad to sell all his rocks to them for the next 5 years. That deal has long since expired but Dad's loyalty to Stellar Steel has not.

He put a crew together with a promise of a share of the take and both guys are still on the board of Sigme today. All three crewmen got a 25% share of the sale of the rocks and Dad's new company (Sigme) got 25% to cover expenses. Dad was a little short when it came time to pay off his loan from Stellar Steel so he offered both of his crewmen 10% ownership in Sigme if they each paid 10% of the loan. Both of his partners went on to command their own ship when Sigme bought its second Spoke and Dad moved into the office. After they retired Dad changed the compensation package to its present format and to say Sigme has prospered is a gross understatement. It is now an extremely well-funded and diversified company. Dad has always said that people work harder and perform better when they are getting a piece of the pie.

When I turned 21, he gave me a 20% share in Sigme in the hope that it would entice me to leave Earth and come to Mars with him. It worked. I wanted to get to know my Dad better and the romance of working in space appealed to me. I worked in the office for two months but I found that I didn't like working that close to Dad. He can be a bit overbearing sometimes so I knocked around on several crew ships before I took the job as Commander for Sigme 3.

We were definitely the heros of the day. Dad grabbed my hand in the firmest handshake I can remember from him and them he gave me an extended man hug during which he told me that Virginia wanted a more private setting and was waiting in the Executive Lounge at the Mars Port Terminal.

He also informed us that they were processing our Gem immediately so we would know the real value of it within a week. Dwaine and Kelly just beamed when they heard that. Dad showed me the way to the lounge and as soon as I touched the door it flew open and Virginia jumped into my arms. If that kiss meant anything she had really missed me. She steeled a bit when she saw Kelly standing there but melted into my body as soon as the door closed. I could feel her whole body next to me and I started to respond to her passion. All of a sudden I was looking forward to our homecoming celebration.

Virginia is someone you would pick out in a crowd but not because she is strikingly beautiful. She is definitely attractive but you would probably notice her posture and confident stride first. She is tall for a woman at 5 ft 8 inches and she moves with the grace and ease of a dancer. Unlike most women of that height she does not seem large because of her slight frame. She could easily be called full-breasted and she has an almost hourglass figure except for a waist that is a little fuller than maybe it should be. Her long trim legs are topped by the firmest butt you could ever want to grasp.

She wears her black hair a little short at just below her ears so that it cups her face. She has a cute almost doll-like face with full cheeks and a perky nose that's turned up just a bit. You don't see her best feature however until you are talking to her. That's when you see the intelligence behind those sparkling black eyes

Dad gave us 10 minutes and then knocked on the door to see if we were decent. Everybody filed into the room and champagne was passed around for a toast. Dad announced that this would be the biggest windfall the company had ever had and that he was going to use it as a springboard to increase our fleet and move out into the Kuiper Belt with robotic spacecraft. Sigme had already staked a claim in sector 3 of rings 4, 5, 6 and 7. This would give Sigme access to a huge block of space from which they could sweep prime rocks. Because of the new rules any uncaptured rock in those orbits was fair game when it passed through Sigme territory so all you had to do was stay in your sector and wait for them to come to you. It was better to claim stacked sectors because the logistics were much better than trying to mine in a circle.

The room came alive when Wes and his crew joined us. This was the first time we had actually met our saviour face to face and Dwaine and I almost shook his arm off. Kelly of course gave him one of her full body hugs that he seemed to appreciate. I noticed that Dwaine seemed a bit uncomfortable with it and that surprised me a bit.

Everybody was transfixed when Wes related the story of our rescue, especially the part where he came in at full speed with lasers blazing. The crew had been taken into custody and would be held until the Interplanetary Council could decide how to handle it. This was the first time a pirate had been caught red handed and there was no precedent to follow.

Kelly and Dwaine were both working the room and were pumping everybody for information about the new rules and the robotic spacecrafts. When Wes finished his story he spotted Dwaine and asked him to tell the crowd how they had managed to corral two such magnificent rocks. Dwaine called Kelly up to the front with him and when they couldn't find me (Virginia and I had slipped out for a few more minutes alone) they started without me. One of the secretaries found us in the hall and practically forced us into the room with the crowd. The crowd was absolutely quiet. Everyone was spellbound by Dwaine and Kellys remediation of the capture of the Gem. There was a room wide gasp when they told the part about releasing the Iron Maiden so we could go get the Gem and a round of applause when we had captured it again. They gave me far too much credit as Commander of the ship and forgot to mention our celebration. They were on a roll so they relayed our side of the story with the pirates and gave a blow by blow of our maneuvers from Ring 10 down onto the Mars Plain.

Virginia was squeezing my hand all through the story and when they were finished she looked me straight in the eye as she said, you're not going back out there again are you? I didn't know that it was so dangerous and I don't want to lose you.

I was starting to answer her when Dad came over and shook my hand and clapped me on the back at the same time.

Well done Wade, he said, I know you need time to decide what you want to do now but I want you to know that any position you want in the company is yours for the asking. Except mine, he added, I'm not ready to retire yet.

Virginia and I were the first to leave and we went directly to our apartment on the fourth tier. I think it's enough to say that our homecoming celebration was a mixture of raw passion and very passionate, heartwarming getting to know you again love-making sessions. Virginia had the next day off and the only time we got out of bed was to eat and go to the bathroom. We just couldn't seem to get enough of each other.

Virginia worked at Sigme in the receivables department and we agreed that she should stay on until we had made our plans. She could have easily gotten the time off but I needed time alone to sort out what I wanted to do. Dad had called twice to see if I was coming into the office and I knew he wanted me to get involved with company management in some form so he could start grooming me to take the reins someday. For some reason I didn't want to be that involved with the company just yet and Virginia was leaving this decision completely up to me. She didn't care what I did as long as we were together and we could start a family.

After Virginia left to go to work the following day, I sat out in the sunroom trying to sort things out. I couldn't believe the passion I felt for Virginia when just a couple of short days ago I was professing my love for Kelly. Is it possible to truly love two women at the same time?

I couldn't seem to focus and looking out over the activity in the crater brought me back to the book I had read on the ship.

As the companies expanded they started to crowd out the living habitants. To start with the habitants were built close to the individual company's operation. As it got more crowded the noise and dust from the plants bothered the people off shift who were trying to sleep and rest. That was when the decision was made to leave two thirds of the wall free for industrial development and put the living quarters all in one place.

The layered canopy design was working so well for the companies it was decided to use it to house the workers. It was possible to modify the design to create individual living quarters with an outside view. Any rock that posed even a remote risk of crashing into Mars had been removed by the miners. Even so, nobody had ever been bold enough to suggest that they built out on the floor of the crater. There were still Rogue Rocks and those pesky Persiod Showers to worry about.

The computer simulations showed that a covering of five feet of waste rock over a three-layer canopy with a 30-foot span had a safety factor of 5 over the worst impact thought possible. This meant that a lot more people could be housed at one location along the wall because the slope could be terraced all the way to the top. The living quarters could be under the canopy and the sleeping quarters recessed into the wall for added security. Five feet of solid rock between the levels was ample strength to support the roof of the sleeping quarters. The living quarters had two carbon dioxide scrubbers that were continuously monitored. When the air exiting from a filter reached 10 PPB of carbon dioxide the air flow is diverted to the other filter and that filter is replaced with a fresh one. The old filter is placed inside the greenhouse so that the plants can clean it. The waste rock from digging out the sleeping quarters and the equipment room from the layer above was used to cover the canopy of the lower level so the living complex could be built from the bottom up and every tier would have the same protective cover.

The most appreciated result was the glassed-in full face of every apartment so you could easily see out and the sun could get in. It looked like an apartment complex on Earth complete with the curtains for privacy. The units had three small bedrooms across the back with shared living space and kitchen. It was big enough for a family or three flatmates could share it. Every unit had its own airlock/entrance and of course the emergency reservoir and equipment compound.

Chapter 18

From my vantage point up here on the 4th tier I can see they have finished building the sealed walkway along each terrace with one airlock at the elevator end. The elevator and the ground transport shuttle are also sealed and pressurized. All are protected by airlocks of course. You can now leave the airlock from your quarters and commute to your work place without having to suit up. A lot of time was lost putting space protection on and off to commute to work so the cost of the pressurized passageway is easily offset by the time saved. This would not have been dreamed of in the early stages of development because air was so scarce and they couldn't take the chance that an accident would drain the system. The excess water from the asteroids changed all that because they can easily make more oxygen now. As a matter of fact, once the passages are filled, there is very little loss of air to the outside because the airlocks are so well sealed.

The solar powered distillation plant that is the source of all the oxygen and rocket fuel for this complex is on the planet surface near the lip on the crater. The solar collectors are in a field half a mile away to avoid getting in the way of the plants operation. There are back-up electrical heaters powered by the fusion reactors in the event the solar panels can't produce enough power. Every chunk of space rock has the water extracted from it before it is passed on to the metal processors at the various manufacturing plants. The water is measured and the appropriate miner is credited with it before it is delivered via insulated pipes to the main underground reservoir constructed into the wall of the crater at floor level.

I'm not getting anywhere here, maybe if I go up to the observation level I can think.

The upper level of the living complex is an observation deck because it isn't buried deep enough to protect an apartment and it also gives the tenants a place to go where they can see across to the other side which gives them an impression of wide open spaces. I admit that I'm more comfortable up here. I like the feeling of freedom.

I can see the steel plants from up here. The entranceway for the Stellar Steel Company is now three canopies wide. They planned this in advance because when they built the first entranceway they cast pockets into both sides of the pillars which made them easily expandable. That kind of planning is the reason Stellar Steel is the biggest company in the solar system.

I can even see the rock receiving terminal on the surface. The rock chunks from the water extraction plant are moved over to the receiving terminal via shuttle. They are feed down the chute to the crushers and then to the hammer mill where they are reduced to a powder. The powder is then sent to a sorting machine that removes the useful metals. The sorting process is very efficient. They first use strong magnets to pull the magnetic ores out of a thin free falling curtain of material. A magnetic roller at the end of a conveyor belt draws the iron ore away from the curtain of material as it is falling past and deposits it on a conveyor belt which in turn deposits it into the iron ore bin. Then various chemical baths and leaching processes are used to extract the remaining metals. Any remaining powder is mixed with the waste rock and is used to make concrete.

The steel companies use the iron powder to cast large steel ingots from the liquefied steel produced in their blast furnaces. As soon as the ingots are cooled enough to hold their shape they are rolled into the various shapes used in the construction industries.

The steel canopy tops are the easiest of the lot to build. The steel plates are rolled out on the plate mill in the plant and put in place with almost no modifications. They have to be cut to the proper length and laid so the joints are staggered. This is done by laying the 16 foot arced plates butt edge to butt edge on the first layer. The next layer is a little longer because the diameter of the arc was slightly larger. They use two half-wide plates to alter the location of the seam between the adjacent plates so that there is no weakened areas on the canopies. They continue in this manner for as many layers as they need to hold the weight. Because this is on Mars with its reduced gravity, four layers are usually lots strong enough.

The pockets cast into the concrete pillars are steel lined to spread the forces out and prevent chipping out of the concrete. The steel plates don't fit tight into the pockets. The pockets are L shaped and the plates rest on the bottom of the L but don't butt up tight against the end until the weight of the overburden flattens the arc of the steel a bit. They are cut so that all the layers would contact the end at the same time and that is what makes the canopy as strong as it would have been with three times the thickness of solid steel. The arcing and flexibility of the steel created a super strong canopy over the entranceway because it can flex under the impact of a big asteroid rather than break.

After two days of pondering I still wasn't any closer to a clear direction for my future. Virginia and I have recommitted to each other but we haven't set a date yet. If anything, our time apart has drawn us closer to each other. We have agreed to abide by the principal of "what happens in space stays in space". We talked about Kelly briefly and I admitted that we had grown close in our working relationship but that didn't take anything away from my love for her. That's my story and I'm sticking to it. She would have liked more details but I insisted that was in the past and I wanted it to stay there. We haven't mentioned it since.

Thinking about that has made me realize that I need to talk to someone to help clear the fog from my head and sort out my options. It was only natural that I call Dwaine and Kelly and ask them to meet in the company cafeteria the next morning. Virginia wasn't wild about the idea but she relaxed when I insisted that she join us as well. After all, we were going to be talking about our future.

Chapter 19

We met in an isolated corner of the cafeteria so we wouldn't be disturbed by well-wishers and where it was quiet enough that we could talk in private. I shook Dwaine's hand and gave Kelly a quick hug and properly introduced Virginia. We ordered a light lunch and were having coffee before the talk turned to business.

I had sensed that something was up with Dwaine and Kelly so when I asked what they had been up to it was like opening a dam. Kelly had really liked the idea of owning her own company especially if she could manage it from here on Mars. She and Dwaine had agreed to form a partnership and were just waiting to see how much money they had to work with before signing the papers. They had already picked the sector in Ring 8 just above the Sigme claims as their choice of location. One of the main reasons to pick that sector was that it was directly above the Sigme claims so they would have a safe route to bring their rocks through.

They asked me if I was still willing to ask Dad to help them get started. They wanted to form a working alliance with Sigme so they could pool their surveillance networks to get a better picture of the incoming rocks. They were also going to ask if they could get the same bonus agreement with Stellar Steel as Sigme has. They were counting of the good-will of

Sigme to get them off on the right foot. They were also going to ask to rent an office from Sigme to keep their overhead down.

I immediately offered to use any influence I had to help them. They offered to make me a partner again but I turned it down. I started to explain to them that I had had enough of space for a while when it hit me like a bolt of lightning. That's what had been bothering me.

I don't want anything to do with space right now. I'm even feeling cooped up here at the settlement because we still are confined to the pressurized chambers.

I didn't realize that I had said it out loud until I saw the look of shock on Virginia's face.

Where did that come from, she asked. You haven't said a word to me about that.

I know, I said, I just realized it myself but it feels right. How do you feel about going back to Earth?

Kelly was looking at me in disbelief as Virginia started to answer. At that exact moment all three of our communicators beeped. The text from Dads secretary read "please call the office as soon as possible".

This sounds serious, I said, as I hit my speed dial for Dads office.

All his secretary would say was that Dad wanted to see all three of us in his office in two hours if that was possible. Kelly and Dwaine nodded their heads so I confirmed for all of us.

Dwaine looked at Kelly and then at Virginia and said, I think you two have a lot to talk about. We'll meet you at the office and they got up and left us alone.

I had forgotten about the bombshell I had just dropped but Virginia hadn't.

What do you mean, how do I feel about moving to Earth, she asked firmly. Where on Earth do you plan on going? What would you do there? How long do you plan on staying? Why haven't you mentioned this before?

Whoa, slow down, I said, I didn't say we were moving to Earth. I just asked how you felt about it. I've been cooped up in one cramped space or another for three years and now that I've said it I have to admit that I'm starting to like the idea of being able to move around freely out in the open.

What would we do with ourselves out in this open, she asked.

I don't know, I answered, this is as new to me as it is to you. How do you feel about it?

I'm warming up to the idea, she said. I used to really enjoy walking in the park and listening to the birds. I can't remember how long it's been since I've felt the wind in my hair and the warm sun on my face. Where would we go? What would we do? What about my job?

Well, let's start with the easy ones first, I said. Leaving your job here doesn't matter because you'll soon be the wife of a major shareholder so you would have to leave anyway. With all the social commitments that go with being the wife of a major shareholder, you could never hold down a day job.

She settled down pretty quickly once she figured out that I was pulling her leg and we started to actually consider the possibilities. We were still talking when my communicator beeped again. It was Dwaine and they were waiting for me at the office.

Virginia jumped up because she was long overdue at her office but I stopped her and insisted she come with me. She hesitated until I reminded her that she was soon going to be the wife of a major shareholder. She cuffed me on the shoulder for that and we left for the office.

Dwaine and Kelly were still waiting in the front office when we got there. I apologized for keeping them waiting and the secretary took us right in. When Dad saw Virginia with me he walked directly over to her and took both her hands in his as he said, I'm glad you're here too Virginia. This will affect you as well and you should be here to hear the news.

He paused and looked from one to the other of us with a strange look on his face. Ok, he continued, I've held this in for as long as I can and I think I'll burst if I don't get it out. We got the final results from the processing of your rocks this morning. Your Gem was far richer than we thought. The center was almost pure Iridium. Added to that is the Iron maiden which along with the usual nickel and iron had a thick seam of Iridium right through the middle of it

All told, the Gem is worth $3,000,000,000.00 and the Iron maiden $1,500,000,000.00.

He paused again to give us time to absorb the news and then hit us with the rest of it.

Your bonus from their sale is $1,000,000,000.00 for the Gem and $500,000,000.00 for the Iron Maiden. That's a total of $1,500,000,000 divided 4 ways. When you do the math that's $375,000,000 each for Dwaine and Wade and $750,000,000 for Kelly plus your normal wages of course.

We were dumbfounded and just stood there like statues when he finished talking until Virginia gasped and that broke the spell. Kelly and Dwaine started screaming and hollering while dancing in a circle and hugging each other. Virginia grabbed my hand as she started to sink to the floor. I caught her and laid her on the sofa in the center of the room. She was conscious but very faint so Dad called for his secretary to bring in a wet towel.

I was tending to Virginia when Kelly spotted us at the sofa and started over to see if she could help. I stopped her with my hand up and she and Dwaine just stood there breathing hard. After Virginia sat up and she could see that everything was under control Kelly cleared her throat and asked very meekly, when do we get the checks?

Dad laughed and said, it'll be about 30 days. Even Stellar Steel can't write a check that big without arranging for financing. If you guys need some money to get by on we'll be glad to advance you some.

Dwaine thought for a minute and asked, would we be able to pick up a cheque for 2 million tomorrow? We've got something that we need to do as soon as possible.

That shouldn't be a problem, answered Dad, if you stop in around 10 tomorrow I'll have the cheques ready. To be fair I should give each of you the same amount.

That would be wonderful, purred Kelly, come on Dwaine, we've got a lot to talk about.

I took the hint from them and told Dad that we also had a lot to talk about. We left right behind them and went back to our apartment.

We talked late into the night and finally fell asleep in each others arms. The next morning I called Dad at 8 o'clock and asked for a meeting at 9 before Dwaine and Kelly showed up. Dad was surprised but agreed when I told him it was extremely important that I talk to him before he met with Dwaine and Kelly

Virginia and I had hatched a plan and I wanted to talk it over with Dad before I mentioned it to Dwaine and Kelly. I could see that Dad just listening politely when I started to talk but he really started to focus as I outlined our plan.

I started by explaining to Dad that I had been in space too long and I needed to spend some time back on Earth but that didn't mean that I didn't want anything to do with space. Virginia and I had agreed that it probably wasn't a good idea for me to be a partner with Dwaine and Kelly because of our close relationship in the past but that didn't mean that Sigme couldn't do business with them. I really liked the idea of robotic mining and I wanted to be directly involved with developing it. I knew that Dwaine and Kelly were good and honest people and they were very component miners. I told Dad that they intended to form their own company and we could benefit from that by forming a joint venture with them. By working with them and helping them to get started we would gain the extra income from the rocks they produced without any direct expenditure by us after the start-up costs and we would become an even more valuable supplier to Stellar Steel. The option was leaving them to work for themselves and then having to compete with them. Dad didn't see why we needed this joint venture until I told him that I wanted to invest $300,000,000 of my bonus with Sigme in exchange for another 5% of his shares to support the change to robotic mining. I wouldn't be in partnership with Dwaine and Kelly but Sigme would be.

I asked Dad to let me propose the deal to them and he agreed with the stipulation that the deal would have to be ratified by the board. I knew that that was just for show. With my shares Dad and I easily controlled the board.

Chapter 20

Kelly and Dwaine were there right on 10 o'clock and Dad asked them to meet us in the conference room. They were surprised to see me sitting with Dad and I saw them glance at each other with a puzzled look on their faces. I asked them to sit down across from us and explained that we had a proposal to put to them. They sat down with an even more puzzled look on their faces.

I explained that I had told Dad that they planned on forming their own mining company and that they were interested in some form of an alliance.

It's called Gem Space Mining Inc, interrupted, Kelly, we're calling our company Gem Space Mining Inc.

May I make a suggestion, interrupted Dad, you might want to change it to just Gem Space Inc.

Why do you say that, asked Dwaine?

Well it's got a lot going for it as it is, it's easily recognizable and portrays the company actives but it could be very limiting.

How so, asked Kelly a little defensively?

Well, added Dad, in the business world it pays to always be looking to the future. You never know when a start-up company like this might grow to become a major conglomerate and you could limit it by identifying it as a mining company. You would always be perceived as a mining company first rather than a diversified conglomerate. That can make a big difference when you are seeking financing.

Dwaine and Kelly looked at each other and Dwaine said, we hadn't even thought of that but we'll certainly consider it now.

I'm glad we got that settled, I said, now where were we? Although an alliance might be quite beneficial to you, we don't see it as a major advantage to us.

Kelly started to say something and I held up my hand.

Hear me out before you jump to any conclusions. Here's what we have in mind. As you know we have already staked our claims and are planning to change most of our operations to robotic mining for a lot of reasons. We will still be maintaining our presence in the inner rings but to a reduced degree. I should tell you this is my proposal and it will have to be ratified by the board before it becomes a formal offer.

I suggest that you immediately stake the next two sectors above us in Rings 8 and 9. I know that's more than you thought you could afford but we will advance you the $20,000,000 from your bonus as soon as you have formed your company. That will mean that between us we can sweep a total of 6 rings.

Hang it there I said to everybody, here's the rest of the plan.

Kelly and Dwaine looked over to Dad and he shrugged his shoulders and said,

I heard this for the first time just before you got here but it is interesting don't you think?

I like it more every time I say it, I continued with a smile. We're not asking for any share of your company. I'm proposing a 50-50 joint venture between Sigme and your company. We're going to take more of a hit going in but we'll get it back after we're up and running because of the 50-50 split.

We will sell you Sigme 3 for $10,000,000. I know Dad, I said, that's well below the market price but hear me out. You will need to purchase another Spoke off the market so you will have one ship for each ring. That will probably set you back another $100,000,000 but that will be cheap once they figure out what we are up to. Sigme will allow you the free use of our maintenance facility and staff here on Mars to modify the ships for robotic control but you will pay for all the equipment and controls. That will probably set you back another $100,000,000 for both ships to be refurbished.

I see what you're up to, interrupted Kelly, you want to be the first one out there so you get your pick of the rocks.

Not me Kelly, I answered, you. I'm not going to be involved in the direct operation of this project. You and Dwaine will have complete control over what happens out in your rings. This is the part where we get back some of our investment. We will receive 50% of the sale value of any rock you mine from your sectors. I know Dwaine, I said, that seems a bit one sided unless you look at the real figures.

Because you are tied to Sigme through this joint venture Stellar Steel will have to extend the same bonus structure to you as well. That bonus is now at 30% above the auction prices so you will only be losing 20 % overall. That's a very good percentage for this type of arrangement. It's also possible that Stellar Steel sweetens the pot even more if this shortage continues and we are able to supply them with the ore they need between us.

This is starting to sound very interesting to me but I think it would be better if we had the free use of an office and control room to go along with it, interjected Kelly.

I'm not sure we could go for the free use part but since this is a 50-50 deal, how about 50% of the normal rental for a period of up to 5 years, I answered.

Kelly and Dwaine looked at each other and nodded. Kelly spoke first,

I think we need to talk this over in private but we're not against it per say.

Dad spoke up and said, I would be surprised and disappointed if you didn't take some extra time to think about this. I believe we have another matter to deal with and with that he reached into the vest pocket of his coat and handed each of us a cheque for $2,000,000.00. That sobered us up in a hurry and drove home the point that we were dealing with real money here, not just a theatrical situation.

Kelly looked at her cheque for almost a minute before she tucked it into her purse.

We do have one more thing we would like to talk about, she said.

Go ahead, Dad said, I have until noon before I have to go for another meeting.

Well, Dwaine said, Kelly and I have decided to make this a real partnership by marrying each other. That's the reason we wanted the advance.

I almost fell out of my chair and I guess my mouth dropped open because Kelly pointed at me and started to laugh.

You of all people shouldn't be surprised about this, she said.

I regained my composure and went over and gave them a long group hug. I couldn't be happier for you, I said, when is this going to happen?

We figure we've already had a long enough engagement, Kelly answered, so it's as soon as we can arrange for a room and a minister. The three of you are invited of course but we'll have to let you know when and where.

I can take care of the where if you will allow me, said Dad. We often clear out the company cafeteria for this type of event and I would be happy to donate it to you at your convenience. Just give us two days notice and it's yours to use.

Kelly and Dwaine looked at each other again and nodded. Kelly went over and gave Dad a strong hug and said, thank you very much, we will definitely take you up on that offer. Now we have to go find a minister.

For a minute I considered suggesting that Virginia and I make it a double ceremony but then I thought that might not be such a good idea after all.

Before you go, Dad called after Dwaine and Kelly, we should set a time to get back together. If you want to go forward with this joint venture then you should stake your sectors as soon as possible before someone else picks them up. I'm going to need at least a day after you give me the go ahead to put this before the board and I need their approval to advance you that amount of money. I will say that I agree in principal with everything Wade has proposed so the next move is up to you. Do you want to book another meeting now?

Kelly paused at the door and stroked her hair before she answered. I think I can say that we also agree in principal with Wade's proposal so we shouldn't need a lot of time. How about we meet in two days at the same time, she suggested with Wade nodding his head.

After they left Dad walked over and slapped me on the back as he said, that was really good Wade, I'm impressed, I guess you have a head for business along with your other skills.

I thanked him for the compliment and took my leave because I had to go talk to his engineers about the modifications I had in mind. After my talk with the engineers I drew up a rough blueprint for the modifications that would turn a Spoke into a remote controlled Space Harvester.

Chapter 21

Virginia was thrilled to hear that Kelly and Dwaine were getting married. She was surprised that the ceremony was going to be in the company cafeteria because she believed that all women wanted a formal wedding. We had finally agreed on our wedding date but decided not to announce it until after their wedding. We didn't want to take any of the attention off of them.

Kelly and Dwaine were on time for our meeting and they brought a copy of their company registration papers with them. They called it Gem Space Inc. They agreed to the proposal without any changes and asked Dad to present it to the board. Dad was all smiles when he told them that the boards approval was only a formality because he and I easily owned the majority of the company shares so we could carry any motion put before it. We shook hands all around and told them that the papers would be ready for signing in a week. Dad let me hand them a cheque for $20,000,000.00 so they could stake their claims.

Kelly stuffed the cheque in her purse and Dwaine took the opportunity to ask Dad if the cafeteria was available for a wedding ceremony in 10 days. When he confirmed that it was they handed us our invitations that they had brought with them. Dwaine asked me to be his best man to which I readily agreed as I bit my tongue to resist the temptation to make the usual smart-ass remark. Just as they were leaving I asked them for a meeting the next day in the maintenance shop to start planning the modifications.

We met at 10 in the shop and I started by explaining that it was the shortage of Iridium that was the bottleneck for building all the new ships on order. Our Gem would alleviate some of that but there was still going to be a one or two year delay for ships being ordered this month. We would need to get started right away to modify the ships that were available now for remote operation unless we wanted to wait that long. The Spokes were the cheapest ships available that could go that far out and tow a load back.

I assured them that these were just suggestions and that everything was open for discussion as I laid a blueprint out on the table. I explained that I had gotten a copy of the construction blueprints of a typical Spoke from the shop engineers and they had made recommendation as to what would need to be done. They both seemed surprised and maybe a little taken aback to see that the blueprints had already been drawn up. I explained that I had asked them to be drawn up to give us a starting point and because Sigme was going to be using the same design for their ships, I wanted to get our engineers involved in the design stage. They only thought about it for a minute before they both nodded their heads in agreement. Kelly suggested and we quickly agreed to keep the design specs for our "Space Harvester" secret so we would have an even longer head start on the rest of the miners.

The engineers suggested we strip as much weight off the ship as possible. All of the life support systems were redundant as well as the rotation and counterweight systems since they would not be carrying human passengers. The operations and living quarters could be stripped of their components and the reactor could be replaced with solar panels and a battery system because it would take so little power to operate the ship with all the systems removed.

Kelly objected to the removal of the reactor because as she pointed out the loss of power was second only to the loss of fuel for a disabling event. Lack of fuel or loss of electricity creates a dead or unresponsive ship. She also pointed out that it would be a good idea to have a heated control room for the survivability of our instruments. The reactor could easily supply the power for that so we left the reactor onboard.

I had already received the go ahead from Dad to start refurbishing Sigma 3 before any papers had been signed because he also wanted to get the jump on the other miners. Sigme 2 was still going to be used to mine the inner rings. As a matter of fact Wes was leaving the day after the wedding to go get our flagged rocks. It seems that the Moon Colonies were expanding and they needed more water to fill their reservoirs. Sigma 1 was destined to be modified after Sigme 3's new systems had been proven.

To my surprise Virginia agreed immediately when Kelly phoned her up to ask her to be her maid of honour. She even volunteered to decorate the cafeteria for the wedding.

I was very pleased with her attitude and I told her so. The wedding went off without a hitch and the after party was talked about for weeks. Martians tend to really let their hair down at weddings. Kelly and Dwaine took a one week honeymoon in the Executive Suites at the Apartments as the living quarters had come to be called. I didn't know until they told me where they were going that there was an Executive Suite in the complex. It was built to house visiting dignitaries and has a vibrating king size bed and hydro bathtub as well as a fully stocked bar. It is ideal for a honeymoon because it also has a fully stocked self-contained kitchen and wine cabinet so there is no need to venture outside until you are good and ready.

They had ordered the instruments and scanner packages before the wedding and they arrived on the Executive Shuttle while they were still holed up. The technicians had stripped everything out of the inside of the Spoke and were getting ready to install the fuel tanks by the time they surfaced. Kelly and Dwaine immediately focused on installing the instrument package while I supervised the work on the rest of the ship.

The elevators and counterweight were even removed. The elevator shafts, storage compartment, operations room and the living quarters were converted into one giant fuel tank. An external port was built for access into the reactor compartment and the Reaction Drive and counterbalance systems were removed. The center housing was welded solid to the docking station so the ship was one entity with no moving parts.

Kelly and Dwaine had ordered the latest and most advanced communication and scanning systems on the market. All the new controls were installed in the old unloading platform including the remote controls for the boost and retro rockets. Four additional retro rockets were installed on the outer ends of the Spoke structure to give the ships added maneuverability. The scanners were mounted at four points; the outer ends of the Spoke structure and both forward and back at the center housing. The ship would be sending all its scanner and flight readouts directly to the control room here at the office.

The three netships turned out to be a blessing. We had only expected to be able to tow one rock at a time but the three netships that came with the Spoke made it possible to capture three separate rocks and transport them back to Mars. We reinforced the docking port so that it was strong enough to handle that kind of a load and we modified the netships cargo hold so that it could be locked solidly together with a rock still in its net.

Each netship could independently capture and hold its rock until all three had captured a rock of its own. This was a major increase in our expected payload and proved to be a huge money maker.

The only major problem we encountered was that the rockets were pointed in the wrong direction. In this case we needed the thrust to be in the opposite direction because we were towing with the docking ports rather than the mainline. We had to split the docking station housing at the bulkhead between the rockets and loading platform. We remounted the rockets over the end of the docking station with support struts out to the center housing framework. It was a tight fit because we had to leave room for the netships to manoeuvre around them but it actually worked very well when we had it finished.

Dwaine and Kelly were on the lookout for a second Spoke to complete their fleet when Kelly spotted a notice on the Space Harbour website that announced the auction of the confiscated Spoke from the pirates. They bought it for $5,000,000 because it was so badly damaged and most of the existing companies were still more interested in keeping their money to buy one of the new robotic ships than repairing a badly damaged Spoke.

Dad was green with envy when he heard about it and he wasn't going to miss a deal like that again. He assigned two of the company purchasers to the task of watching the markets and finding their own bargain. They found an old Spoke that the owners had been trying to sell for a year because it needed a complete internal refurbishing including the reaction drive control system. They picked it up for $10,000,000 and Dad now had the core he needed to build our own Harvester with the added benefit that we would not have to take Sigme 1 out of service.

That was still a good deal because the word had already got out that we were modifying Spokes for remote operation and several other companies were also looking for a cheap ship to convert. We had an advantage because we had our blueprints already and they would have to start over from scratch. It was a good thing that we had decided to keep our plans secret because if they had become public knowledge then the price of old Spokes would have skyrocketed. Stellar Steel was concerned about this as well because a drop in orders for new ships would seriously affect the price of Steller Steel.

Chapter 22

The conversion went really well and Gem Space was ready to launch the first Harvester in two months. Nobody was surprised when they named it Gem 1. After a few test runs in high orbit around Mars they were ready to actually try to capture some rocks remotely. Dad gave them permission to use Ring 10 rather than go all the way out into the Kuiper Belt.

Everything went surprisingly well. They powered out to Ring 10 in one week instead of the usual one month and the ship flew well. The scanners had enough range so they could easily avoid the rocks and other ships they passed on the way out. This was essential because the trip out to the Kuiper Belt was so far that unless they were able to manage a high speed flight most of the time would be spent in traveling rather than mining.

Kelly had done a super job of programming the capture and recover sequences for the netships. After she had designated a rock to be captured, the onboard computer took over control of the operation. It controlled the timing of the launch of the netship, its path to intercept the rock, the deployment of the net, the rocket bursts necessary to bring the rock under control, the reconnecting of the two compartments and the docking with the Harvester itself. These operations had to be all managed by the computers because of the time lag in the signals between Mars and the Kuiper Belt.

Kelly was in charge of the test flight and Dwaine and I forged ahead with the refitting of the pirate ship now called Gem 2. Dwaine talked Sigme into parting with the new rockets they had in inventory rather than wait three months to have them delivered from the moon. Sigme could wait the three months to restock their inventory and Dad wanted to see how the ships would work together before he spend the money to refurbish our ships.

Kelly had collected three iceballs from Ring 10 and delivered them to the moon before we had finished our refit. She didn't even bring the ship back to Mars. Apparently it caused quite a stir when their remotely controlled ship flew into the moon's Spaceport. Almost everybody in the space industries knew that someone was refitting a Spoke for remote operation but this was the first time that anyone at the moon base had seen one and everybody wanted a close look at it.

Kelly didn't waste any time in port and after refuelling and a few minor programming changes she sent Gem 1 on its way to their claim out in the Belt as it had come to be called. Even at high speed it was a one month flight out to their sectors and they wanted one ship flying while one was mining.

There was a party that rivalled their wedding reception the day Gem 1 left the Moon's orbit on the way out to the Belt. As far as anyone knew Gem 1 would be the first Harvester out there and we were all very pleased about that. There isn't a lot of champagne on Mars but there is a flourishing distillery in the industrial sector. They use the leftover fruit from the residents' kitchens to make a kind of a wine and then distil it to make a high-octane alcohol called Grappa. The wine is almost undrinkable because of all the different fruits that go into it but the Grappa that comes out of it has a very pleasant taste and it will knock your socks off if you get carried away with it. Martian Grappa has been blamed for a lot of misbehaving at more than one celebration.

It was time I moved on. My job was done because the engineers at Sigme were now more than capable of refitting Gem 2 and our newly acquired Spoke. Dad also ordered two of the new Harvesters to add to the converted Spoke to complete our deep space fleet.

Virginia and I had decided to have a double reception wedding. We would get married on Mars because it would have been unfair to ask the people there to take the time away from their work to travel back and forth from Earth for the wedding. The wedding would be telecast to Virginia's friends and Aunt Irene on Earth. We were willing to use the Executive Shuttle to bring them to Mars but some of them weren't up to the trip. The Executive Shuttle made the normal three-month trip in one week with a full days burn on each end. The G-forces were quite extreme during the full day's burn to bring the shuttle up to speed and then to slow it down again.

Stellar Steel offered to let us use their cafeteria because it was bigger than Sigme's. That worked out very well because Virginia wanted our wedding to be unique to us rather than a duplicate of Dwaine and Kelly's. I was really glad that I hadn't suggested that we have a joint wedding. Virginia left her job and devoted full time to planning and arranging the wedding.

We made the announcement after Gem 1 was launched and I kept myself busy and out of the way by working on Gem 2.

I was pleased when Virginia asked Kelly to be her maid of honour so I of course asked Dwaine to be my best man. We weren't surprised when Virginia's parents chose not to endure the shuttle ride from Earth and that meant that the only guests present were from Mars. The wedding went off without a hitch and the after party will be remembered for a long time. The only people on Mars who weren't at the reception was the skeleton crews necessary to keep the systems running at the various plants and the life support facility The good news is that there were none of the fights or marriage break-ups that used to be common at Martian wedding. It isn't unknown for a partner to stray during one of these after parties but that has become a part of the Martian culture so most couples have adopted a forgive and forget attitude. Most people see this as a direct parallel to the Cabin Fever parties that used to happen in the more remote gold mining camps of the 1800's. Time may move on but people tend to remain the same.

Dad and I have had several heart-to-heart talks and he finally understood that I needed some time to myself before getting involved in the operation of the company. Dad still owned the ranch near Lethbridge and he was very happy to find out that we wanted to make it our home on Earth. He even transferred the title to us as our wedding present. We stayed until Gem 2 was launched and we left for Earth the next day on the Executive Shuttle. We were both anxious to start our new life on the ranch but it was hard saying good-by to all our friends. To be honest both of us were in tears. Kelly started to melt into me but she caught herself and settled for a quick peck on the cheek. Virginia didn't say anything afterward so I don't think she noticed.

The shuttle ride to Earth was quite dramatic for Virginia. She had never had a high G trip before and it took quite a toll on her. She didn't exactly kiss the ground when we landed at the Spaceport in Winnipeg but she was very glad to get out of that ship. We decided to have the reception for the Earth family members at my Aunt Irene's place in Calgary. We telecast the reception back to Mars mainly for Dad's benefit and he had a great time visiting with his old friends. I think he wished he had come with us but this would have been a really bad time to leave Sigme. With me gone, he was deeply involved in getting our Harvesters ready as well as getting everything in order for this new direction we were taking.

Chapter 23

Virginia was almost ecstatic when she saw the ranch house. It was a true ranch style house and had been built in the 1950s. It was still liveable but it needed a major refurbishing inside and Virginia immediately took this as an opportunity for us to build her dream home. She loved the wide open prairie and even as a little girl had dreamed of living in a big ranch house with her garden and the kids playing in the front yard.

As far as the ranch itself was concerned it had been allowed to go to seed and the roof on the machinery shed had fallen in. The good news was that the silos and grain storage buildings were still in usable condition. Dad had sold off all the machinery when he left so there was nothing to work with on site. The neighbour, Robert Hathaway, who had leased the property from Dad had retired and moved to Calgary so the fields had gone back to their wild state. The good news is that the irrigation system was still in place and operational. The dam on the Old Man River had not been drained because it was an irrigation dam and had never been used to generate electricity. With the switch to Fusion Powered Generators a lot of the Hydro Dam reservoirs had been drained to create farmland because they were no longer needed to generate electricity. Even our irrigation ditches at the ranch had been well maintained because there are still several ranchers in the area who used the network.

Our ranch covers four sections so we had 2560 acres to work with. This wasn't a very large ranch as ranches go but it was definitely big enough to support a family. It would take a lot of work to bring the fields back so they could produce a viable crop but the rest had done the soil good. With irrigation it would produce a bumper crop of not only hay but most of the food grains as well. With the warmer summers and longer period of frost-free days because of global warming we could even grow seed corn. Global warming has made Canada a much more pleasant place to live except for the severe wind and thunderstorms. Severe storms were now the norm on most of the planet with tornados now common as far north as Edmonton. The plus side to this is that Canada now has a growing season capable of producing bumper crops of both food grains and vegetables as far north as the Yukon and Territories border. The Canadian Prairies and the Russian Steppes are now the breadbaskets of the world.

Virginia chattered all the way back to Calgary about changes she wanted to make to the house after that first visit. I'm sorry to say that I didn't listen very well because I was planning the changes I wanted to make at the ranch. I couldn't stand the thought of that much fertile land lying dormant when food was so scarce in a lot of places on Earth. Neither of us wanted to live in the city so we decided to move in first and then change the house one room at a time. Virginia quite understandably insisted on buying a new bedroom suite for the master bedroom before we moved in but other than that we made do with what was there. The kitchen appliances were the next things to go and then the bathroom got a complete makeover before every room in the house got a facelift and new paint job. I was more than happy to leave all this to Virginia as I occupied my time by getting ready to plant a crop and find some cattle. The most exciting thing for both of us was that Virginia became pregnant with Ruth sometime during the refurbishing of the bathroom.

It's amazing how much I did not know about ranching. You need to grow your own feed for the winter months for your own animals and most ranchers also grow a cash crop just in case the cattle market turns sour. You had to know what machines to buy and how to prepare the land for the crop after you decide what crop you wanted to plant. If that wasn't bad enough, you had to know how to operate the machines so that you didn't tear up the land you are trying to plant and the seeds actually germinate. It wasn't long before I started to question my decision to become a rancher and if Virginia hadn't been so happy with the house I think I would have quit and gone back to Mars. As luck would have it, on one of my forays into town looking for information I was introduced to Jim Stevens who had lost his ranch. He had sold his ranch as part of a divorce settlement but he really liked the lifestyle so he was working as a ranch hand part-time for several of the other ranchers.

Jim and I got along right from the start and it wasn't long before I offered him a job as our ranch manager. He was a little sceptical when I first asked him to be our manager because we were so small but then I told him that I had plans for expanding the ranch. Robert Hathaway had put his farm up for sale when he retired and it was almost the same size as ours. He still had his water rights and most of the machinery he had used so it could be a win-win situation for us. Jim and I toured his ranch and found that the machinery was still usable and the land hadn't turned completely wild yet so I made them an offer.

Now that we were the proud owner of a large ranch, I had a lot of work to do. We started on the Hathaway homestead or Lot 2 as we had renamed it because his land had only sat dormant for three years. The plan was to plant our crops on Lot 2 and pasture the cattle on the home ranch. Jim and I had our first disagreement at this point. He had figured out that I had lots of money to work with so he wanted to trade the machinery in on some newer pieces and I wanted to try my hand at reviving the older stuff. I had to insist before Jim relented but luckily it wasn't long before he caught the bug himself. Mr. Hathaway had kept his machinery in good condition so we were able to get them all up and running within a week. Both of us got a great deal of satisfaction from resurrecting something that others would have thrown away.

Jim was an excellent farm manager and I turned out to be a passable mechanic so it wasn't long before we had one crop in the ground and were working on the rest of the fields. I was even turning into a decent operator under Jim's stern tutlage.

We had enough hay planted to feed our intended stock through the winter so Jim and I started to hang out at the cattle auctions. We were using one irrigation system for the crops and one for the pasture. When we sowed grass seed onto the pastures and added water the grass literally sprang up almost overnight. We bought 200 yearling heifers because that was all our pastures would support until the grass had a chance to grow more. We rented the services of a couple of good bulls with excellent bloodlines and by late fall we had 200 pregnant cows.

Both ranches had been part of the National Wind Farm Network and we had 5 windmills on each property. The windmills had been neglected so I undertook to repair them and bring them back online. Even with the fusion powered generating plants, wind power was still a major part of the energy supply system. The total energy collected from the entire system negated the need to build three reactors and the frosting on the cake was that they didn't need to build any extra transmission lines because every producer was already connected to the grid via the supply network.

The Canadian Government had funded the development of a 3000 watt windmill that was cheap to build and could be mounted on a much smaller version of the towers that carry high voltage transmission lines. The components were mass produced in Canada through a crown corporation and were only available to a Canadian company that had registered as a windmill manufacturer. It didn't take the electrical industry long to recognize this as an opportunity to create some much needed extra business and before long there were windmills being built all across the country. Because the components were mass produced the windmills were a lot cheaper to buy and parts were readily available so they started to spring up in farmyards and on top of industrial buildings all over the country. This was a win-win situation for everyone involved. One 3000 watt windmill would take a residence almost completely off the grid and even in a moderate wind there was a net surplus at the end of each day that could be feed back into the grid. This turned the household into a producer instead of a consumer and the energy they didn't need from the grid was also available to be used elsewhere. Even one windmill would pay for itself in 10 years with the money saved and the income earned from the surplus. Most farms and even the industrial buildings had several windmills because the cash flow just kept on coming every time the wind blew.

This is still a win-win-win system. The government gets the Carbon Credits to help offset our environmental footprint, the ranchers and other producers get the income from the energy produced and the utility companies get enough energy to replace three generating plants. It wasn't long before the utility companies recognized the benefit of a continuous supply of electricity regardless of what part of the country it was coming from. When the change was made to wireless electric meters they were able to tell the exact location of the producing windmills and accurately predict the volume from the storm fronts as they sweep across the country.

By the end of the first spring the new calves had doubled our herd to 400 head and the pastures sprouted full of new grass. It's amazing how fast time can pass. Daniel was born in year three and we were both enjoying our lives as ranchers. I admit that some of the fire had gone out of our lovemaking but Virginia and I agree on almost everything important and we had settled into a very comfortable lifestyle that we were in love with.

Dad came to visit his grandchildren every January and was proud as punch to be a grandfather. He soon began hinting quite strongly that he might be ready to hand the reins over to a younger man. I had to sit him down and explain in no uncertain terms that I had no intention of moving back to Mars. Virginia and I had talked it over and she assured me that she was perfectly capable of managing the ranch if I wanted to go back. That was her gentle way of telling me that if I went to live on Mars, I would be going by myself. The ranch was now making money and with my shareholder payments from Sigme we were doing very well.

Life is good.

Chapter 24

I had been keeping in touch with the happenings on Mars through my link in the office so I knew Sigme was also doing extremely well. The three-rock loads that the Harvesters brought back with them and the 50% share from Gem Space's rocks were a big part of that.

Dwaine and Kelly were also doing extremely well. For the first two years they rotated their two ships back and forth from their sectors and they were bringing in a steady supply of rocks. The main shortcoming of that system was the one rock per net limitation. Dwaine was able to change the programming of the netships so they would not dock with the Harvester after it had captured its rock unless it received a separate command from the office. He programmed them to remain in place with the net still stretched out between the two compartments. When a suitable rock came their way they would then capture the second rock with the same net and in some cases would even grab a third one. It's easy to see that you could triple your payload with this type of system and that it was feasible to grab the smaller rocks that you wouldn't normally have wasted a net on that far out in the Belt. The bottom line is more tonnage for less time spent and that made a very positive addition to the company's bottom line.

Kelly, being a person who is never satisfied with the status quo, decided that they were losing too much time in transit and therefore losing rocks that travel through their sectors while it was unattended. She talked Dad into reworking the towing mechanism on Sigme 1 so that they could connect up to six tow-lines at one time. The Harvesters have proven to be very dependable so it wasn't necessary to bring them all the way back to Mars every time. Sigme 1 was going to be a tugboat. Gem's 1 and 2 would be collecting their rocks and they would rendezvous with Sigme 1 at the bottom of Sector 4 where they were safe inside Sigme's claim. The crew on the tug would refuel the Harvesters and transfer the nets to the tow-lines. They would reload the netships with fresh nets and then all three would go their own way. Sigme 1 would haul the empty fuel tank and the rocks back to Mars while the Harvesters returned to their stations out in the Belt. Dad was quick to adapt the same strategy because this allowed the Harvesters to spend more time mining and that more than offset the loss of Sigme 1 as a mining ship. There are so many rocks available out in the Belt that you can literally pick and choose the ones you want, rather than sit patiently and hope something good will come your way. Sigme 1 was spending all its time towing rocks in and fuel out and Sigme 2 had also been reconfigured as a tug and was being used to pick up the extra loads if Sigme 1 fell behind.

We were actually bringing rocks in from the Belt two years ahead of the rest of the miners because we had got the jump on them by being the first to modify our Spokes into remotely controlled Harvesters This has been very good for both Gem Space and Sigme because when the other Spokes were taken out of service in the Rings it created a shortage of rocks for the steel plants who were operating at full tilt trying to fill their orders. The prices at the Rock Auctions remained high because of the shortage and anyone still bringing in rocks did very well. It wasn't long before someone figured out that it was more profitable to steal a load rather than to collect their own rocks. The pirating was first noticed when several Ring Miners reported that rocks that they had left for later pick-up were missing. It was noticed that a few of the miners who brought rocks into the auctions were bringing in more than their normal volume but nothing could be proven. All the rocks had the proper tags on them but a few did have some very suspicious burn marks on them.

Stellar Steel has bought every rock we brought in whether they needed them are not. For a short period the price of Steller Steel dropped when a few miners cancelled their orders so they could convert their Spokes into remotely controlled Harvesters. Then the price skyrocketed again as they all put in their orders for their second ship at the same time. Most of the miners continued to work in the rings while they were waiting for their ships to be built and they all needed good loads to pay for these ships. Emotions would run really high when a valuable rock started to loop and more than one miner was after it. They would literally be waiting at their claim boundaries to grab it and some of them may have been a little too quick on the trigger. The rings were quickly being picked clean of good rocks to fill the orders from the factories.

I was working in the machine shop trying to repair one of the windmill generators when I got the call. It was from Kelly and she was frantic. Sigme 1 had picked up a load from the rendezvous point at the bottom of Sector 4 to tow back to Mars. They were about halfway in when a ship came out from behind Jupiter with its lasers blasting. All she knew was that it was a conventional Spoke and that they had disabled Sigme 1 and stolen their rocks.

Sigme 2 had been dispatched to go tow the crippled ship in and she thought that the rocks were probably being towed to the auction at the Moon. There were more rocks than normal being brought into the Moon Auctions and it was generally accepted that that was the preferred place to go to get rid of any questionable rocks. The authorities couldn't find any proof of wrongdoing because the rocks were properly tagged when they arrived and even if it looked like the tags had been removed and replaced with a new one, they needed proof. The Space Patrol had put several suspicious ships on their watch list but they didn't have the manpower to patrol out in the rings so all they could do is check the loads as they were coming in.

Kelly had been a little paranoid about something like this happening because of our incident on the way in with the treasure rocks. She believed that it was inevitable for the pirates to eventually try to grab one of our loads. She spent a lot of time studying ways to ensure the security of the rocks and she couldn't find anything available that looked tamper proof. She was haunted by the thought of someone else stealing their hard earned loads so she and Dwaine put their heads together and quietly designed a unique two-stage flagging probe. Their final design was a shaft that splintered so that the splinters fanned out into the base rock on impact. Two seconds after it splintered a second projectile was fired from the middle of the shaft and it imbedded itself further into the rock. If the main probe was cut or pulled out, the second was still left imbedded in the rock with it's own identity code that could only be read by a special wand frequency.

They immediately began to use it on their rocks but they kept the design to themselves. Even Dad didn't know about it and so far nobody at the steel plant had found one because by the time the rocks had been processed the probes were just another piece of the rock. All the rocks in the stolen load were flagged with a two-stage probe so if I could find them, I could identify them.

Kelly wanted me to go to the rock auction at the Moon to try and identify their rocks. It was a good bet that the pirates didn't know about the probes so all I had to do was go to the auction and wait for them to bring the rocks to me. I booked passage on the next shuttle to the Moon and I was waiting at the rock auction site a week before they were to take place. Kelly had transmitted the frequencies for the hidden probe to me and I had programmed my wand to search for them before I left Earth.

I identified myself to the Space Patrol at the Spaceport as soon as I arrived and we set a trap for the thieves. I wasn't known at the Spaceport so it was easy to disguise me as a security officer and place me into one of their normal patrols.

I would be present when they did their normal paperwork as the rocks came in and I would scan the rocks as I checked their tags. Everything seemed perfectly normal so nobody was the wiser and everyone carried on the same as usual.

I hit the jackpot on my second day. A load had come in with what looked like burn marks on their rocks and a small blackened section on the ships hull. I knew within 5 min. that these were Kelly's rocks because my wand lit up like a Christmas tree as soon as I got close to the load. We had agreed to play it cool if I did find our rocks because we wanted to see if anybody at the Spaceport was in on the scam. There had been a lot of new people hired lately due to the increased volume of the traffic at the Spaceport. The rest of the Security Patrol thought I was just another new recruit training for the job so nobody suspected a thing when I took a little longer than normal to inspect the rocks.

The pirate commander went directly to the office of Ralph Krammer rather than stop at the desk to do his paperwork. Mr. Krammer cleared him through the port without even a cursory inspection of the rocks despite the fact that they were supposed to be on high alert for the stolen load. There are usually burn marks on the rocks if the tags have been removed and replaced with a different one. The inspection officer is supposed to check for any sign of tampering on the rocks when they first come in but this guy didn't even get out of his chair. The tags must stay on the rocks until after they are sold so the proper miner gets credit for his rocks. It doesn't matter if there are flags on the rocks or not as long as they are properly tagged because not all rocks are flagged before they are captured.

The auction went off without a hitch with the rocks receiving a very good price. We had arranged with the auction office to secretly trace the money through the system. The auction house issued their credits one week after the sale and our commander hung around to pick up his money. When he took possession of the sales receipts he and his crew were arrested on the spot and their ship was confiscated. There was a surprise disbursement listed on the sales slip to a Krammer Services Inc. that we later confirmed was owned by the same Ralph Krammer who is the receiving officer at the Space Authority Office. He had been receiving a third of the sale price from any rocks that he waved through the system so he was arrested along with the others

In the meantime Gem Space had applied to seize the funds from the sale of the rocks and Sigme had laid a claim against the pirates Spoke to cover the expenses of repairing their ship. As soon as Sigme 2 had delivered Sigme 1 to our repair shop on Mars it was assigned to tug duties out in the Belt as a replacement for Sigme 1. We were going to have to make do with one ship for a while.

Chapter 25

After the sale I was quite popular with the other miners because I had helped catch the pirates. By then they had learned that I was a partner in Sigme and they were eager to learn about mining out in the Belt. We swapped a few stories and I started to hear rumours about big things coming for the Moon. There were no solid facts but I heard the same rumour from several different sources.

I had been away for two weeks in total and I admit I was anxious to get back to the ranch. Victoria and I may have been an old married couple by then but I missed having her around even though I hadn't been gone that long. It's amazing how well suited to each other we are. To say we are comfortable with each other would not be fair to either one of us. It would be far more accurate to say we are comfortable around each other but there is still lots of fire in our romance. I can't imagine not having her in my life.

It didn't take long for Kelly and Dwaine to decide that it would be only appropriate if the ship that stole from them should belong to them. Dad didn't care who bought it as long as he got the money to repair Sigme 1 so Kelly made the trip from Mars to the Moon to be at the confiscated equipment auction the next month. I'm sure they expected to get a deal because they had got the last one so cheap but that wasn't going to be the case. The other miners had already converted any spare ships that they could find into Harvesters and were always on the lookout for more. The pirates ship was fully operational and had already been converted as a tug so it generated a lot of interest and Kelly had to pay $120,000,000.00 for it. That was half the price of a new one but there weren't any more available and they didn't want to wait for a new one so it was worth the price. They hadn't got as good a deal as they had hoped for but it was still a good deal in that market. Kelly told me later that she would have gone as high as $200,000,000.00 if necessary. They had a good cash reserve because they still hadn't spent all the money from the treasure rocks and Gem Space was doing really well. The extra cost for the Spoke was partially offset by the price they had gotten for the stolen rocks. Kelly told me that the market on Mars was softening a lot because of the number of ships coming in from the Belt with multi-rock loads. The supply was quickly outstripping the demand and even Stellar Steel was talking about limiting the number of rocks it would accept.

I insisted that Kelly come and visit with us since she was already almost on our doorstep. She agreed to come and stay for a week and I really enjoyed catching up on the latest news with her. She and Virginia seemed to get along really well and our kids took to her like ducks to water. I have to admit that it was a little weird having both women that I loved in the same house. I knew I still had very strong feelings for Kelly when my heart skipped a beat as I saw her step off the shuttle at the Spaceport in Winnipeg. She and Dwaine are very happy together but I could feel her warmth toward me every time we got close to each other. I think it was a good thing that Kelly didn't stay longer than a week. Virginia mentioned to me that she had noticed that I seemed to change when she was in the room. I brushed it off as familiarity with each other and a common interests thing but I heard the warning loud and clear. She was willing to let the past stay in the past but the present had better stay uncomplicated. Dwaine and Kelly had decided that they were going to focus on expanding their fleet rather than start a family but I could tell that being around our kids had made her realize what they had given up.

The sale of the confiscated ship was an opportunity they had been looking for. They loved being on Mars and were determined to be one of the major players out in the Belt. There were a lot more Harvesters out in the Belt now and they could see an opportunity to diversify and form their own towing company. They had already lined up two customers so along with their own loads this ship was fully committed even before it went into service.

Gem Space had built a small factory on Mars to produce the two stage flagging probes and now they were going to expand into a towing company. Dad was proven right again. Gem Space had taken the first steps to becoming the diversified conglomerate that he had predicted might be possible.

After Kelly left I went back to being a rancher but something had changed. I had gotten a taste of the excitement of being on the frontier again and although ranch life was busy, it had lost its challenge. I really enjoyed being on the ranch with my family but I couldn't shake the feeling that I needed to do more.

I started digging into the rumours I had heard at the auction and I quickly found that there really was something big in the wind. Virginia was a little surprised when I got myself invited to the Space Industrial Council meeting in Houston the month after Kelly left. The germ of an idea was starting to grow in my head but I didn't want to tell her about it yet. I told her Dad had asked me to go and represent Sigme which wasn't exactly a lie since I had told dad that I was thinking of going and he thought it was a good idea. I didn't learn anything specific but you could almost taste the optimism in the air. The consensus was that there would soon be a major announcement concerning the Space Industries and everyone was sure that it would be very good for business. I was now on their contact list so I would know as soon as anything happened.

I finished repairing the windmills and helped bring in the crops but the ranch didn't really need me anymore. Jim was a first rate manager and everything went as smooth as clockwork whether I was around or not. He had already hired a part time helper to take my place when I wasn't around. We had given Jim full authority to make any decisions regarding the running of the ranch and a substantial raise as well as the house on Lot 2 rent free as a bonus and that turned into another win-win situation. He had his own place again where he felt at home and he was always around to watch over things.

I found that I was spending more and more time in the office going over the reports from Mars and even talking to Dwaine and Kelly every now and then. Virginia had noticed that I had seemed a lot more antsy than normal lately so she suggested I find a project to keep me busy.

I had been planning on resurrecting the old Gravity Irrigator in the back of our ranch so I started on that.

A Gravity Irrigator is exactly what it seems to be. It uses the force of Gravity to power the pumps that force the water in the tank out through the pipes to the irrigation towers scattered about the field. It is really a very basic machine that serves a necessary need so it was usually used in areas that had a limited water supply and little or no electricity. It was almost always used in conjunction with a wind driven water pump but could also utilize solar panels to power the charging pump. The charging pump delivered water to a vertical water tank. The water tank housed a float that was connected to as many as four external weights via a locking pin arrangement. The float raised with the water level until it reached the stops at the top of the tank where it would then trip the locks that secured the weights to the float. The weights were attached to a chain and pulley that powered the irrigation pumps when the weights were allowed to free-fall. The float followed the dropping water level until the weights rested on the stops at the bottom. At that point the charging pumps would start replenishing the water in the tower and when the float started to raise again it would again lock the weights to the float. The cycle is repeated as often as the water level is replenished from the charging pump.

This system was normally connected to stationary irrigating towers approximately 20 feet high and placed about 40 feet apart in the area to be watered. A rotating head mounted on the top of the towers had two 10 foot arms attached to it. These arms rested against the tower structure until they started to turn. As the water pressure from the irrigating pumps reached the head at the top of the tower it would force the head to rotate. The arms attached to the head would then pivot outward and begin spraying water on the surface below. When the head reached its operating speed the arms would be fully extended and they would be throwing water outside of their radius as well as watering the ground directly below. When the water flow stopped they would fold back down out of the way against their rests on the tower. In this way the towers are unobtrusive in their dormant state but would spread water over a very large area when they were rotating.

The system is built to operate with a very minimum of maintenance so they are ideally suited to isolated areas with a limited water supply. In our case it was used to irrigate a small piece on the very back of our property that was outside the sweep of our pivot style irrigation system. Without water the only thing that grew in these areas was some stunted grass and weeds.

My new project was keeping me busy but not so busy that it took my mind off of what was happening on Mars. In January when Dad came for his annual visit we had several heart to heart talks again and I have to admit I was quite torn. On the one hand I loved my life at the ranch and didn't want to do anything to jeopardize our happiness there and on the other hand I wanted more and more to be involved in what was happening out in the Belt.

It was a surprise to us when he announced that he had started a serious relationship with Helen Humbolt. She was born on the Moon to one of the first families that had moved there to help build the first mining complex.

Dad had met her at one of the infamous wedding receptions being held in the Sigme cafeteria. Dad was feeling particularly lonely and she had just filed for a divorce from her first husband and was in a partying mood. They went home together that night and the relationship built from there. They have been seeing each other off and on for three years and this last year it has gotten more serious. She loved the Mars lifestyle but she knew how easily you could be consumed by the never-ending challenge of working there. With that thought in mind she had convinced Dad that he would have to cut back on his workload so they could have some time together if this relationship were going to evolve into a shared life. Dad didn't mention marriage but I could tell he really didn't want to lose her.

We were both happy that Dad had found someone to share his life with and Virginia made him promise to bring her with him the next time he came. At the same time it did put more pressure on me to take a bigger share of the load in running Sigme so Dad could have a life other than work. I promised

Dad that I would try to take some of the load off him but I had no idea how I would be able to do it.

We talked about the softening of the rock market on Mars and Dad wasn't worried about it. So far Stellar Steel was still taking all the rocks we could bring in and even if they did decide to cut back, it wouldn't affect us much because we were their prime supplier. He admitted that Stellar Steel had been caught off guard by the amount of rocks we had been delivering but they had compensated by buying less from the other contactors. The two new Harvesters had been delivered so we now had three ships harvesting and together with the two ships from Gem Space it was everything that Sigme 1 could do to keep up. As a matter of fact most of the other contractors from Mars now delivered their rocks to the Moon unless they had a specific order from Stellar Steel.

He agreed that it wasn't a good time to be expanding and he was a little worried for Dwaine and Kelly because of their plans to diversify. He also downplayed the excitement about the expansion of the industrial base on the Moon because he didn't see how that could benefit us.

Just before he left Dad pointed out to me again that I had been enjoying the benefits of being a major shareholder but I had not held up my end of the bargain by contributing to the company. He was right of course but Virginia was still adamant that our home was here on Earth and that she had no desire to move. When Dad left at the end of January we still had not come to any kind of agreement that we both could live with. I brought up the subject again of the growing excitement coming from the Moons industrialists and he admitted that it was interesting but he still couldn't see how that would benefit us. I told him that I was working on a plan that would mean it could do us a lot of good but I needed more details before I was ready to talk about it. We left it at that but I could see that I had piqued his interest.

I quickly fell back into my ritual of perusing the company records from my office at the ranch and found myself talking more and more to both Dwaine and Kelly when I caught them in their office. Their office was still in the Sigme complex but they were looking for a new place to call home. The nice thing about mining by remote control is the sensors will warn you of anything that needs your attention. That leaves you with a lot of free time that can be used for other things as long as you are electrically connected to the control panel. Unless something special is happening they actually leave the control room unmanned overnight so that they can live a normal life together but at least one of them usually hangs around the office during the day.

It was fall by the time I had finished the Irrigator and I was spending my extra time talking to Dwaine and Kelly again. Luckily the orbits of Earth and Mars were converging so we could talk almost normally. There was only a 10 second delay between transmissions. I guess I was whining a little bit too much about Dad putting a lot of pressure on me to take more of the load at the office when Kelly blurted out "why don't you sell us your shares?"

You should have seen the look on Dwaine's face as he did a double take and stared at Kelly with his mouth open. I guess I must have had a shocked look on my face too because Kelly immediately apologized.

I don't know where that came from, she said, that was incredibly rude of me. Please don't be offended.

I'm not offended, I said, I'm sorry if I've been crying on your shoulder too much. Have I given you the impression that I wanted to sell out?

No, no, Kelly said, I have no idea why I said that. We're glad that you feel you can talk to us and we like to hear how you are doing. Can we forget I said it? Please call us anytime you feel like talking especially if you need to vent a bit. I'm sure you realize that we have a special relationship. I didn't realize how special it was until after I talked to some of the other girls who had taken a contract on a ship. I wasn't the only one who ended up with a bad taste in their mouth after a term out in the rings. Every girl I have talked to has ended up being quite resentful because they felt they were either taken for granted or taken advantage of. It's quite unusual for them to even keep in touch with their old crewmates. The friendship we developed is obviously very unique because all three of us go out of our way to keep in touch. Please keep calling because it rekindles our feelings for each other every time you do.

That goes for me too, added Dwaine, I like feeling that you trust us enough to share your thoughts with us and I consider you one of my closest friends.

We signed off shortly after that but I couldn't get the idea out of my mind. Maybe that would solve my problem after all. It was a week before I told Victoria what Kelly had said and she was as shocked as I had been at first. She knew that I had been stewing over my talks with Dad but she hadn't even considered the possibility that we should sell our shares. It was obvious to her that I had been getting more and more restless and she took the opportunity to lay her cards on the table. She admitted that she was worried that I was going to leave her and the kids and go back into space again and she was upset that I had spent more time talking to Dwaine and Kelly about it than to her. She had me there so I had no choice but to tell her what I was thinking about even though I still didn't have a firm plan. To my surprise she didn't try to argue with me or talk me out of it. She had known for a long time that ranch life wasn't enough for me and she just wanted to keep us together. She admitted that she was willing to move back to Mars if that was what it took and she was relieved to find out that I didn't want to move. We had a real heart to heart talk for the first time in a long time but the only thing we accomplished was that we agreed that we didn't want to sell our shares.

Virginia is as resourceful as they come when it comes to sorting through a problem. We talked until daybreak and I had to reassure her several times that I was happy with my life with her and I did not want to move to Mars. We finally had a plan that we thought would work but I had a few things to check out before we presented it.

In business, timing is everything when it comes to taking advantage of an opportunity and as luck would have it the Space Industrial Council issued an advance notice that the WGC Intergovernmental Committee was going to make their plans known at the conference next month. The World Governing Council had replaced the old United Nations after the member countries had finally realized that it was a toothless tiger. The veto system granted to the members of the Security Council actually rendered is helpless when it came to holding the permanent Security Council members accountable. In the end the final structure of the WGC looked a lot like the United Nations it had replaced. They replaced the Security Council with an elected Council that held office for 5 years and were elected on staggered election dates from the general membership. The vote of the panel was binding and there was no veto for anyone. They kept most of the organization that the United Nations had created because they were doing so much good.

I couldn't find anyone who knew what the announcement would be and that in itself was unusual because government bureaucracies are notorious for leaking like a sieve. Virginia and I agreed that I needed to be there to get as much information as I could first hand. It's amazing how much more you get from interacting with the people at a conference than from a dry formal announcement. I left a day early to be sure I had a place to stay and that proved to be very prudent because everybody and his dog in the space industries community was there.

Chapter 26

This wasn't a major announcement; it was a bombshell. The WGC had been meeting secretly over the previous two years and they had hammered out a joint venture agreement to build and launch a three wheeled Interstellar Space Ship. Their mission was to find a habitable planet and establish a settlement there. I couldn't help but wonder if this was a replay of the settlement of the new world by the European Nations in the 15 and 1600s. Time may move on but the human spirit remains the same. We have an insatiable appetite for exploring and pushing our boundaries to the limit in the hope of finding something better.

The outer rings of the two outer wheels would be the habitant rings and they would each be the home of 2500 people. The ship could easily hold more people but they thought it wise to leave room for the population to expand because 10 generations could easily come and go during the journey.

The rings on the center wheel will be the biggest because they will house the life support and food compounds. Everything from greenhouses to "small animal" farms to raise some real meat and supply the genetic foundation for the new settlement so they could be self-sufficient would be housed there. Most of the meat consumed during the journey would be cultured protein that looked and tasted almost like real meat so the breeding stock would survive to seed the new settlement.

The Ship is going to be 2-miles in diameter and is going to be constructed in Moon orbit with most of the materials coming from the Moon factories. This was as big an opportunity for us as it was for the Moon based industries because they were going to need all the raw materials they could get their hands on and that was the business we were in.

There was some very intense reaction to the announcement to build the Ship from a lot of different sources. To say that the announcement was greeted with incredulity and utter amazement would be a serious understatement. The consensus of the objections was that the squandering of so much money and effort on a space station that would only carry a minuscule number of our species to an unknown destination was ridiculous in the extreme. That amount of money could improve the living standard of every person on Earth. This same subject had been at the core of innumerable in depth debates in every government on Earth before the decision was made to build the Ship.

After the initial furor toned down the WGC published the scientific evidence that had forced them to even consider this kind of a drastic action.

It had been confirmed that our Sun would undergo a midlife burp in about 400,000 years and that burp would burn off our atmosphere and leave the Earth a barren smouldering rock. If our species were to survive we would need to transplant as many of us as possible to a different solar system with a younger star. The nearest known planet that appears to be capable of supporting our kind of life form is 125 light years away. Even with the Ion Drives we will be traveling roughly 500 years just to get there and it will take another 125 years for us to receive their arrival announcement. They will be using rockets for a faster start and to stop at the other end but the Ion Drives will supply the main thrust after they are well underway. They will also need large retro rockets so they can maneuver quickly to dodge rocks that come too close. If for any one of a thousand reasons the planet is not habitable then they will have to continue their search. During that time frame we will send more ships out in different directions to improve our chances of success. Just knowing that we are capable of surviving for that long in space will be a major achievement in the quest to spread our seeds aloft.

In the galactic time frame 400,000 years is little more than the blinking of an eye and the timing of the midlife burp of a star is far from an exact science. Added to that, the evolution of the event was not known. It was impossible to know when we would start to feel the effects of this change and how the Earth would be affected by the preliminary build-up to the actual burp. Any number of things could render us helpless to the ravages of a runaway sun. In the end, the decision makers were left with one indisputable fact.

The sun in a very short galactic timeframe will burp and render the Earth and probably our entire solar system completely lifeless. The obliteration of every life form on Earth seems inconceivable to us but it wouldn't even cause a ripple in the ebb and flow of the Cosmos. It's impossible for us to know how many times this may have happened in the past. Millions of stars have been born and died a fiery death since the big bang and if life did evolve on one of their planets we would have no way of knowing about it because all evidence of their existence will have been wiped out. The survival of our species is not assured in the Galaxy. If we do nothing then we will very likely simply disappear. This event could happen anytime but definitely within the next 400,000 years. It is far better to be premature in our actions because being late will be too late. I think the realization that if this started to happen tomorrow all evidence of our existence could disappear before we could do anything about it was the final straw that left them with no choice but to start now. Just the launching of one ship will be a major step toward ensuring our self-preservation. Luckily we are at a time when with our present technology and resources we are capable of building a prototype ship and launching it through Interstellar Space toward a new home.

I freely admit that I didn't see the logic or understand the reasoning behind the spaceship idea until they released these facts. As soon as I read them I knew they were on the right track and they would be going ahead with their plans regardless of the public uproar. We now know that things can change fast in space and even a seemingly minor event like the close passing of two planets or an impact from any medium sized rock could wipe us out forever. The stripping of the atmosphere off of Mars and the killing of the dinosaurs is ample proof of that.

Chapter 27

During all this turmoil I gathered all the facts I could because I knew that the early bird gets the worm and we would need to move fast if we were going to really capitalize on this opportunity. I called Dwaine and Kelly in the morning while I was fresh because I wanted my wits about me when I proposed this to them. I got lucky because she and Dwaine were both in the office and I jumped right in after we exchanged pleasantries by saying.

I think there's something we need to talk about.

Oh my god, cried Kelly, you ARE upset with me aren't you? Is that why you haven't called us for over a month? I've been really worried that you won't want to talk to us anymore. Honestly, I was about to call Virginia to find out what was going on.

No Kelly, I'm not upset with you, I assured her, but you did strike a nerve the other day and I needed time to check a few things out.

Please Wade, she said, I didn't mean to say that.

Relax Kelly, that isn't what I wanted to talk about exactly.

What you mean exactly, she asked

As usual Kelly, I said, I think you may have hit on something that we need to explore a little more. Were you just talking or is this something you would consider?

What you mean consider, Dwaine asked.

I mean, would you consider being true partners with Sigme?

This is weird Wade, are you saying you're willing to sell your shares, asked Kelly.

What I'm saying is that there may be a way for all of us to work together if that would interest you.

I saw the light come on in Kelly's eyes and she shifted into business mode.

What did you have in mind Wade, she asked?

Can you be in Dad's office tomorrow afternoon for a secure video call, I asked?

They looked at each other and nodded so I set the time at 2 o'clock. Next I had to put in a call to Dad and after a very long discussion and several adjustments to our plan he agreed to the meeting in his office at 2 the next afternoon.

Virginia was with me when we made the call and after pleasantries were exchanged Dad said,

It's your move Wade; tell us what this is about.

Ok, Dad, have you told Dwaine and Kelly what we have been talking about?

No, I thought it would be better if I left that to you.

Ok then; let's start from the start. I've had this germ of an idea growing in my head almost from the first time Dad told me he wanted me to get more involved with running the company. Even then I liked the idea of all of us working together as partners and when Kelly suggest that I should sell my shares I started to put things together.

Virginia and I have talked about his at length and I'm sorry Kelly, we don't want to sell our shares and Dad's right, it is time I got more involved with the company. My urge to work the land has been satisfied and my trip to the Moon made me realize that I miss the excitement of working in space. Having said that and as Dad well knows, I like my life here at the ranch and I don't want to leave my family and go back into space. When Kelly inadvertently made the offer to buy our shares it set us on a new course and I think I've found a way that we can all get what we want.

Enough Wade, interrupted Kelly, you're kill us here. We know you've conjured up something that involves us so what is it?

Sorry Kelly, I know you like to get right to the point but I thought it was important that you know what we were thinking before you hear this.

Virginia and I own 25% of Sigme, Dad owns 55% with Chris Crater and Robert Aikens each owning 10%. Sigme is not listed on any stock market so we are free to consider any offer that comes our way. We haven't mentioned this to Chris and Robert yet and you should know that they will have to agree to this before the deal is final. They are Dads former workmates who hung in there when he needed them and Dad won't do anything that changes the structure of the company without their approval.

Ok Kelly I'm ready. I'm suggesting that Gem Space buy a 25% share in Sigme from Dad for 500 million dollars and a 10% share of Gem Space. At the same time I suggest that you make an offer for the shares of the other board members who Dad assures me are ready to retire. I'm sure you realize that Sigme in easily worth $100 billion dollars so that is a really good price for you and it will leave you with 45% of the shares in Sigme with only Dad and I on the board with you. This could be a win-win situation for all of us. We would expect that as the major shareholder you two would assume the positions of CEO and Director of the Board at Sigme and Dad will be available to assist you at your request and to act as liaison with Stellar Steel. Dad's responsibilities will be cut drastically so he will have more time for himself but he would still like to be involved at least in the short term with the decision making process. Gem Space will be the biggest and most powerful company in the Belt and will control a huge chunk of the rings to sweep rocks from. Virginia and I will still receive our income from our shares in Sigme in return for which I am willing to look after our operations here on the Moon. By that I mean I will manage our refueling and repair facility as well as attend the monthly auctions to oversee the cataloguing and sale of our rocks. I have heard that the monthly auctions will soon be changed to bi-weekly.

That brings me to another subject that could be even more significant than the merging of our two companies. I'm sure you have heard by now that the new Interstellar Space Ship is going to be built in orbit around the Moon. They are going to need all the rocks they can get their hands on and if we play our cards right, we can be their prime contractor.

With our combined Harvesters and all three Spokes doing duty as tugs we can bring a steady stream of selected rocks in from the Belt. I would like to suggest that Gem Space claim two more sections above the current six now held by the two companies to increase out sweep of the rings.

You guys are awful quiet over there Kelly; what are you thinking?

Speaking for myself Wade, answered Dwaine, I'm doing just that, thinking. You've outdone yourself this time and that's a lot to absorb all at once.

I know it's a lot to spring on you at one time but with this new space station contract in the offing I think we need to move fairly quickly. Did you hear anything you were opposed to Dwaine?

No, not off the top of my head Wade but I need time to sort this out in my head before I can form any kind of an opinion. When are they letting the contracts for the rocks?

The final plans are just being drawn up but they know enough to be able to start construction and to order the materials from the factories. That's where we come in. We will have to double or even triple our mining operations to supply the factories with the ore they are going to need. The Moon is definitely going to be a beehive of activity for at least the next 50 years. I'm sure they will have to sub-contract a good part of the mineral extraction work to the factories on Mars as well so Space Based Industries are going to be booming for at least the foreseeable future.

They are accepting proposals starting the 15th of next month and I think if we are ready to make a supply commitment to them then we should be able to get a preferred price as well.

Dad has suggested that we sub-contract some of the harvesting to start with to help us meet our commitments if we manage to land a big supply contract.

That's enough for now Wade, interrupted Kelly, my head is spinning and we definitely need time to talk about this. I have to ask; Mr. Frederick; do you agree with all of this?

I admit that it took me a while to warn up to it but I think this could work out really well for all of us in the long run. Wade is firmly against moving back to Mars and I know that you two are honest and trustworthy with a good amount of ambition thrown in so I know I'll be putting Sigme in good hands. In answer to your question Kelly: yes, as the present CEO of Sigme, I am in agreement with this proposal.

Well, Dwaine said, I know that we need to take some time to think about this so how about we get together again in two weeks. I think it would be a good idea if you told your other board members what we are considering Mr. Frederick.

Yes, Dwaine I thinks that's only fair. May I suggest that we meet in the boardroom here so everybody can be present.

Great idea, Kelly said, How about we work up an offer for them by the end of this week so they'll have time to think about it.

Ok, then it's settled, said Dad, I'll call a board meeting tomorrow and tell them what we're talking about and I'll pass your offer on to Chris and Bob when you're ready. I think we've got lots to think about for now so I suggest we all go to our corners and meet again in two weeks.

The Starship is going to be something else and it is going to take at least 50 years to build. They are sparing no expense in its construction. The outer hull is going to be made entirely of Steller Steel and it will be self-sustainable in both fuel and food production. It will carry its own fleet of netships so they can capture their own ice balls to replenish their supply of rocket fuel and water. There will be a reduced gravity ring built ½ way out on each of the outer wheels for storage of the food and supplies. All three wheels will have three rings, one very close to the center for storage and very low gravity work stations, a ½ gravity ring for the hydro phonic gardens and anything else that didn't require full gravity to develop normally. The third or outer ring on the center wheel will be a double size ring that will house the animals and other food production facilities.

The Starship will be too heavy to turn around easily so the rocket thrust will be redirected instead to allow the ship to decelerate when they want to orbit the new planet. The living compounds interior floor design is not a true arc. It has three equally sized flat floors offset so that the residents can live in a normal gravity sensation regardless of what the ship is doing. The rearward floor is for accelerating, the center for traveling and the forward floor for decelerating. It will be a simple matter of rearranging the furniture when the ship changes from one mode to another. The ship could be in each of these conditions for years and probably generations at a time so it is crucial that gravity feels normal for the human body to develop properly both before and after birth.

Each outer ring on the outer wheels will house 2500 people and each living space will be protected by an air lock. To get from one home to another a person will have to go out through a doorway into a walkway and then pass through an airlock to get into the walkway for the next home. The airlocks will be left open for convenience but a drop of pressure of 5 p.s.i. between any compartment will automatically close all of them until the control is manually reset.

The most likely planet that could support a human settlement is orbiting a star 125 light years away so this is going to be a trip of at least 500 years presuming we can eventually reach 1/4 light speed. That will mean that up to 10 generations of humans will live and die before we reach it. For that reason this ship must be completely self-reliant and self-sustainable. We will be receiving regular updates as they go along so if they have a system failure or discover some serious flaw we will know about it and correct it in the next ships. The plan calls for the building of several ships over the next two hundred years and sending them off to different locations. If the burp occurs prematurely them we will have at least saved enough people to ensure that our species will survive.

Some astronomers are now theorizing that there may be a quicker way to reach the distant stars. It is still thought to be impossible to reach speeds even close to the speed of light but there may be a way to cut years off the travel time. It has been proven that the stars in the universe are moving further apart with time and they appear to be accelerating as well. One astronomer had compared this to the spots on the skin of a balloon that is being blown up. This has fostered a search to see if we are actually living on the skin of a space-time bubble that was created when the big bang blew our universe into being. The big bang is generally considered to have been an eruption into the fabric of space-time similar to the eruption of a volcano here on Earth. It is now thought that is may have been an explosion rather than an eruption and that could have created a bubble that would be spherical in shape rather than coned shaped. If we are actually living on the relatively thin skin of a giant bubble that is still expanding then it may be possible to cross through the interior of this bubble rather than travel along the outside of it. If the edge of this skin can be identified and the barrier crossed with a space vehicle; then it would be possible to travel across the sphere on a chord-like trajectory and therefore cut years off the time it would take to travel around the outer skin of the bubble.

That was one of the longest two weeks I have spent and I knew even before Kelly said a word that we had a deal in the making because I could see it in her eyes.

After we exchanged pleasantries Dad started off by saying

I should bring you up to speed Wade. We have had a chance to talk before you called and Dwaine and Kelly have some interesting changes to make to your proposal. I'll let Dwaine have the floor.

To start with Wade: I want to assure you that we like the idea of merging our two companies. Having said that, there are some things we would like to change that could make this a little more workable for all of us.

Go ahead Dwaine, you've got my full attention.

Our first concern is with money. Don't get me wrong, the price you have proposed is more than fair but if we laid out that kind of cash we would be cash poor and not able to take the steps necessary to take full advantage of current events. We agree with you that this is an unprecedented opportunity but we have to be able to prepare for it. To do that we will need all the cash we can get our hands on so here's what we propose.

We will tender Mr. Frederick 15% of Gem Space if he will credit the $500 million back to Gem Space as a shareholders loan payable in 5 years. That will allow us to keep enough cash to claim two more sectors in the rings directly above our current claims so that every rock in the inner eight rings of the Belt will eventually have to pass through one of our claims. We will also commit to buying two more Harvesters and one more Spoke to be used as a tug so that we can properly mine all of the sectors.

Before you answer Mr. Frederick; we would also like you to tender an extra 6 percent of your shares to Gem Space so that we will be free to make any necessary changes as we go along.

Let's deal with that first, interrupted Dad, I don't have any objection to the shareholder loan idea but I don't think I can agree to the extra shares and here's why. I have built this company from the ground up and I'm willing to give up a good portion of its control but not to one entity. I think I still have a lot to offer as an adviser and my advice in this case is it is much wiser to have a board where a consensus is required before any major changes are made. I can tell you from experience that it can save a lot of money from mistakes or rash decisions.

Is this going to be a deal breaker Dwaine?

No, Mr. Frederick; we thought you might feel that way and we're still willing to stay with the 15% share offer because we think you will be a valuable asset to the company and you can take some of the operational load off of us.

That's fine by me Dwaine, I guess we can move on then. What other concerns do you have?

As you know we have tendered a cash only offer to Chris and Robert. It will eat up some of our cash reserve but we don't want to dilute our ownership of Gem Space any more than necessary. How do you feel about that?

Before you answer that Dad, I interrupted, do you mind telling me what that offer was Dwaine?

Dwaine looked at Kelly with a puzzled look and said, I guess not Wade but why do you want to know?

Virginia and I would like to buy their shares instead and tender them to Gem Space for a straight across trade of shares so we would have a 20% interest in Gem Space. This will save more of your cash reserve and we both like what you have done with Gem Space and would love to be part of it.

Dwaine looked at Kelly again who still had a startled look on her face when she smiled and nodded her head. Dwaine nodded back as he said

We're very pleased to hear that Wade. Kelly and I have been wondering what it would take to entice you into our company because we work so well together. The only fly in the ointment is that you will be getting a disproportional portion of our shares compared to your Dad. How do you feel about that Mr. Frederick?

That OK with me answered Dad. I'm really glad to see Wade taking a serious interest in space again. I can see a potential problem with Chris and Bob. I think Wade should tell them what he intends to do with their shares. It might help them understand why they haven't been offered any shares if you explain why this offer is only open to you. I was supposed to announce today that they both had accepted the offer but I think this changes things enough that they should have a chance to reconsider. It is never good business to create bad feelings with your business partners. I suggest you offer them a signing bonus when you approach them Wade. I think they are ready to retire and will take your offer as long as they don't feel they are getting the short end of the stick. We closed the meeting pending a decision from Chris and Bob and Virginia and I put together an offer for them.

They were surprised when I contacted them about a conference call but they agreed to a meeting the next morning. They were curious and a little cautious when we first started the meeting because Dad hadn't told them anything except that there was another offer for their shares that they should consider. Virginia and I had decided to sweeten the pot for them by $500,000.00 so I started by telling them the offer they had from Gem Space was still valid and there would be no hard feelings if they decided to accept that instead. I explained that we expected to gain an advantage from buying their shares and because of that we were willing to pay a premium price. They were a little dubious about the share trade until I explained that Dwaine and Kelly had been looking for a way to bring me into the company. They were very aware of our previous working arrangement and only thought about the offer for a couple of minutes before they accepted it. Dad had been right when he said they were ready to retire and because I had been so straight with them they were actually happy that we were able to leverage their shares into a position on the board of Gem Space.

This was the final piece of the corporate puzzle that we needed to put everything together so within a week we were a lot poorer and board members of Gem Space. After the dust settled Gem Space owned 45% of Sigme with Dad at 30% and Virginia and I at 25% and Gem Space also had two new owners with Virginia and I owning 20% and Dad 15%.

The first order of business after all the papers were signed was to elect the company officers. Dwaine was elected as CEO of Sigme and Kelly was Chairman of the Board with the roles reversed on Gem Space with Kelly as CEO and Dwaine the Chairman of the Board. Dad and I were minority shareholders on both boards which Dad found to be a little weird at first but his duties were greatly reduced so he would have more time to himself. Dad's main job was to be a liaison between both of our companies, Stellar Steel and the various government agencies. My responsibilities were to take control of all operations relating to our Moon Terminal and the rock auctions. Kelly and Dwaine were of course responsible for directing all of the companys business and all the mining operations.

The first thing Dwaine asked Dad to do as the company liaison to Stellar Steel was to negotiate a change in our exclusive deal with them. We were now capable of supplying more rocks that they could use and with the softening market on Mars we needed to be able to sell our rocks on the open market at the Moon. That turned out to be a much easier job that Dad had expected because Stellar Steel had started construction of a new plant on the Moon and only asked for priority choice of any rocks we brought in at either port. They guaranteed us the same bonus structure that we had enjoyed on Mars so this was a win- win deal for both of us. We will be getting top price for every rock we bring in regardless of where we sell it and they will have a guaranteed supply of rocks regardless of what happens at the auctions.

We decided to focus all of our mining efforts out in the Belt but we didn't want to lose our Ring 10 claim so Dwaine suggested that we stay in Ring 10 as long as we could when we were traveling back and forth to the Belt. That more than satisfied the occupancy requirement of our claim and also reduced the danger of an accidental collision with rocks on another claim. The plan calls for us to power directly to Ring 10 and then stay there until we are positioned to jump to the next destination wither it be the Belt, Mars or the Moon.

All three Spokes will be used as tugs and they will use their time in Ring 10 to scan for new rocks and even capture an easy one if it comes their way. The Spokes still carry a full complement of netships just for this occasion and most of our supply of iceballs and ice-iron rocks will probably come from there. Iceballs were becoming more and more valuable because of the expansion happening on the Moon and the iron is always in demand. Gem Space and Sigme are ideally situated to take advantage of this. We will have a huge volume of new rocks passing through our sectors in the Belt that we can scan and choose from so we can virtually guarantee to fill any order we get.

Chapter 28

Things were going really well until the astronomers pushed the panic button. The long-range scanners had identified a huge rock only three years out that had come out of an obscure orbit in the Belt and it was dead on track to collide with Earth. This was a 20 kilometer wide rock that was classified as a CEV (civilization ending event) because it was twice the size of the rock that killed the dinosaurs so it would definitely destroy almost all life on Earth. A rock that size might even crack the crust if it hit land and that would most certainly kill every living thing on the planet. Even if it landed in one of the oceans, the atmospheric damage and the Tsunamis could make the Earth uninhabitable for humans and kill almost everything in the oceans. The news media had named it the Nemesis because it could kill us all unless we did something to deflect it.

Everything came to a screeching halt while the Planetary Council tried to come up with a plan to divert it. The first option they looked at was to deploy a Gravity Tractor. A Gravity Tractor is just what it sounds to be. A Space Vehicle big enough to exert a gravitational pull on an asteroid is placed close enough for it to exert a slight pull on the asteroid. Over time the trajectory of the asteroid is changed enough that it misses Earth and goes merrily on its way into interstellar space. This rock was already too close for a Gravity Tractor to have time enough to pull it off course so they decided that the next best approach was to ram it with several old ICBM rockets. There was a heated debate on the merits of arming them with nuclear warheads so they decided to try knocking it off course first to avoid the danger of creating several chunks that could still be big enough to cause major damage here on Earth. Then we would have several chunks to deflect rather than just one.

The rockets proved ineffective because the Nemesis was tumbling so fast that it deflected them off into space before they could exert any significant push on it. That also cancelled the thought of using warheads because the same thing would happen to them. Time was more and more our enemy because with every minute that passed the Nemesis was getting closer to Earth and therefore it would need a bigger course correction to steer it around us.

Kelly called an emergency meeting of the board on one days notice and I could feel her excitement as she called the meeting to order.

I want to be clear, she said, this could very well be a make or break it operation. It's not only risky, it's dangerous as well but the pay-off could be huge.

She paused to give us a chance to absorb that and then went on to say;

Because we are such a new company and we will be risking the assets of both Sigme and Gem Space we have decided that we will need the full boards approval before we go ahead. The good news is that the full board members of both companies are present so we should be able to decide today.

Come on Kelly, I interrupted; now you're killing me. I'm almost scared to ask but what have you come up with now?

She started by saying that she and Dwaine (mostly her I knew) had come up with an extremely bold and risky plan to not just deflect the Nemesis but to capture it as well. She admitted that she not only needed our permission to go ahead, she needed our input as well to come up with a workable plan.

Dad was never one to walk away from opportunity but when Kelly sketched out her plan it almost blew him away. I was more used to Kelly's ideas and it almost blew me away as well. Before dad had a chance to say anything I suggested that we fine tune it a bit before we made any decision.

It was like old times again with the three of us feeding off of each other and coming up with solutions to problems that would never have been possible by ourselves. The time delay between Earth and Mars was now almost a minute because the planets had passed each other and the distance between them was increasing each day. It was frustrating at first but it eventually worked in our favor. It gave us time to think through what the other person was saying before we responded. Dad was almost spellbound as he watched and listened. We threw one idea after another onto the discussion table and then proceeded to take some part of one to put together with another idea until we had a plan that seemed feasible. We did this over and over until we had solved all the problems we could think of.

Dad had pretty well stayed out of the idea free-for-all and when we were finished he complimented us by saying,

I'm impressed and pleased to be involved with you three and I'm glad I was here to see you working together. There doesn't seem to be any ego involved when you are trying to put a plan together. You aren't a bit self-conscious about throwing an idea out for consideration and you don't care if someone tears it apart or grabs some good part of it to complement another idea. It's obvious now how you were able to bring in both the Gem and the Iron Maiden when another crew would have had all they could do to just bring in one of them.

Kelly called for a vote and we all approved the operation without any hesitation.

We confirmed the next day that the Nemesis was considered a rogue rock and informed the Planetary Council of our intention to capture it. The council was dead against any plan that hadn't been approved by them until Dad pointed out that we were the only company that had the assets to pull this off and that we were ready to go now. The clincher was when he pointed out that we couldn't do any harm because it was already on a collision course with Earth. Two of the members were still worried that we might be wasting assets that could be better used later but they didn't have the authority to stop us so they gave us their blessings and offered us any help we might need.

Virginia was not happy at all when I told her what we had in mind and that I had to leave immediately for the Moon. She changed her mind a bit when I reminded her that unless something was done it was inevitable that three years from now the Earth would be struck a blow that could kill all life on the planet. She still didn't understand why I had to go and why someone else couldn't do it. I tried to explain that we had the best chance of success because of how well we worked together but in the end I had to take a firm stand. She almost lost it when I informed her that the decision was made and I was going with or without her approval. I got a better understanding of her objection to my going off onto this wild goose chase as she called it when she quizzed me about where we were going to be living during the trip out and back. I had to reassure her several times that Kelly and I were both happily married now and the previous arrangement would not be reintroduced into our onboard life. I'm not sure she entirely believed me but that did seem to make her feel better about it.

I left the next morning for Winnipeg after a tearful and passionate good-bye from Virginia and the kids. They didn't understand the danger of the situation but they could tell that their mum was upset and that I was going to be gone for a long time. Even under full power it would take two months to reach the Nemesis and if our plan worked we would be twice as long getting back.

Gem 1 was in port at the Moons spaceport and Sigmes 1 and 2 were in the Mars port with Sigme 3 coming in to the moon from the belt with a load of rocks. I took the Executive Shuttle so I was on the moon the next morning.

I immediately readied Gem 1 for the trip by reworking our nets and the netships for their new role. I knew Dwaine and Kelly were doing the same on Mars and we were going to rendezvous in Ring 10 on the way out. The plan called for each of us to take a fully loaded Spoke complete with all its reworked netships and to tow a full fuel tank with us as well. Dwaine will pull another extra fuel tank with him and we will top up our fuel tanks in Ring 10 and then leave the spent tank there for pick-up by Sigme 3 on its way in. Our experience with the Iron Maiden had taught us that you need brute force and a lot of fuel when you are dealing with a heavy rock and this rock was heavier than anything that had ever been captured before so we weren't taking any chances of running out of fuel. It was probably going to take all of the fuel in the netships just to slow the Nemesis down so it wouldn't collide with Earth. Capturing, controlling and transporting it was another matter altogether.

We rendezvoused in ring 10 as planned and decided to use Dwaine's ship as our control so we linked the other two ships to his computer and Kelly and I moved over to his ship. It was a bit uncomfortable when we met in the control room the first time. All three of us hadn't been alone together since we landed on Mars with our payload of the Gem and the Iron Maiden.

As usual Kelly took the initiative by saying

I'm really looking forward to the three of us working together again but I think we all realize that things have changed since the last time we were together.

She looked directly at me when she said.

We are both happily married now so things can't be the same as it was.

I glad you brought that up Kelly, I said, I'm sure you realize that I have very strong feelings for you but I have stronger feelings for Virginia and I can't do anything to threaten our relationship. I fully expect to be the third man out on this trip.

I appreciate you saying that Wade but Dwaine and I don't think that's fair so we have decided to take separate compartment for the duration.

That's not necessary or fair to either of you, I protested, all that's going to accomplish is to create three frustrated people trying to work together and that's a sure recipe for failure if I ever heard one. Please don't do that.

Dwaine and Kelly looked at each other and nodded and Kelly said

Ok Wade if that's the way you want it but if you start to get snarky we're going to throw you into a cold shower

Deal, I said.

I took the first shift while Dwaine and Kelly made their nest and we automatically settled into our previous work mode. We were powering through unfamiliar territory so there was a lot more to watch for and the shifts passed fairly quickly. Kelly avoided being alone with me at first until I objected to being ignored. I made a point of calling Virginia at least once a week and she gradually became more comfortable with Kelly and I living so close together.

The time passed quickly and we were approaching the Nemesis in just under the two months we had allotted. We started to change our shifts to four hours each so that when we pulled alongside of the Nemesis we were all fresh and ready to tackle it. It looked a lot more dangerous up close and the word tumbling didn't do it justice. Careening through space totally out of control seemed much more appropriate. We scanned it from all four sides and couldn't identify a rotational centreline or any consistency to its motion. It's no wonder the rockets were thrown off into space because even a direct head-on hit would be instantly deflected. The only thing that was consistent was its flight path and our computers confirmed that it would indeed score a direct hit in the northern hemisphere of Earth.

The number one priority for us was to slow it down so that the Earth had time to move past its insertion point into Earths orbit before the Nemesis got there.

To do that we would have to hold our netship rockets in contact with the rock long enough for the thrust to have an effect on it. The problem with that idea was that the way this rock was tumbling it would just twist our nets into a knot and then probably throw both the netships and the net off into space to suffer the same fate as the ICBMs.

Chapter 29

Our original plan called for the three netships from one Spoke to all be linked together and stretched out in its path in a conventional capture scenario. The rockets were to be fired when all three netships were in contact with the surface. That approach was obviously not going to work here so we modified the plan. The new plan called for all three netships to be linked together as before but in a "C" configuration with a radius approximately the same as the rock. From our experience with the Iron Maiden we knew that we had to use all the power we had if we were going to accomplish anything. In this new plan we will fire all 6 rockets on the three netships just before first contact was made. We figured that this would keep the nets from being twisting into a knot because they would be forced against the rock and basically become part of it. The rockets would still be twisting about in space but they would be stationary on the rock. The rockets would fire continuously but they would alternate between full power and ¼ thrust subject to the input from our beacon so the power bursts would at least slow it down and maybe even change its course a bit. The ¼ power burn would still hold the rockets against the rock so the timed power bursts could slow it down and counteract the tumbling motion as well. Our simulator told us that all six rockets firing at full power would be enough to slow the rock and stabilize it some.

Part of the plan worked. We did slow it down some and we did stabilize it some but not enough of each so that we could call it a success. The Nemesis would now miss the Earth but there was a good chance that the Moon's gravity would pull it into it. If it missed the Moon it would certainly strike Earth on its return flyby in 30 years because we had also changed its orbit.

We did learn that the netship rockets weren't powerful enough to really control this thing. The good news is that our netships were thrown off into space when we shut them down and Kelly was able to retrieve them.

We had to do better and that meant that we had to make a new plan from scratch. We pulled out all the stops on this one.

When we threaded the towlines through the nets of the three netships on each Spoke they were connected in a continuous line as well as being connected to the frame of the netships. We had done this because we were worried that the center netship might have been torn apart with all the rockets firing. That little bit of precaution probably saved our butts.

When we analyzed our data from the first try we realized that our rockets were too close together to have any kind of effective stabilizing effect on the rock. Even with all three netships connected together we weren't even 25% around the rock so the mass of the rock was easily overpowering the stabilizing tendencies of the rockets. It was clear that if we were going to gain control of this rock we needed to change our tactics.

We connected the remaining six netships together with the first three so we had one continuous net and then we released the spare fuel tanks from the other two Spokes. Dwaines Spoke might be the only one to survive this but we would still be able to get home even if we were empty handed. We tied all three fuel tanks to our command ship and positioned the other two Spokes at each end of the extended netship array. With the towlines from the Spokes fully extended we now had a basket that extended almost half way around the Nemesis so our rocket thrust from the two Spokes was now outside the diameter of the rock and should be much more effective.

We deployed the net in the same configuration but we only fired the rockets on the two Spokes to catch the rock. As soon as the rock was firmly in the basket we went to full power with both ships and then tied their rocket bursts to our computer so it could time the alternating burst to stabilize the Nemesis. This took most of the tumble out of it but it was still rotating and tumbling too fast for us to handle. The good news was that we had slowed it down enough that it would sail harmlessly past both the Earth and the Moon. The bad news was that we were almost out of fuel on the Spokes and we still didn't have control of the rock.

We shut the rockets down and trouble started immediately. With the rockets shut down the twisting forces coming from the tumbling rock started to wrap the tow-lines around the rock which in turn was pulling both Spokes into the rock. We had no choice but to restart our rockets and keep then at low power to protect our ships. Even at low power we only had one hour of fuel left in the Spokes. Kelly almost jumped down my throat when I suggested that we cut our ships loose and let the Nemesis go on its merry way.

You can't seriously be thinking that, she said. We've got all nine of our netships and most of our nets tied to that rock. On top of that we've spent a fortune getting out here and the last thing I intend to do is to go home empty-handed and broke!

Be serious Kelly, I said. We've still got one ship here and we can save the other two if we act before we run out of fuel. We're already heros on Earth for diverting the Nemesis so I'm sure they'll be glad to replace the equipment we lost. How do you feel Dwaine?

Well, I think Wade might be right.

WHAT!!!!, Kelly hollered

Dwaine took Kelly by the shoulders, and said quite firmly, hear me out Kelly before you jump to conclusions. Wade is right when he says the smart thing to do it to cut our losses and salvage what we can from a bad situation. I just had a wild thought that might work so let's see what we can do with it.

Right now would be a great time for a good idea, I said, I don't want to go home empty handed either. I was just stating the obvious.

The way I see it, continued Dwaine, our most pressing problem is that we are fast running out of fuel on the Spokes so let's tackle that first to try and buy us some time. We have enough auxiliary tanks on each of the Spokes to refuel the netships twice. If we can get onboard the Spokes we can pump that fuel into the ships and buy us a couple of more hours.

I love it, Kelly blurted, if we use that fuel to stop the tumbling altogether we'll be able to tow it anywhere we want.

Not so fast Kelly, Dwaine said, we don't have that much fuel on board.

Yes, I know, answered Kelly, but we will still have the extra auxiliary tanks that we can jettison off the ships. We can collect them with our rocket packs and refill them so we can replenish the fuel in the Spokes.

It's going to be tricky enough getting onboard the ships with the rocket packs let alone trying to manoeuvre the auxiliary tanks as well, I said.

I know, Kelly answered, but by the time we burn up the fuel from our first refuelling we will have slowed it down even more and it will be easier to get on and off the ships.

First things first, interrupted Dwaine, if we don't get some fuel into those ships soon it'll all be all over but the crying. I guess I'm the primary on this one. Both of you are better with the rocket packs than me. I'm sure I don't have to tell you how dangerous this is. If you get hit and injured trying to get onboard we may not be able to get to you in time to help. Are we all agreed on this?

Yes, answered Kelly emphatically.

Let's do it, I said.

Chapter 30

By the time we got into our suits and the rocket packs we only had ½ hr. of fuel left in the Spokes and that didn't leave us with much time to synchronize our trajectory with the tumbling, rotating Spokes. We each carried a safety line with a grab hook on the end so we could snap onto the docking port before we tried to get inside. Even if we did get hit and knocked around by the wobbling docking port the line would prevent us from getting thrown out into space.

Dwaine dropped us both off at the midpoint between them and we rocketed full power toward our respective Spoke. Kelly made it onboard on her first try but my timing was off a bit and I took a hit on the side of the rocket pack. Thank god for the safety line. I made it the second try and scrambled out of my pack. Luckily we had strapped the extra auxiliary tanks to the loading dock after we had filled the storage compartment. My heart was racing as I connected the first one to the pump. I knew we must be running on fumes and I fully expected the engines to sputter and quit at any second. It took almost an hour to pump all the tanks into the ships tank but when we were done we had almost ¼ tank of fuel to work with.

Kelly was finished a little ahead of me and she was about to start throwing the empty tanks off when I stopped her.

Hello Kelly, have you thrown your tanks out yet.

I just released the first one but it won't take me long to chuck the rest off as well.

Don't do that yet Kelly, I just had an idea. What if we tie them all together before we set them free? We can use the tie-straps that held them to the loading dock and they'll be a lot easier to find and recover.

I love it Wade, that will save us a lot of time and we can use the same method to reload them back onto the Spokes.

You guys are on a roll, interjected Dwaine, hurry back. We need to make a plan to bring this baby under our control.

Hold on a minute Dwaine, Kelly said. Wade do you have any fuel left in your rocket pack?

As a matter of fact, I was about to switch it out for a new one from this ship Kelly. Why do you ask?

Let's tie our used packs to the tanks as well so we can use the remote emergency system to fly them home. They can follow us in and we can grab them as soon as we get into the docking station.

Great, I said, we can refuel the packs as well and use them to fly the tanks back to the ships.

Awesome idea Kelly, added Dwaine. Why don't you refuel everything before you get out of your suits so we'll be ready to move quickly when we need to refuel the ships again. I need a little more time to finish these computer simulations anyway.

We were finished refuelling everything and in the control room in just over an hour. Dwaine was waiting for us with a grin on his face.

You look like a cat that just swallowed a canary, was the first thing I said when I saw his face.

Yea, he said, I think I have some good news to share. I've been running several different simulations and I think we have been going about this the wrong way. According to the last three simulations I ran we should stop the rotation first so our anti-tumble efforts can be more effective. It will also make reboarding the Spokes a lot easier.

How is stopping the rotation going to make a difference, asked Kelly?

We need to do a little more than just stopping the rotation; we need to turn the Nemesis so that it is tumbling on the centerline of the direction of travel. That way both the forward motion of the rock and the center-line of its tumbling motion are in the same plane. When that happens we can accurately predict when to fire our power bursts and they will have a much more dramatic effect than if they were off-center. According to these simulations we can stop the rotation with the fuel we have on board and have some to spare.

That sounds good to me, chimed Kelly, it's easy to see how that will them a lot easier to board.

Ok Dwaine, that sounds like a step in the right direction. What do you need us to do, I asked

We need to reposition the two ships so they will counteract the clockwise rotation of the rock. That's going to be a lot easier to do because of the stable centerline of the tumble geometry. We will be pulling at a 45% angle to the rock rather than straight back toward it so that half our thrust will be used to slow the rotation. The computer says that a two-minute burn should stop almost all its rotational inertia. The bad news is that its solar orbit will start to degrade even faster than it is now and if we let it pick up too much speed we might not be able to pull it back. We could lose everything into the sun if we aren't careful.

I think I see a way to help with that, I said. After we stop the rotation we should still have almost an hour of fuel left in the tanks and that's lots of fuel to do a staggered burn.

Ok Wade, I think you've finally lost it, interrupted Kelly, what on earth is a staggered burn.

Yea, I said, I just thought up that name. I may have invented a new manoeuvre because I don't remember ever hearing of it being done before.

Come on Wade, you're killing me here and we don't have time for games; please get to the point, blurted Kelly.

Ok Kelly, here goes. After we stop the rotation we still have to leave the rockets at low power to keep the towline tight. By keeping the towline tight we are also holding the netships and the nets against the rock so they will be gripping the surface. If we go to full power on only one of the rockets it should swing the tumbling centerline about its axis. In actuality we will swing the centerline around so that when we use our power bursts to stop the tumble we will also be slowing the orbit degrade as well. With the tumbling slowed down it should be easy to tow the auxiliary tanks over the ships with the refuelled rocket packs and pump in enough fuel for us to stop it altogether. With the tumbling stopped we can shut down the rockets so we can refuel them directly from our spare tanks. With full tanks the Spokes will easily pull our friend out there up into a higher orbit that will take us out to Ring 10.

Why Ring 10, asked Dwaine, why not Mars?

I don't think the Planetary Council or the Mars Space Authority will allow us to put a rock this size that close to Mars. To be honest, I wouldn't be comfortable about it either. What if we lost control of it when we start to cut it up. We wouldn't have much time to react if we're that close to the planet. Ring 10 is friendly territory and we may not want to sell all of it to the Mars factories and we can easily access either Mars or the Moon from Ring 10.

Kelly walked over and gave me one of her amazing full body hugs.

Welcome back Wade, she said, we are unbeatable as a team.

Chapter 31

Amazingly enough everything worked like clockwork. The two-minute burn almost completely killed the rotation and we let it drift until the ships were in the right orientation for the staggered burn to stop it completely. The staggered burn worked like a charm to swing the Nemesis around and we still had enough fuel for one strong burst to slow the tumbling inertia.

We had a bit of a problem getting the auxiliary tanks back onto the ships. They were still tumbling enough that we couldn't get the string of them on board without them swinging back into the side if the docking station. It was Kellys idea to untie the back tank first and bring them onboard one at a time. It took a little longer than we had planned but we soon were up to ¼ tanks again.

Dwaine used the refueled ships to good advantage when he tied the firing control to his computer again. The simulation had been right and it only took three bursts to bring the Nemesis dead in the water so to speak. With the ships powered down it was childs play to move the spare fuel tanks alongside each ship and pump them full of fuel.

As soon as we were back on board Dwaine powered up both ships and it took a three-minute full power burn before the Nemesis started to climb higher in its solar orbit. It was a good thing we had brought as much spare fuel as we did. It was going to take a lot to spiral this baby out to Ring 10. We had stopped the orbit degrade with that burn so we powered down and let them coast while we collected the spare tanks. After that it was just a matter of plotting our course and then powering up to speed to put us on the path to Ring 10.

To say we were heroes on Earth was a gross understatement according to Dad. He said they spoke of us as if we were gods and they were falling all over themselves to find some way to show their appreciation. I was glad we wouldn't be back for three months so they would have time to get that out of their system.

Dad had already made arrangements with Stellar Steel to use their big laser to cut the Nemesis down to size. He offered to rent it but when the Interplanetary Council heard that we needed one, they insisted on buying one for us. They ordered us the biggest and best that was available and promised to have it on site in Ring 10 by the time we got there. We already had orders from Stellar Steel and the Moon factories for everything we could supply.

Virginia was ecstatic when I called and she said the reception she was getting everywhere she went was unbelievable. The press had stormed the house after the monitoring stations had announced that we had diverted the rock and it would no longer hit Earth. They were making such a nuisance of themselves that she had to ask them to give them some privacy and to leave the property. She was full of questions about how we managed to capture it because nobody had expected us to actually do it. I promised her a full disclosure when I saw her in person but only after we had taken care of some very pressing personal business.

She had a confused look on her face until I said, ok, I'll start first and slowly removed my shirt.

I could hear the change in her voice when I said that and I swear that if she could have crawled through the video link I would have been in for the treat of my life. As it was, thanks to a secure channel and the privacy of our individual rooms we had a very intimate conversation. We had to improvise more than a bit to compensate for the 20 minute lag between sending and receiving mode. After a clumsily start, the time lag actually made out time together more interesting.

My calls to her had been getting more and more intimate on our journey outward but this time we went all the way. It wasn't the same as actually being together but it was the next best thing. We both knew that this wouldn't be the last sexting date we would have.

The three months it took us to get to our destination in Ring 10 were uneventful except for the two stops to top up the fuel tanks on the Spokes. We had to keep the rockets burning continuously to maintain a steady pull on the Nemesis in order to break it away from the sun's gravity. We also had to be very careful about crossing paths with other rocks because we were far too heavy to be doing much manoeuvring. We were always working on the outer edge of our sensors range so we could predict any potential collusion hazards and several times we had to shut the rockets down and coast awhile so that a rock could get out of our way.

The time went surprisingly fast and true to their promise, Wes was there with Sigme 3 and our new Rock Laser to meet us. We wanted to stay and collect our netships and nets but Wes wouldn't hear of it. There was a welcoming committee waiting for us on the Moon and Wes assured us that he would probably be lynched if he delayed us even one hour. As soon as we had the Nemesis secured in its orbit we released our fuel tanks and rocketed full power to the Moon Spaceport.

We were kidnapped as soon as we stepped onto the landing pad at the Spaceport. The spaceport personnel were out in full force and they literally carried us on their shoulders to the terminal building. There was hardly room for us to get through the door because the entire lower floor was packed solid with well- wishers and dignitaries. There was a raised platform in the center of the floor and I spotted Virginia and the kids immediately because they were in the front row alongside Dad and Helen.

The room exploded with noise from the clapping and cheering as they let us down just inside the door. Our honour guard from the Spaceport formed into a spearhead pattern and they burrowed through the crowd to the steps of the center stage. As soon as I reached the top of the steps Virginia broke away from the line up and almost knocked me back down the steps when she ran into my arms. She held nothing back as she melted into me and kissed me with a passion that almost burnt my lips. We had to break it up because the others had taken their que from Virginia and swarmed around all three of us.

Dad managed to elbow his way over to us and gave me the strongest man hug I have ever gotten. He was full of praise for all three of us as he led us to the center of the stage.

It seemed like every dignitary from the Moon and Mars was there to share in the glory but during the first speech from the Mayor of the Moon base the crowd started to migrate toward the stage and it was obvious that they could not be held back much longer. If they swarmed the stage we would have been trampled in their push to get to us. Dad recognized the danger and he actually took the microphone out of the Mayors hand to announce that the bar was open at the back of the hall and the drinks were on the house. That eased the pressure on the stage and the rest of the dignitaries wisely decided to forego their speeches. They did however insist of congratulating us individually and it was an hour before we could break away and slip out the back door. We were afraid to venture out into the crowd even though they seemed to have forgotten about us.

The party that ensued rivalled anything that ever happened on Mars even though there wasn't any grappa to get them going. The free drinks did almost as good a job and that party will be the topic of conversation for a long time as much for its revilers as for its rowdiness. Everybody there was bursting with energy and enthusiasm and could hardly contain themselves. We were the catalysts that released all the pent up anxiety from the past few months and that sense of release resulted in a party atmosphere that was so strong that you could almost taste the energy in the room.

The three of us along with Virginia and the kids followed Dad and Helen to their penthouse suite in the Lunar Hilton where we started our own celebration. Dwaine and Kelly left for their room just down the hall. Dad and Helen volunteered to baby sit the kids if we wanted to make use of the honeymoon suite he had reserved for us.

Despite the pleasure we had enjoyed from our intimate phone calls over the past few months there is nothing that can take the place of feeling the passion from a warm and anxious body next to you.

Life is Good.

Chapter 32

The next couple of months were a blur of activity. After our wonderful stay in the honeymoon suite. We said our good-byes to Dwaine and Kelly who left on the Executive Shuttle to Mars the first thing in the morning. We spent the day with Dad and Helen and took the evening shuttle to Earth. It was the normal commuter shuttle so it was a three day trip and that gave us lots of time to talk and exchange stories about the events of the past 6 months. We were all glad to be back on Earth and together again.

We stayed for the welcome home ceremony at the Space Port in Winnipeg before we made a dash for home. Jim had the ranch purring like a kitten but I joined in with the chores just to get my feet back on the ground. After a week donated solely to ranch life I had to start paying attention to my responsibilities on the Moon.

Sigme's 1 and 2 had to be refurbished and the nets and the netships returned to their original configuration before I could send them back out so there was lots for me to arrange to have done at the Space port on the Moon.

It soon became obvious that I couldn't get it all done from the ranch so I told Victoria that I would be gone for up to 2 weeks and jumped on the Executive Shuttle. It's amazing how much more cooperative people are when you are looking them directly in the eye. Tele-communications will never replace direct personal contact.

I had to draw on some of the residual good-will left from our Nemesis expedition and I was able to get us priority designation at the repair facility. There is only one repair facility on the moon and they were booked solid for the next year. Their other customers were actually anxious to do us a favor so they allowed us to go to the front of the waiting list. Gem Space also needed an office on the Moon so I rented a penthouse room at the hotel for our exclusive use as both an office and sleeping quarters.

Gem Space was starting to deliver the cut off pieces from the Nemesis and I had to tend to them as well. We were cutting 200 ton chucks off and using the Spokes to tow them in three at a time. Wes brought the first load in with Sigme 1 so it could be refurbished. He left Sigme 3 on station in Ring 10 so we could rotate the others into port for refitting. I had Sigme 2 ready to go with its new crew and a new crew for Gem 1 when he arrived with Sigme 1. Wes immediately transferred to Sigme 2 and left with them for Ring 10 to take command of Sigme 3 again and return to his tugboat duties. We needed all our Spokes back in service as soon as possible because we not only had to tow in the loads from the Nemesis, we also had to service the other miners we had contracts with.

The Nemesis was 10,000,000 tons of mostly nickel and iron so there was very little of the PGM metals needed to produce the alloy steels so much in demand. This was good for both Gem Space and the other miners because the capture of the Nemesis had not affected the price of anything except iron. They concentrated on capturing only the higher value rocks and they still needed the tugs from Gem Space to bring them in. Sigme 3 had barely been able to keep up to the towing contracts with the other miners while we were gone so Sigme 2 was also transferred to tugboat duty until the backlog was cleared up. After that Sigmes 1 and 2 will bring in the chunks from the Nemesis with Sigme 2 available to help with the contract work if needed. Gems 1 and 2 will revert back to deep space tugboats for our own rocks.

Delivery of the PGM rocks was now becoming more important than iron because of the glut of iron from the Nemesis. Kelly had reactivated the Harvesters out in the Belt again shortly after arriving back on Mars so we needed Gem 1 back in service so it could rotate with Gem 2.

I was back home in a week and a half to Virginia's surprise and within 2 months everything was back on an even keel. All the Spokes had returned to their rotation schedules and the rocks were coming in at a steady pace. I was easily able to keep up with the paperwork and arrange for the ships to be resupplied and refueled from my office at the ranch. I knew it wouldn't last but for the time being my job was looking pretty cushy.

Things weren't going that well for the Lifeboat Program though. Someone had coiled the phrase Lifeboat when referring to the Space Ship during one of the multitude of debates that sprang up all over the planet after the initial announcement. The media immediately adopted it and the name has stuck.

The formula created by the negotiators to fund the Lifeboat Program was tied to the Gross National Product and the population of each country. Every country on the planet was committed to contribute to the Building Fund according to this formula because this had been passed unanimously by the Council as the WGC had come to be called. Enough countries did meet their initial deposit so that the Building Fund Managers felt confident enough to let the supply contracts. As a result existing factories were expanding and new factories were being built to meet these contracts. The Procurement Committee was mandated to fund the construction or expansion of any factory that was supplying material to the Lifeboat Program and it was not allowed to borrow to obtain the capital. That left the Building Fund as the only source of income and if the money wasn't on deposit then they had to collect it or stop production until they got it.

Funding turned out to be a major problem right from the start. Several of the countries who had signed the memorandum of agreement failed even to post their initial deposits into the Building Fund. This had been anticipated by the WGC so they had formed a Collections Division to deal with the problem. Their mandate was to negotiate first but they had the power to freeze the international assets of the delinquent countries leaders and to stop any international trade with any country that hadn't met its commitment.

This was supposed to ensure that everyone paid their fair share but in reality it had little effect on them. At first a few of the countries found the money to pay their dues when they were pressured but it wasn't long before someone figured out that the Collections Division was another toothless tiger. They realized that because of the time lapse that it took to initiate the sanctions, the people responsible will have moved on. Most of them felt that it was less painful and easier just to leave it for their successors to deal with. In the meantime the fund was empty and they could not meet their payment schedule.

To make matters worse, the furor over the project had not abated and the governments that had made the initial decision to build the Lifeboat were in danger of being replaced. Discontent was running very high in the bigger democracies because of the amount of money being taken off of social programs to meet their Lifeboat commitments. Politicians just naturally attack the social budgets first because they consider them the least critical to the national economy. The smaller governments had simply not been able to justify spending such large sums when the problems at home seemed far more relevant than a probable future catastrophe. To make matters even worse several of the dictatorships had flatly refused to contribute any funds unless they could be assured that at least some of their offspring would have priority placement in the crew of the Lifeboat. Surprisingly, the very rich throughout the world had adopted the same philosophy. They were using their influence within their respective governments to limit or refuse any future funding until they could be assured of a special standing on the Lifeboat. It wasn't long before the news media got wind of these demands and they began to refer to the Lifeboat as an elite "members only" club. Several even went so far as to proclaim that the poor and unimportant had no chance of ensuring the continence of their genetic lines.

Needless to say everything came to a screeching stop in the space industries until they had some real assurances of being paid. The bigger companies like Stellar Steel were able to absorb the loss and divert their operations to smaller contracts but the small companies and miners had no choice but to stop altogether. The WGC issued an order preventing the seizing or sale of the assets of these companies until this could be resolved.

Gem Space actually came out of this reasonable well. We had gradually scaled back our operations until we had three Spokes in stationary orbit in Ring 10 and we had stopped giving credit to anyone. Any miner that failed to pay his bill for the last load we brought in was immediately taken off our list of clients. I had argued that this was too harsh a stance until Kelly pointed out that we were actually doing them a favor. By limiting their credit we were preventing them from going so far into debt that they wouldn't be able to recover even after the Lifeboat Program was reinstated.

We were still of the belief that this was just a temporary setback that would soon be ironed out by the politicians. We began to rethink that as future events unfolded.

To the surprise of no one, the dormant troublemakers in every country seized the opportunity to exploit this crisis in an attempt to gain power and/or significant influence with their own governments. Of course the naysayers and disablers of the world were quick to proclaim that the working class was again being expected to bear the brunt of the cost of a project without even the possibility of receiving any of the benefits. This group who are a far less than silent minority in every country was soon joined by the politically hungry opportunists as well. The individual groups eventually joined together and formed a worldwide organization called "The Workers Movement" under the banner of a workman stooped over and carrying a heavy pack on his back. They protested the building of the Lifeboat and raised a great hue about the exclusion of the general population from the hypothetical "Elite Club" membership. They masterminded riots and demonstrations in dozens of countries at the same time and literally brought several economies to a standstill. The WGC had no choice but to publically recognize their concerns and offer then a vote in any final resolution.

It wasn't a great surprise to the elected politicians when The Workers Movement announced that they now considered themselves the representatives of the working class and they therefore represented a majority of the worlds population. They followed that up by insisting that they should have the deciding vote or in reality a veto over any final agreement in the event that the Lifeboat Program actually did go ahead. As you can imagine this infuriated the legitimate world governments and they immediately withdrew any further support of the program until this matter could be settled.

We had been following these happenings closely and had discussed them at several Monday morning meetings. We were all in agreement that things were now much more serious and the Lifeboat Program itself could be in real trouble.

Through his contacts with Stellar Steel Dad found out that some of the construction companies had not been paid for the preliminary work they had done. They had no choice but to cancel their orders for supplies (including steel) until they found out why the money was so slow in coming. They also could not pay for the supplies and steel they had already received so that left the coffers of the supply companies empty or dangerously low. This left the smaller steel mills with no choice but to stop taking rocks before they themselves went broke.

This went a lot deeper than just the industries on Mars and the Moon. Hundreds of earthside companies had over-extended themselves in order to bid on supply contracts for the Lifeboat Program and they were now on the brink of bankruptcy because they hadn't been paid.

This combined with the political situations in several of the smaller countries was beginning to create a lot of instability in several governments and that was leading to a situation where revolutions are born. The new Workers Movement was smelling blood and were doing their best to create an uprising of the common people against their governments. If that happened the political structure of the entire world was at risk.

I can tell you that we were more than a little concerned when we got this news but try as we may we couldn't think of any way to help the situation. I personally believed that building the Lifeboat had been a good call but if it was going to destroy our governing system and create chaos then the big question was "Is it worth it".

I was in my office on Friday when the call came in on our private line. Dad had received a high priority request as he called it. He had been summoned to a meeting of the board at Stellar Steel and they impressed on him the importance of their request. They were passing along an invitation from the Government for me to attend an in-camera meeting within the next week if at all possible. He didn't know anything more about it but he had no doubt that it was extremely important that I accommodate them. I agreed to try and get a flight the following Monday as soon as they let me know where I was supposed to be. The four minute delay hadn't even elapsed after he had hung up when I got an email informing me that I would be picked up at 7 AM at our ranch house on Monday morning with a Canadian Military Harrier Jet. That made a bigger impression on me than anything my Dad had said.

When I came into the kitchen for a coffee Virginia almost dropped the dish she was putting away. She took one look at my face and gasped

My god! What's wrong?

I don't know was all I could say.

What do you mean, you don't know, she asked with a puzzled look on her face.

I seemed to snap out of a trance because I stopped and looked at her with an equally puzzled expression on my face.

I just got an invitation or rather a summons to appear before the Government on Monday, I said meekly.

The Government? Do you mean "The Canadian Government", she mouthed.

Yeaaa, I almost whispered, and the Canadian Army is picking me up here in a Harrier Jet.

My god, are you in trouble, she asked.

I haven't the foggiest idea, I answered in bewilderment, but I can tell you they think it's important. I don't mind saying that I'm a little worried. As far as I know we haven't done anything wrong but I can't imagine what could be so important that they would send a military jet to come and get me?

Virginia and I spent the rest of the weekend going over scenario after scenario but we didn't come up with anything that made sense. The whole family was standing on the porch to watch the Harrier land in our front yard. The kids were impressed with their dad being picked up with a Harrier Jet but they were wondering what was going on because they could see that we were uncomfortable about something.

Chapter 33

I was flown to Calgary where I was met by a plainclothes RCMP officer who confiscated my cellphone before we boarded a plane to New York for my meeting. When I questioned why we were going to New York for a meeting with the Canadian Government, he just smiled and went back to his book.

He also didn't tell me that as soon as my plane was out of sight of the ranch a caravan of plain cloths Military Police appeared at the ranch house and informed Virginia that the ranch was now under a security lockdown. No one was to be allowed to leave or communicate with anyone outside of the normal stream of events. They impressed on her that any calls that came in would be monitored and if they suspected that she had passed on any information relevant to the current situation, they would also put the receiving parties under lockdown. She was required to call the school and explain that the kids were needed at home for the next couple of days so they wouldn't be attending school. Virginia was close to hysterics but she managed to make the calls without incident. She is no dimwit and she could tell by their actions that they were dead serious about this and at the same time were no threat to them unless she forced them to take action.

I questioned my escort quite sharply when he asked for my phone. He was very polite when he answered and at the same time very firm when he asked for the phone the second time. The only thing he would tell me is that he had explicit orders that nobody was to know that I was here or where I was going so they didn't want anyone tracking my phone. Virginia got the same "I'm just following orders" type of an answer when she started asking them questions. It didn't help her temperament much when they refused to tell her why this was happening.

I found out later that they didn't know. Their job was to simply secure the premises. Luckily we hadn't called anyone over the weekend because they had also been monitoring our phone and internet communications. I called Dwaine and Kelly on our company line and told them of course but they had already been briefed by Dad and couldn't shed any light on the reason for the "request" either. This made the security guards jobs a lot simpler because all they had to be concerned about was me and the ranch. What happened on Mars was not their problem.

I was met at the airport by not one but two smartly dressed security guards and they whisked me away to a penthouse suite at the Waldorf. I was told that the phone had been disconnected but all I had to do was ask if I needed anything and they would get it for me. I had resigned myself to this kind of treatment by then so I settled in for a comfortable nights rest after a gourmet meal in the room by myself.

After a similarly lonely breakfast I was delivered to the WGC headquarters somewhere in the center of New York. I admit that I was starting to feel more than a little testy about the way things were going so as soon as the door was closed behind the guards, I demanded an explanation for the way I had been treated.

Well, said the meeting chairman, let's make that the first order of business as soon as the introductions are over. I am Christopher Meade and I chair this assemble. These other committee members are the heads of every important department concerned with finance and constitutional protocol of the World Governing Council.

Mr. Frederick, he continued, we had a very good reason for the precautions we took in bringing you here.

I'm very anxious to hear it Mr. Chairman, I answered. I have been treated like a dangerous criminal and I don't appreciate it.

Trust me Mr. Frederick, he answered, if we thought you were a criminal you would not have been treated with such kid gloves.

That may be so Mr. Chairman, I said, but to practically demand that I come here and them to put me under so close a guard does nothing to make me believe that I'm an honoured guest.

We have heard that you are a man that doesn't mince words, he answered, so maybe you should listen to our explanation before you judge us too harshly.

I'm sure you have been following recent events on the world scene, he continued. We believe that we have come to a tipping point Mr. Frederick. We either have to salvage something good out of this Lifeboat enterprise or scrap the whole thing and hope we can manage to keep the world from descending into political chaos with all the turmoil that will go with that.

My partners and I have come to the same conclusion, I said. We have been following the recent events very closely and unfortunately, we haven't been able to think of anything that might be helpful.

I'm very sorry to hear that Mr. Frederick, continued Chairman Meade. We were hoping you and your partners would be our saving angels. That was the main reason for all the secrecy and the tight security for you and your family.

For me and my family, I interrupted. What have you done to my family?

I'm sorry Mr. Frederick, answered Chairman Meade, I thought you had been told.

Been told what, I asked quite sharply.

Please don't be alarmed Mr. Frederick, answered Chairman Meade calmly. Your family and anyone they may have talked to have been placed under a security lockdown since you left the ranch. No, please let me finish, continued the chairman, we consider this to be the gravest of situations. The very fabric of the World Government is at risk here as well as the financial well-being of almost every country on Earth. We did not take this step without seriously considering every option that offered even a glimmer of hope to turn things around.

It is our collective opinion that you and your partners offer us the best chance of success. We considered it crucial that you, as well as we, be free to consider our options without being pressured or harassed by all the different individuals, organizations and last but certainly not least the news media, all of whom would most likely go to extreme ends to influence your decision.

Chairman Meade. I Interrupted, I insist that I be allowed to contact my family before we go any further.

Yes, by all means Mr. Frederick, answered the chairman, please put your mind at ease. We are going to need your full attention if we are going to salvage anything good out of this situation. You can use a booth at the back of the room so you will have some privacy.

I walked briskly to the closest booth and dialed my house.

Virginia answered a little meekly on the third ring. As soon as she heard my voice, I could hear the relief drain out of her.

Thank god it's you, she said. Are you all right? Why didn't you call last night? I've been so worried and nobody will tell me what's going on. Are you on your way home?

I started by saying, I'm sorry Virginia. I didn't know they were going to lock you down but they obviously believe that secrecy is paramount now and I have to say is does make some sense. To that end please don't say anything on the phone about where I am and who I'm meeting with. These people are just doing the job they were ordered to do and have no idea what's it about any more than you. As a matter of fact you probably know more than they do so there's no need to make it harder for them.

The only thing I can tell you on the phone, I continued, is that I am in no danger at all and apparently not in any trouble either. I'm in the middle of my meeting now and as soon as I learned that they had locked down our ranch, I insisted on calling you. Are you all right? I assume that they have just sequestered you on the ranch.

We're all right now, she said, they gave us all quite a fright when they showed up and took over. The kids are here at home and they're starting to treat it like some kind of a game and I have adjusted to the fact that for the time being this is necessary. They've been nothing but polite and kind to us except that we aren't free to go anywhere except on the ranch. Jim isn't happy with the permanent guard but he is making good use of him as a helper.

I never thought about him I said, he's a very capable fellow so I'm sure he has adjusted well. I have to go back to the meeting now and it will be a lot easier to concentrate knowing that guys are safe. Don't count on me being home too soon, it looks like it might take a couple of days or more to get this ironed out.

Thanks so much for calling Wade, she said, I feel a lot better now and the kids will be happy to know that this is just business. It is just business isn't it?

I reassured her again that everything was all right and then broke the call off because I could see that the committee members were getting restless. Virginia sounded very composed when we said our good-byes and that made me really glad that I had called.

As soon as I made it back to my desk Chairman Meade called the meeting to order again and started by saying, we apologise for any anxiety our actions may have caused you and your family Mr. Frederick and I hope you will find our explanation satisfactory.

Thank you for allowing me to talk to my family Mr. Chairman, I answered, it made us all feel better. Now, how do you think we can help and why aren't my partners here if you feel they are that important to this problem?

The committee felt, he answered, that there was too big a risk of a security slip-up had we tried to bring you all here so we are going to have to count on your powers of persuasion should you decide to help us with this.

We are very aware of the chemistry between you three and that is precisely why we feel you are our best hope, he continued. Your team is already universally respected because of your success in not only diverting, but capturing the Nemesis. If anyone can convince the public that this program is worth saving, it is you three.

I'm afraid Mr. Chairman, I interrupted, that you have over-estimated our abilities. It is true that we do work well together but as I've already stated, we do not have even one suggestion that might be useful to you.

But do you have any suggestions that would help you Mr. Frederick, he asked.

I'm sorry Mr. Chairman, I answered, I don't think I understand the difference.

The difference Mr. Frederick, answered the chairman, is that you would have complete control over all changes to be made to the program.

Chairman Meade, I interrupted quite sharply, are you looking for a scapegoat to blame the failure of the Lifeboat Program on? If so, I have to tell you that a shallow offering of praise is not going to accomplish your goal and to be blunt, I am insulted at the attempt.

Please Mr. Frederick, interjected Chairman Meade admit a roll of surprised mutterings from the committee members, you dishonour us by your suggestion.

Perhaps I misunderstood you Mr. Chairman, I answered still quite sharply, but you clearly stated that as a group you consider the Lifeboat Program to be on the verge of collapsing and your offer to transfer control of a failing enterprise to us does not project an image of a solution, rather it sounds like an attempt to slip out from underneath a landslide of blame.

Forgive me for being blunt Mr. Frederick, said Chairman Meade a little sharply himself, but I fear it is you who have misjudged us.

The members of this committee as well as myself believe very strongly in this program and consider it the only viable course of action to insure the continuance of our species. We feel so strongly about this that we are willing to step aside if there is any reasonable hope that the program will proceed. I admit that we are grasping at straws Mr. Frederick but I assure you our intention is honourable. Please allow us to sketch out our concept of how this might work before we break for lunch.

It is our intention, he continued, to give you a free hand as long as you can produce a plan that appears to be feasible.

After lunch perhaps we can produce a draft that outlines the perimeters of the final plan.

By the time I had finished lunch with my ever present guards I had calmed down and actually started to think about ways that we might be able to help. When I entered the meeting room and took my seat I must have had a bit of a confident stride because Chairman Meade called the meeting to order and started by saying.

It appears as though you have put your lunch time to good use Mr. Frederick. We would be very pleased if you would share your thoughts with us.

Gentlemen, I began, I freely admit that I am intrigued by the possibility that we might in some way actually be able to help save the Lifeboat Program. As I stated earlier, my partners and I are of the belief that this is the most logical way to ensure the survival of our species regardless of what happens in the future. I have to admit however that there is some question in my mind as to whether or not we should consider taking responsibility for it.

Mr. Frederick, began Chairman Meade, we must have a firm commitment for you

Excuse me Mr. Chairman, I interrupted, this is too big to be considered on the spur of the moment. Will you gentlemen agree to an adjournment to allow me time to get together with my partners? I think we need to talk about this together so I'll have to go to Mars to consult with them.

Mr. Frederick, interrupted Chairman Meade, now might be a good time to inform you of another action that we initiated in the belief that you would at least entertain our proposal. We have anticipated that you would want to consult with your partners and to that end we have already made arrangements to bring Mr. And Mrs. Franks to Earth. I believe your father is going to take over their responsibilities while they travel to Earth on an urgent business trip. We know you told them that you had been called away and through our friends at Stellar Steel we were able to impress on them the necessity of this trip.

They were hesitant at first until we made them aware that this was directly connected with your summons to appear before the government and their help could be very beneficial to you. When they heard that they readily agreed to jump on the first Executive Shuttle to Earth.

I don't know what to say Mr. Chairman, I said, it appears that you have made a lot of assumptions about what I will or will not do. Is there anything else that I should know?

As a matter of fact Mr. Frederick, we did take one more liberty on your behave. Mr. And Mrs. Franks will be arriving at your ranch Friday night. It seemed like the most logical place for you to meet and we already have it secured so you won't be disturbed.

I paused for a long minute before I said, well, I guess I had better hurry home to meet them. With your permission Mr. Chairman I'll use your phone again to let my wife know that we'll be having company.

By all means Mr. Frederick, agreed the chairman, your escorts will make the arrangements for your immediate return.

I'm sure you realize that they will also be accompanying you until the Canadian contingent takes over for them.

Yes Mr. Chairman, I answered, I guessed that and I have to agree that it was a very necessary step for you to take. If we are to going to try and sort this out, distractions are the last thing we need. With your permission I'll take my leave of you gentlemen for the time being.

By all means Mr. Frederick, agreed Chairman Meade, but please be aware that time is of the essence. The very fact that we were so presumptuous and so forceful in our actions should be good evidence of that. We would like your plan of action in one week if at all possible. You will be given a number to call when you wish to be picked up.

We'll do our best, I answered, and with that I went to the booth at the rear of the hall to call Virginia. I could see one my escort on his cellphone and I presumed he was making our flight reservations.

Virginia was surprised to hear from me again so soon and delighted when I told her Dwaine and Kelly were coming. She could tell by my voice that I was holding something back and all she said was that I had better have a good story to tell when I got home.

Apparently you get priority booking privileges and seating when you are flying on the governments ticket. We flew first class and I was home by Wednesday night. I vetoed the Harrier in favour of an undercover SUV because I didn't want to draw any more attention to our meeting at the ranch than had already been accomplished. I'm sure some of the neighbours must have noticed the Harrier come for me but nobody had called to ask about it so I thought it was best not to push our luck.

The security contingent had been told to co-operate with me unless my actions were likely to compromise their mission so they let me arrange to have Dwaine and Kelly picked up by limousine as if it were really a business meeting.

Even Jim came over to the house to meet me when I got home to be sure that everything was on the up and up. I reassured him that everything was all right and told him that he might have his helpers with him for a few more days. He was happy with that because one of his guards had grown up on a large farm in Manitoba and was a great help to him. Apparently he was a better machine operator than me.

The kids were excited to see me and full of stories of the fun they had playing with their new friends. They were satisfied with my explanation that this was just another business venture that we were starting and were delighted to hear that Dwaine and Kelly were on their way.

The best part of going away is the homecoming and Virginia seemed quite anxious to get me alone so we put the kids to bed early and retired to our bedroom. She and I had been assured that there were no listening devices in the house other than on the telephone and internet communications.

That was important to us for two reasons. We could enjoy our intimate time together without fear of being photographed or recorded and almost as good, we could talk freely about my trip and what they expected from us. She was shocked to hear that the Lifeboat Program was on the verge of collapse and twice as shocked to learn that they wanted us to try and save it.

Dwaine and Kelly arrived from Calgary late Friday night. After our welcomes were said I cautioned them about saying anything in front of the guards. I tried to put off any business talk until morning but they would have no part of it.

There's no way that I'm going to be able to sleep a wink until I find out what the hell is going on, Kelly said. The kids had gone to bed so we moved into the kitchen for a cup of coffee and Kelly started by saying.

Can we talk freely in here?

Yes, I said, I had the house checked again this afternoon for bugs and not even the security detail knows what is happening in here. This is not going to be a five minute explanation, I said, are you sure you wouldn't rather wait until morning?

You know us, Dwaine said, we didn't have any trouble sleeping on the shuttle and the suspense is killing us. The first question we have is when did you hire a security team for the ranch? What kind of trouble are you in anyway?

Chapter 34

Ok, that's a good place to start, I said, they are the Canadian Military Police and they are here to keep us confined as much as they are to protect us and I have to agree with their being here now that I know the whole story.

What do you mean confined, demanded Dwaine.

Relax Dwaine, I said, it isn't what it appears to be.

Kelly was quite exasperated when she said, we were told you were in trouble and needed our help but this sounds really bad.

Yes I know what you were told, I said, and I'd like to clear that up. First you need to know that I had no idea what was going on either until I got to New York.

"New York", Dwaine asked, we were told you had been called to Ottawa.

This will go a lot faster if you guys will just listen until I finish telling you the whole story I said, so I'll start by explaining that. This is a top secret proposal orchestrated by the Finance Committee of the WGC.

"The" WGC, interrupted Kelly. I nodded my head and schussed her before I continued. They took great care to ensure that nobody in the general public had any hint that they were talking to us as can be verified by the fact that we were grossly misled and manipulated into having this meeting. Virginia is already up to speed and I have already talked to you two about a lot of this so I'll give you the shortened version.

The Council Members know that the Lifeboat Program is in serious trouble and that if it fails, it could affect the stability of not only the Financial Markets but of several of the major governments as well. They are also very much aware that the same special interest groups who have created this crisis will go to great lengths to prevent the Lifeboat Program from succeeding. Does that cover the reasons for the tight security and secrecy?

Dwaine was the first to speak. Ok, he said, where do we fit into all this?

That's the kicker, I said. Apparently they have examined all their options and they are convinced that we are the best hope of saving the Lifeboat Program.

Where in hell did they get that idea, Kelly asked?

They are banking on our popularity because we saved the Earth from the Nemesis to help turn the tide of public opinion in favor of the program, I answered.

Kelly couldn't contain herself any longer as she blurted out. They're going to need a lot more than popularity to save that program.

I was coming to that, I said. They are also counting on us to be able to come up with a plan to save it.

Just for the sake of clarity, Kelly interrupted, they want to use our good name and our ideas to pull them out of this hole that they have dug for themselves. Is that right?

It's more serious than that, I said. Things are falling apart fast and they need our plan by next Friday. They are willing to give us complete control over the implementation of any plan we come up with as long as they approve of the plan.

Ah, the plot thickens, injected Dwaine, me thinks they are looking for someone to blame for the failure of the program.

That was my first thought as well Dwaine, I said, but when I questioned them the real truth came out. They are desperate to save the program to avoid the ramifications that go with its failure and are completely at a loss about how to do it.

How can they possible think that we can save it if they can't, asked Kelly.

They were so impressed with the fact that we were able to capture the Nemesis when nobody could even come up with an idea to divert it that they think we can figure something out by brainstorming.

That's crazy, said Kelly, for one thing we didn't have to deal with an army of bureaucrats, we had complete control over everything when we went after the Nemesis.

Before we even get into how we might do it, I said, maybe we should talk about whether we "want" to do it.

Wow, said Kelly, that's a good point. How do we do that?

I have no idea, I said, but I'm open to suggestions.

I wasn't part of your earlier discussions so maybe it would help if we started with all of us just stating our opinions, suggested Virginia.

That's a great idea, Kelly said, who wants to go first?

You have the floor Wade, suggested Dwaine.

Ok, I said, I believe that it's worth doing mainly because the cost of not saving the program will be catastrophic not just for the worlds economies but maybe for our species as well.

How do you figure that, asked Dwaine.

Well mainly I agree with their premise that it is doomed to failure if things keep going in the direction that they are. The entire organization is so mired in bureaucracy that they can't even decide what to have for lunch at a meeting and the special interest groups are so involved in their quest to wrestle political power out of the hands of the legitimate governments that they don't care what happens to the rest of the world.

That makes a lot of sense Wade, Kelly said, but have you looked at the other side of the coin. What about all the money being spent on the program that is desperately needed for programs here on Earth and the difference that could make in the quality of live for hundreds of thousands if not millions of people.

That's a good point Kelly, interjected Dwaine, and I think that's what Wade meant when he said that the survival of our species may also be at stake. There will always be serious problems that need to be solved and there will never be enough money to address them, if this program is allowed to fail, who or when is it likely to be reattempted. My guess is not until it's far too late to do anything about it because the naysayers will be able to point to this failure as a justification for not trying again.

There's something else to think about, added Virginia, what if the Council stops supporting the program as soon as they have someone to blame the failure on. I know they assured Wade of their complete co-operation and support but do we dare to trust the word of a group of politicians.

All right you guys, I interrupted, I think that's about enough for tonight. Let's try and get some sleep and meet in the morning. Breakfast will be served whenever you get up and we'll continue this tomorrow. Agreed?

It was almost noon before Kelly and Dwaine came wandering into the kitchen. The kids had been pestering us all morning about when they were getting up so they stayed close until mid-afternoon when I shooed them away so we could have a business meeting. We didn't get anything significant accomplished at all the entire day. All we did was to rehash the previous nights comments because as soon as we started to get into a serious discussion we would be interrupted by the kids. We finally put off any discussions until after the kids went to bed. We talked until the early morning hours again and still didn't make much headway. The only thing that did appear apparent was that if we did decide to accept responsibility for the Lifeboat Program we would be putting our personal credibility and perhaps a good portion of our money on the line. When we broke for the night I suggested that we make a final decision when we reconvened in the morning. We were running out of time and would need what time we had left to make an action plan if we decided to go ahead.

We started our meeting in my office after lunch and the first order of business was the decision making vote. I was surprised when even Virginia voted to take on the responsibility of trying to save the program. She was still quite concerned about the continued support of the politicians after they had someone to blame but as she said "our personal well-being is really unimportant if we have even a slim chance of saving the program". We hadn't been able to include Dad in the discussions but he had cryptically told us that he would go along with the majority so that made it unanimous.

In the meantime Virginia and I had a serious talk about how we should proceed. We both felt that she should be involved in the discussions and that she was definitely contributing some very useful input. If she was to continue to be part of the discussions she would have to be involved with the complete process with no breaks for her duties as a mother and hostess. The only way we could achieve that was to have someone else take over her responsibilities in those areas. After more than a little soul searching we decided to ask our guards for a chef and a tutor for the kids so we would be free to explore our options without interruptions. I got a funny look from the Sergeant when I asked for the help but he agreed to have them there the next morning. I'm sure he thought we were putting business ahead of the kids and maybe taking advantage of them as well but he didn't know what was at stake.

The Sergeant was true to his word and when we got up with the kids in the morning there was someone else in the kitchen to the surprise and delight of the kids. They had never seen anyone else cooking in our kitchen and they made a big thing about having their own chef. They weren't quite as pleased about the tutor/nanny and they both groaned when they heard that part of her responsibilities was to see that they got their homework done. We took them aside and explained that we were involved with something extremely important and for the next few days neither of us would have much time to spend with them. They weren't especially excited about that but they did accept her without any objections.

With that behind us we started to go through dozens of different scenarios to try and come up with something/anything that looked like it might be feasible.

The breakthrough came on Thursday when Virginia said.

Something Kelly said has been eating at me all day. I think she said that the difference between your mission to capture the Nemesis and this program is that you had complete control over all aspects of your mission. What would it take to have complete control over the Lifeboat Program?

We already have complete control once the Council approves of our plan, I said.

No, Virginia said, I mean over everything.

Everything, asked Dwaine, you mean the entire finance department?

No, answered Virginia, I mean everything. That's the big stumbling block here. Even the best plan in the world can't fix a problem if it's not implemented properly. We would have to have complete control over financing, staffing, priority planning, and even the building of the Lifeboat itself. Everything!!!!

The only way we could have that is if we owned it, Kelly added. Are you suggesting that we somehow buy it and then pay for everything?

This would take billions and billions and billions of dollars, interrupted Dwaine. There's no way we can afford that.

I think we should explore this a bit more, I said, it does make more sense than anything else we have considered.

We stayed at it all night and we almost gave up a couple of times but by morning we had a plan that I could submit to the Council. I called the number they had given me and asked to be picked up immediately if they thought they could still get me to New York to meet with them today.

They must have had the Harrier on stand-by because I had just finished breakfast when it arrived. I was flown directly to Seattle where I was met by the now customary two escorts who took me immediately to first class accommodation on the Super Commuter to New York. It was only a three hour flight so it seemed like I had just got to sleep when they woke me up for the landing in New York.

Chapter 35

I was given the option of going directly to the meeting or having a quick lunch at the Waldorf before going to meet with the council. I chose the quick lunch since I had slept through the food servings on the plane and I didn't want to face the council on an empty stomach. I tend to be a little short tempered when I'm hungry and that would not be a good thing in this instance.

We arrived at the meeting just after 1 and Chairman Meade called it to order as soon as we had exchanged greetings.

Chairman Meade opened the meeting by saying, thank you for coming today Mr. Frederick, the situation has worsen this week. I fear our opponents have got the smell of blood and are anxious to press their advantage. Do you have some good news for us?

I started with a formal recognition of the committee members so that they would realize that I considered this to be a formal meeting rather than a gathering to talk about ideas.

Chairman Meade, ladies and gentlemen of the committee, my partners and are ready to respond to the challenge you presented us with. I would like to start by saying that after hours of discussion my partners and I have decided to accept your offer to allow us to take responsibility for the Lifeboat Program.

Excuse me Mr. Frederick, interrupted Chairman Meade, I believe our offer was for you to take charge of the financing of the Lifeboat Program.

Thank you for bringing that up Mr. Chairman, I said, that was the focus of most of our discussions. We finally realized that we were trying to save a system that had already failed.

There was a rumble as everyone on the committee tried to talk to the person beside them. Chairman Meade called the meeting to order with a loud bang of his gavel.

Mr. Frederick, he said, I think you had better explain yourself to the committee.

Chairman Meade, I began, what you asked of us is impossible.

I had to speak louder as the rumble again echoed through the room.

Mr. Chairman, I shouted, will you hear me out?

It took three raps of the gavel to re-establish order and Chairman Meade spoke very firmly when he stated.

We will extend the same courtesy to Mr. Frederick that he gave us when we first approached him. I insist that there be no further interruptions until he has finished saying what he has to say.

Thank you Mr. Chairman, I said as I continued, my partners and I are convinced that this program was doomed from the start. Government run projects are inheritably slow to respond to changing situations and almost impossible to manage effectively because everyone in responsibility is afraid to make the tough decisions necessary to run a successful project. Inevitably they revert to governance by committee so that no one can be blamed for the failure of the project. To make matters even worse the Lifeboat Program as it now stands requires the co-operation of dozens of governments and their bureaucracies before any major decisions can be made and by the time these decisions are made the problem has worsened considerable or is no longer relevant to the situation. We feel that the present political climate has just hastened the inevitable demise of the program.

Having said that Mr. Chairman, I think you should know that we also feel that the program can still be saved. We also accept the premise that the future of our species could well be at stake here and that this committee does appear to have a serious desire to ensure that the Lifeboat Program is completed. To that end we propose a drastic change in format.

Before we can do anything constructive we have to change the very structure of the program and raise it above the political quagmire that it is mired in.

Mr. Frederick, interrupted Chairman Meade a bit sharply, perhaps you could dispense with the rhetoric and allow us to know your plan to save the program.

Mr. Chairman, I continued, I'm sure you realize that one week is an impossibly short time to formulate a complete plan for a project this big. I have been trying to show you that the present system has already failed and will collapse from political pressure in the very near future. I'm sure that if you are willing to look beyond your emotions you will see the truth in this statement. Your response to what I have to say next will reveal your true intentions with regard to the Lifeboat Program.

My partners and I have come to the conclusion that our personal reputations and creditability are secondary to the completion of the program. Put another way, if we can contribute to the saving of this program we are willing to risk our own futures as well as that of our companies. We are of the firm opinion that if this program is to be saved some very drastic changes will have to take place.

To that end we propose that the Lifeboat Program be reinvented as an as yet unnamed non-profit corporation. I apologize for not having a name to give you but time was very short and we thought there were more important things to focus on. This new company will be structured with myself as a permanent CEO and Chairman of the Board. My partners Dwaine Franks, Kelly Franks, Virginia Frederick and James Frederick will also be appointed as permanent members of the Board of Directors. Let me be clear ladies and gentlemen, I am talking about taking full responsibility for the entire Program from beginning to completion.

The room erupted with thunderous statements of surprise, indignation and denial.

It took a full minute for Chairman Meade to restore order and he practically shouted as he said.

Mr. Frederick, do you seriously believe that this committee will allow you to hijack this program for your own personal gain.

There was another rumble of conversation around the table and I waited until Chairman Meade had restored order again before I answered him.

Mr. Chairman, I began with a strong voice, perhaps you have not understood what I have been saying. There is nothing to hijack here. The program is on the verge of collapse and to be blunt you have no idea how to save it. When that happens it will probably take several of the worlds governments down with it and certainly affect the credibility of the WGC as well.

We believe we might be able to save it and we believe that strongly enough to put our personal reputations on the line. As far as personal gain is concerned we have everything to lose and very little to gain. I can assure this committee that we are doing quite well in our present ventures and quite to the contrary, if we do take on this challenge both our company and our individual worth will almost certainly be negatively affected. May I suggest that we take a short break to recompose ourselves. I fear our emotions may be getting the better of us.

An excellent idea Mr. Frederick, said the chairman, we will reconvene in 2 hours.

I found a quiet café for myself and the ever present escorts and we lingered over several coffees and a BLT sandwich. I made my way back to the meeting and watched as the grimed faced committee members came back to their seats.

Chairman Meade called the meeting to order and asked my indulgence while he made a statement.

Mr. Frederick, he started, we are willing to admit that there is some truth to the premise that it may not be possible to save the program. What we don't understand is why you would be willing to take it over.

Mr. Chairman, I answered, you may very well have taken the first step toward saving the program. My partners and I believe that given a free hand we may be able to overcome most of the obstacles presently killing the program.

Would you care to enlighten us as to how you intend to do that, asked the chairman?

Mr. Chairman, I answered, I freely admit that we do not have a firm plan in place but we are willing to try. If we are able to succeed then we will have made a mark in history that will long outlive us. If we fail we will be in disgrace and maybe banned to the outer reaches of space to live out our lives.

For you, the present leaders of the world, the pendulum swings in the opposite direction. When you transfer responsibility to us you will be taking all the wind out of the sails of the special interest groups and the political radicals that have caused so much turmoil. You will be free to focus on todays problems and the individual governments who were feeling the pinch of trying to fund the program will find themselves with some extra money that should go a long way to quell the unrest in their countries.

Mr. Frederick, interrupted Chairman Meade, we have not weathered this storm just to walk away from the program. We are still very concerned that the loss of the program could spell the extinction of our species and we will need some assurance that the program can and will be completed before we consider transferring control to anyone.

I looked around the table at each member of the council before I spoke.

Mr. Chairman you have admitted and we agree with you that the program is doomed to failure unless something is done. We have just made you an offer that allows you to unload this white elephant onto us and at the same time will very likely facilitate the return to normalcy of the world political systems. If you have a better offer then I urge you to accept it.

No, please let me finish, I said, as the room started to reverberate with conversation again. We will give you our solemn promise that we will leave no stone unturned to try and save the program. We are exploring several options now but we do not have a firm plan of action at this time. There are a lot of individuals out there who believe as strongly as we do about the program and a big part of our plan will be to reach out to the general public for our funding.

Before we can do that, I continued, we must have something to offer them and part of that offering will be a much leaner organization with a strong responsive leadership at the top.

There are three conditions to our offer Mr. Chairman.

1— We require complete control over the entire Lifeboat Program as well as the transfer of all the blueprints and any other documentation that is relevant to the program to the Board of Directors of the new company.

2— All outstanding accounts must be paid up to date so that we are starting fresh. As far as the delinquent accounts from the countries that failed to contribute to the building fund are concerned, they are no concern of ours.

3--- We will need a public admission that the present system has failed and a strong statement from this Council that reaffirms that this non-profit company is the only hope of saving the program.

Mr. Frederick, began Chairman Meade, that sounded very much like an ultimatum.

Not an ultimatum Mr. Chairman, I began, simply a statement of fact. We are absolutely convinced that the biggest risk of failure to the program lies with the inability to make firm and immediate decisions. The second greatest risk is that the program is a slave to funding fluctuations caused by changes of government in any one of the member countries. These constitute almost as big a threat as the political unrest that is presently threating to destroy the program. If we are to have any hope of success these pitfalls must be corrected. I believe our past performance qualifies us to state that we can provide the necessary leadership and the political interference will be eliminated by transferring responsibility to the new company. To that end, Mr. Chairman, if we are to attempt this task we insist that these three conditions be met.

Mr. Frederick, began Chairman Meade with a sharp tone in his voice, I think we have accomplished all we can for today. We did not ask you here to be dictated to. Perhaps you would like to return to your ranch to reconsider your position.

Mr. Chairman, I answered, you are correct when you say you invited me here. You also tasked us with an almost impossible mission because as you yourself have said, the program is on the verge of collapse and you have no idea of how to save it. We have offered you a solution that is very likely the only one that has a chance of being successful considering the state of the world today, so yes, thank you, I would like to return home now. Before I leave I would like to say one more thing. This committee has professed to be concerned about the survival of the Lifeboat Program yet you attack me when I state the obvious. I think that it is you who needs to rethink your position. You need to ask yourselves this question "is control over the program and your public image more important to you than the completion of the Lifeboat Program"? You know where to find me should you decide to accept our offer.

I marched directly to the door and burst into the lobby. I caught my escorts by surprise when I asked to be flown home immediately and for the second time in one day I found myself on the Super Commuter.

Chapter 36

They flew me from Seattle to Lethbridge where I was met by the Canadian escort contingent and we drove to the ranch in another black SUV. I arrived at the ranch around 10 PM and I was handed a cup of coffee on the way to our office. As soon as the door was closed I was besieged by three people asking questions.

I held up my hands asking for silence and started by saying, I'm sorry to tell you that I think the meeting was a complete loss. I guess I should have had more rest before I went into the meeting but when I had to keep repeating myself to even get them to consider that the program had already failed I became a little testy with them and they in turn didn't like my attitude. They particularly didn't like being told what they must do if we were to take on this challenge. When they accused us of seeking personal gain, I'm afraid that I lost my temper with them and we did not part on very good terms.

Trust you Wade, said Kelly with a grin, to tell off the WGC when they get out of line. I have to be honest with you. I'm actually not sorry to hear that. We don't really need to do this and it would probably end up costing us if we tried.

I agree, said Dwaine, but I do hate to see the Lifeboat Program fail. I'm glad you stuck to your guns Wade, if they aren't willing to give us an honest chance of success then why should we put ourselves at risk?

I second that Wade, added Virginia as she gave me a hug. The fact that they aren't willing to trust us is an indication that their motives may not have been honourable so the only chance we had of success was to remove them altogether from the equation.

It's been a long day, I said, so let's finish this in the morning.

With that we all went off to our beds and I'm not sure about them but I tossed and turned all night. I was up early in the morning and had breakfast with the kids. They were missing their friends and I assured them that they would be able to go back to school within a couple of days. Virginia actually went back to sleep after I got up so she arrived in the kitchen just after Dwaine and Kelly. She ordered a big breakfast from our "chef" and lamented while he was cooking it that she was definitely going to miss this part of our confinement.

We spent the day just visiting and talking a bit about the future of Gem Space. Both Kelly and Dwaine were anxious to get back to Mars because they were finding the gravity on Earth quite tiring and there was lots to do at the office. We talked to Dad and he was pleased to hear that they were coming home in the morning. He had enjoyed being in charge again but he also had other things in his life now. I'm sure we all thought about the Lifeboat Program but we didn't mention it even once. I think we were adjusting to the reality that it would fail and there wasn't any sense in talking about it any further.

We were up early again the next morning because Dwaine and Kelly wanted an early breakfast before they left. Virginia insisted on cooking them their last breakfast, as she put it, and she had just put the food on the table when there was a knock on the door. I wasn't particularly surprised to see Sergeant Taylor standing there and I invited him in.

I'm sorry to eat in front of you Sergeant, I said, but my food will go cold if I don't.

That's all right Mr. Frederick, he said, I've already eaten. I'm sorry to interrupt your breakfast but I was instructed to give you a message as soon as you got up.

That's all right Sergeant, I said, I imagine you're here to tell us you guys will be leaving us today.

As a matter of fact, he said, I did think we would be leaving but instead we've been ordered to stay on station and to give you this message.

Everyone stopped eating as he continued, apparently you have a guest on the way and he didn't want to surprise you. He is supposed to be here shortly after lunch.

And who is this guest, I asked.

I'm sorry sir, answered the Sergeant, I wasn't told that but apparently he is coming from New York.

After the Sergeant left, I looked at Dwaine and Kelly and suggested that it might be a good idea if they stayed for a while. They both nodded their heads and we all returned to eating our breakfast albeit a lot slower.

No one was surprised that it was Chairman Meade who got out of the SUV when it arrived shortly after 1 PM.

I greeted him cordially and introduced him to the others on the way to our office. As soon as we were seated he asked if he could start by making a short statement. I nodded my head and he began by saying.

We had a very robust discussion that lasted well into the night after you left Mr. Frederick. The fact that you were so abrupt with us and would not change your position was the deciding factor. It was after midnight before we realized that the very thing that had upset us was the kind of leadership that was required to get this job done. We also realized that it was impossible for us to supply that kind of leadership for precisely the reasons you were trying to explain to us. Our hourly reports shows that the political situation continues to deteriorate and may well be accelerating. We are left with no choice but to take a leap of faith and place the fate of the Lifeboat Program in your hands.

I'm sure you have already guessed that we have decided to accept your offer and transfer complete control of the program to your new company. I wanted to deliver the news in person and to apologise to all of you for any anguish we may have caused you.

That's very kind of you Mr. Meade, I said, I'm sure we will have some of those robust discussions ourselves now that we have a job to do. How long do you think it will take to have the papers drawn up?

Thank you for asking that Mr. Frederick, that brings up another topic we need to discuss. We would like your permission to announce these changes to the program at a media wide news conference Monday morning.

We all became very quiet and after a full minute Kelly spoke.

Mr. Meade, she said, I hope you will forgive my bluntness but all hell is going to break loose as soon as the media gets wind of this. If we don't even have a signed contract to show them then neither of us will be believed and that could cause more havoc than waiting at least a week so we could put a preliminary plan together. We don't even have a name for this company yet.

I understand your point Mrs. Franks, said the chairman, however I'm afraid that the situation is so dire that we must take immediate action. We have learned that the Workers Movement is calling another worldwide strike to protest the lack of results from their last action. With the present world economic condition we are very much afraid that will trigger a worldwide depression and may even topple the governments of more than one of our biggest democracies.

If I may continue ladies and gentlemen, added the chairman, to impress you with the urgency of this request I have brought with me a memorandum of agreement signed by every member of the Council Finance Committee. We recognize that this in not in the final legal language but it is a legal document that sets forth the conditions and terms of the transfer of authority to the new company and it binds both parties to the signing of the final documents when they are completed.

Whew, whistled Dwaine, you guys are really serious about making that announcement.

All we need is the name of the new company and your signatures answered Chairman Meade. I'm sorry to pressure you this way but time is paramount and I have to be back in New York for the news conference.

That may not be possible Mr. Chairman, commented Dwaine, there is one member of our team not present and you will need his signature as well.

We have anticipated that Mr. Franks, answered the chairman, and we have taken steps to make that possible. We have asked our friends at Stellar Steel to invite Mr. Frederick to a meeting in their communication complex. Their complex is the most secure line of communication with Mars. Most people do not even know that they have a secure dedicated line to the WGC head offices.

He had barely finished speaking when his communicator started beeping.

That will be Mr. Frederick now he said, I left instructions not to put anyone else through. May I put it on open communication mode?

By all means, I said, is that you Dad and have you been briefed on the present situation.

I've been briefed, he answered 4 minutes later, are you still of a mind to accept the offer?

We had talked briefly during the 4 minute delay for the signal to travel both ways and we had reaffirmed our determination to make a difference if that were possible.

Yes, I answered, but things are happening really fast so the real question is "are you still in favor of going ahead with it and with the announcement Monday morning"?

We had another discussion during the delay and Virginia took the opportunity to suggest that we draw up the announcement ourselves. Chairman Meade was a bit taken aback by the suggestion but he accepted the proposal when he saw that the rest of us thought it was a good idea. I guess Virginia wasn't the only one that still didn't trust The Council.

Dad's answer came back on time and he voted in favor of both proposals. As he put it "there are times when you have to do what's right even if it might cost you".

Dad signed his copy of the incorporation papers in front of the Stellar Steel lawyers who immediately copied the documents for transmission to the WGC head office. They promised to send the originals off to New York on the morning Executive Shuttle. We signed our papers with Chairman Meade present (he happened to be a lawyer) and he left immediately to catch his plane back to New York. He left us his encrypted phone so we would have a secure method to send them the company name and the announcement.

We sat in silence for almost ½ an hour before Dwaine finally spoke.

Well, he said, that changes things doesn't it?

Yes, I said, I was just getting used to the idea of going back to our normal lives. We may never be able to do that again now.

Are you sorry, asked Virginia?

No, I'm not sorry, I said, but I can't help wondering how this will change our lives. This is going to affect all of us.

You know, I continued, we still have a lot of work to do before morning but I think it would be a good idea if we broke for dinner first to collect out thoughts.

We broke for dinner and not one of us mentioned the Lifeboat Program until we reconvened at eight o'clock. We still had two jobs that had to be done before that announcement in New York. We had to come up with a name for the company and we had to write the announcement that introduced this new company to a very sceptical world.

The announcement turned out to be the easy part, it was the company name that took most of our time. The name had to be instantly recognized as a separate entity and at the same time produce an image in the public's mind that captured the hope that had been the reason the Lifeboat Program had been started.

It was 6 AM in New York when we placed the call. It was answered on the first ring and I was put right through to Chairman Meade. I'm sure I heard relief in his voice when he answered the call. He was already getting ready for the news conference and he was obviously happy to hear from us. He was pleased at the brevity of the announcement and promised to read it verbatim. He wasn't as pleased when we insisted that he not give out any details other than those included in the announcement.

The news conference started on schedule and true to his word the chairman cleared his throat and read the announcement without any preamble

Ladies and Gentlemen, he began, as you are aware the Lifeboat Development Program has not been well accepted by some segments of our society. It is now clear that there were some serious flaws in the original plan and recent events have compelled the Council to make some fundamental changes to the Lifeboat Program.

To that end, this Council has authorized the creation of an independent corporation to be named Interstellar Lifeboats Incorporated. ILI is a not-for–profit corporation under the permanent directorship of the same team that captured the Nemesis.

The purpose of ILI is to remove the entire Lifeboat Program out of the political arena and place it under the stewardship of the Board of Directors of ILI. Let me be absolutely clear on this point, the responsibility for the entire program from operational planning to the actual construction of the Lifeboat now rests with the Board of Directors of ILI.

The Lifeboat Building Fund will be paying all outstanding debts that were incurred up to this date in the very near future. Let me also be absolutely clear on this point, from this day forward no new monies or resources either from individual governments or the Lifeboat Fund will be allocated to the Lifeboat Program. The Lifeboat Building Fund will be dissolved as soon as the current outstanding debts have been paid.

The Board of Directors of ILI is in the process of developing a new operating plan and will announce their plans as they see fit. Please note ladies and gentlemen that there are no representatives from ILI here today. This is their way of making a strong point. ILI has moved beyond the influence of the political arena and any future announcements will come from the Office of the Board of Directors. All questions or requests for information should be directed to their head office in Calgary, Alberta, Canada.

There was a hush in the room for almost a moment before it erupted with noise as almost every reporter demanded more information at the same time. Chairman Meade was hard pressed to re-establish order but after five minutes he had control of the situation again and he did an excellent job of not answering any questions about ILI.

Chapter 37

To say that the members of the media were infuriated with the lack of information and extremely frustrated with their inability to get any direct quotes or interviews with one of us would barely explain the situation. We had anticipated a flood of calls so we had reset all our different communication channels to go to a recording that simple stated that we were in the process of finalizing our plans and would be making a public announcement soon. Virginia had suggested this as a way to give us a little more time to think and to garner public interest in the new company. The airwaves almost overheated with the tremendous volume of calls we received and when that didn't get them any real information, they started to speculate. For the next week ILI was the lead topic on almost every newscast worldwide and we were a household name.

By the end of the week we were ready to make our announcement so we invited the media to the Calgary Stampede grounds for a news conference.

We had arranged for a meeting room in the main lobby but so many reporters showed up that we had to move to the stadium and it was almost filled to capacity. There were so many news cameras set up that the stadium had to use their emergency generators to meet the demand. We were tremendously pleased with all the free advertising.

It had been a short but very significant week. The announcement that the World Governments were no longer financially responsible for the Lifeboat Program was every bit as effective as the WGC had hoped. The demonstrations and the general strike that the Workers Movement had planned both fizzled. The optimism projected by the sitting governments due to the extra money they would be able to allocate to social programs took all the wind out of their sails. Governments worldwide were openly enthusiastic about the future now that had been released from their commitments to the Lifeboat Building Fund. The financial markets almost immediately rebounded and instead of dire predictions of a crippling depression, the news media were now projecting economic growth in almost all areas.

We kept them waiting until they were starting to get restless and then I led our team onto the stage in single file. At the same time Dad's image was projected onto the stage monitors at each side of the stage. The crowd quieted down as soon as we started to walk on stage and by the time we were all at center stage an expectant hush had settled over the stadium.

I began by saying, ladies and gentlemen, please allow me to introduce you to the Board of Directors of ILI.

We know who you are, shouted a reporter from the front row. What we want to know is what you are up to.

I paused to look directly at the heckler before I answered. I am going to answer that question sir but not because of the rude way in which it was asked. I will answer it because I believe that is the very question on the minds of most of the people here.

Our goal is to fund and construct at least one Interstellar Starship that will be capable of traveling to another star system. It will carry with it a huge sampling of the great variety of the human genetic lines from Earth so that our species will be able to survive the pending catastrophe here on Earth.

Ladies and gentlemen, the evidence is undisputable. Sometime in the next 400,000 years our sun will burb and expand its corona to engulf all of the inner planets and bombard the rest with extreme doses of radiation and plasma. After that event there will be no live left here on Earth or anywhere else in this solar system. Our species could be eliminated from the universe in what is little more that the blink of a cosmic eye. This could happen tomorrow or next week or 200,000 years from now but if we put off doing anything until after we see it starting to happen, it may well be too late to save anyone.

We believe that our species is worth saving and that we may possibly be able to have some part in saving it. That ladies and gentleman is our sole reason for accepting this challenge and we mean to do everything in our power to complete this task.

My heckler started to shout out another question and I stopped him in mid-sentence by beckoning to the security guard who had moved to his location while I was talking.

I looked him directly in the face again as I said, sir, this is a private news conference and you are here at our invitation. If you or anyone else interrupts me again you will be forcible removed from the stadium. He reluctantly sank back into his seat and I returned to my introductions.

Ladies and gentlemen, I began, it is very possible that most of you know who we are but you do not know what function we perform.

I am Wade Frederick and I am the CEO and Chairman of the Board of Directors of ILI.

A hush fell over the crowd again as my heckler stood up and cautiously raised his hand.

I raised my hand to stop the security guard who had started to move toward him.

Sir, I said, may I know your name and the name of the paper you represent?

Certainly, Mr. Frederick, he answered, I am Patrick Roy and I am a freelance journalist. Thank you for recognizing me and I apologize for the interruption again but there is still one glaring question that needs to be answered. Why did you buy the Lifeboat Program and who are the real owners?

Mr. Roy, I answered, you ask excellent questions and had you the patience to wait a few more minutes you would have had your answer. As it is, I'm afraid you will have to ask one of your peers that question because you will not be here to hear it. Guard, please remove this person.

I waited until he had been escorted from the stadium before I continued. As I said, Mr. Roy does ask excellent questions.

There are no owners of ILI other than the Board of Directors. Please let me be clear on this point. ILI is the owner of ILI because complete ownership rests with the Board of Directors as an institution not the members of the Board of Directors. There are no shareholders and never will be. We, the first members of the Board were appointed by the Incorporation Documents but any future directors must be accepted by the unanimous vote of the sitting members. We are permanent members and can only be removed by a unanimous vote of the other members, death or resignation. This is a private "not –for –profit" Corporation and it will be operating according to the principles of a private "for-profit" company. By that I mean that we will be making our decisions based on what is the best direction to go to achieve our goal, not on political expediency or under any form of political interference.

To further separate ourselves from the previous Lifeboat Program we have decided that a change in name is also appropriate. We believe that the term Lifeboat does accurately describe the future Starship so we will keep it and refer to this endeavor as the Lifeboat Project. We feel this name more accurately describes the seriousness and scope of this new endeavor rather than that of a failed government experiment.

Having said that and to avoid any more impromptu questions, I continued, we have chosen to forgo any salaries at this time. Again, to be clear, none of the members of the board will be receiving any remuneration of any kind. That may change in the future when future members are appointed or our duties start to take too much time away from our own companies. We will however be reimbursed for any out of pocket expenses we incur. To begin with, we will be using funds advanced interest free by Gem Space and its partner Sigme Corporation and those funds must be returned as soon as possible.

Now that we are on the topic of funding, I would like to introduce you to my wife Virginia who just happens to be the head of our Finance Department.

There was a polite applause as Virginia took the microphone from my hand.

Thank you ladies and gentlemen, she began, I am not as good at impromptu speaking as Wade is so I will read from a prepared script if I may.

Ladies and gentlemen, funding will always be the primary focus of our efforts because we must remain solvent or stop short of reaching our goal and that is not an option. Let me emphasise, we WILL pay our bills and we WILL launch a Starship out into the cosmos.

There was a brief applause before she was able to continue.

Our first fund raising effort will begin immediately. We will be drawing on a tried and proven concept. We will be selling space on the walls of the corridors throughout the entire ship. The wall space will be divided into 1 square foot sections so that a name can be inscribed in it. If you are a person of means and you believe that it would be a good idea to be able to ensure the survival of your genetic line then you would be well advised to purchase a building block. These building blocks will be available from the close of this conference onward. As well as your name being engraved into the walls you will also receive a Survivors Certificate and your name will be recorded in the official records as a sponsor for the construction of the Starship. In addition you will receive a lapel pin with the word survivor on it and you will be asked to wear it throughout your workday so that we and everybody else can see that you are a sponsor of a Lifeboat to the stars.

There is still another good reason for us to be able to recognize you as one of our sponsors. We are going to need supplies and to find contractors to perform a multitude of tasks. We will support those companies and individuals who support us. Everybody is welcome to bid on these contracts but only those applicants who are sponsors of record will be considered as a potential contractor. To be clear, ladies and gentlemen, if at least one individual from the Leadership Team of a bidding company is not a holder of a Survivors Certificate, their bid will not be considered. If you want to profit from doing business with us then we must profit from doing business with you.

This is a very significant journey we have started and it will be years before it is completed. It is going to take huge sums of money to bring it to fruition and it is our intention to raise that money from the general public in return for services rendered. Every person on Earth will have the opportunity to sponsor the building of this Starship in one form or another. Similarly, every person on Earth will also have the opportunity to have their genes on board this starship when it leaves. I will also be assuming the job of Communications Officer so I will be announcing future funding programs as the need arises. We will post the details of this and every future funding program on our company website.

Thank you for your time ladies and gentlemen.

I stepped up to the microphone just as Virginia was finishing so she handed me the microphone and walked back to her place during the again polite applause.

Ladies and gentlemen, I began, part of my duties will be to oversee all Earth-bound operations so I would like to introduce you to Dwaine Franks. He will be overseeing all off-Earth operations.

Dwaine walked to center stage during the courtesy applause and accepted the microphone from me.

Thank you ladies and gentlemen, he began. Please note that we are all wearing our lapel pins and yes for the skeptics among you, we did pay for them out of our own pockets. We have purchased the first building blocks and have chosen to have our names inscribed beside the entrance door to the bridge. You will note when you purchase your own block that you may choose to locate it anywhere that has not already been taken.

My responsibilities will be two-fold for the duration of this project. I will oversee the construction and operation of any facilities we may need on the Moon and I will oversee the construction of the Space Dock that will be used to build the Starship. As soon as that is ready, I will also oversee the construction of the Starship itself. The first contract will be put out to tender within a week of this news conference. The applications should be submitted to our head office in Calgary or my office on the Moon.

We will be moving the head office of Gem Space from Mars to the Moon and we will be using it as the off-Earth office of ILI as well. This will eliminate any difficulty with communications between the board members. The varying time delay associated with communicating from Mars would have made normal conversations impossible. As you may know, we operate as a team so it is imperative that the board members be able to contact each other quickly and to be able to formulate plans effectively.

My wife Kelly has accepted the responsibility of overseeing the operations of both Sigme and Gem Space as well as acting as a consultant on the Board of ILI. My role with respect to Gem Space will be reduced to that of a consultant. We will both be actively involved with each company because it is necessary for them to remain solvent. As you heard earlier, both Gem Space and Sigme Corporation are our fallback bankers in the event we encounter a short term gap in funding between promotions. The other member of our team is James Frederick and he is here with us via a live video feed.

Just then the screen flickered and Dwaine yielded the floor to him.

Ladies and gentlemen, he began, I'm glad I was able to be here with you today. My colleagues have asked me to come out of retirement to help with this very worthwhile project. I want to add my personal endorsement to proceed with all haste to complete a lifeboat to carry our genes out into the cosmos. Those of us who make our living in space are very much aware of how fleeting life can be and how quickly it can be snatched away from you. Living on a planet with an atmosphere to protect us has kept our species alive so far but that atmosphere could be torn away in the blink of an eye and without the Lifeboat Project our species would simple disappear. My retirement lifestyle pales in comparison to the importance of this project. I look forward to working with my colleagues to make the Lifeboat a reality.

As soon as Dad signed off I closed the meeting by reminding everyone that we were still in the process of making a complete action plan so we would not be taking any question at this time.

The stadium roared with questions from every direction as we walked off the stage. We had a helicopter on stand-by on the roof and we lifted off in full view of the crowd to return to the ranch.

Every line in our communications room was lite up by the time we reached the ranch. We had deliberately failed to mention the price of the Survivors Certificates and the $100,000.00 price tag did discourage a few of the callers but sales were brisk anyway. The biggest selling feature seemed to be the option of selecting the location for their name to be displayed. The most encouraging part was that the pace of the incoming calls did not taper off for at least a week.

Chapter 38

We were especially pleased at how well our heckler deception had worked out. The media reported the incident as proof that we were a no nonsense leadership team. We were even more pleased that we were able to promote our Survivors Package free of charge and it had received worldwide exposure.

Virginia was surprising adept at finding ways to keep our names to the forefront in the world media. It was she who suggested that we limit the amount of information we gave out at the news conference in New York and that proved to be very much in our favor. That and the heckler incident was proof positive for us that we could benefit tremendously with a little bit of manipulation of the news media. The trick would be to keep the media hungry by giving them enough information that they would report it as news but not enough to stop then from speculating about what was coming next.

There was one unexpected result of our news conference. The reference that Virginia had made about a person of means was causing quite a stir. The recently idled members of The Workers Movement seized on those words and were presenting them as proof that the program had been designed to benefit only the rich all along. They also accused us of accepting kickbacks because of the requirement that contractors must purchase a Survivors Certificate. We were a little slow to realize that the media can be a two edged sword because they tend to focus most of their attention on negative news.

Our Military Police squad had left us the day after the New York news conference and we had made arrangements to have them replaced with our own team. Our guards were under constant siege as the news media tried every conceivable means to get to any one of us. Even Dad had received a visit from an inquisitive reporter on Mars looking for more information.

We were worried about the change of focus caused by the negative coverage from the news media regarding the accusations made against us. Our sales dropped off sharply and we had to take action or lose access to our focus group. We knew that there was a huge reservoir of money out there under the control of a relatively few people and our first promotion was aimed directly toward them. We decided to take a chance and pull another rabbit out of our hat of tricks so we agreed to an on camera interview from one of the news networks. It was not a coincidence that the CEO of that network had recently purchased a Survivors Certificate.

The interview was with Conrad Chow, the head reporter for World News Service (WNS). It started off politely enough until Mr. Chow insinuated that we had shown blatant disregard for the law by openly accepting kickbacks. Virginia was almost condescending when she reminded him that the definition of a kickback was monies repaid to the contracting organization in return for having received the contract. She became more firm in her language when she reminded him that there was no privilege extended to the contract applicant and certainly no monies returned to ILI after the contract was let. The requirement for the purchase of a Survivors Certificate was at worst an application fee and at best a statement of belief in the Lifeboat Project. After all, she said "owning a Survivors Certificate does not guarantee you will be the successful bidder".

I realize, she continued, that this not a normal business practice but this is not a normal business venture and we must garner support from every possible source. I would point out that your CEO Gerald Tibadoe purchased a Survivors Certificate last week before all these accusations became public and that is one of the reasons we chose to grant this very interview to you.

Let me address the rest of the accusations being bandied about. I am referring to the suggestion that the Lifeboat Project is being undertaken to benefit only the rich. The rich have a lot more money than the common folk so it is only right that we offer them more if we expect more from them. To that end we are offering one other enticement to people of means. When the time comes to select a crew for the Lifeboat, individuals who are registered as owners of a Survivors Certificate will be given the first opportunity to fill these positions. Please notice that I did not say that they were required to be part of the crew or even that every one of them would be selected. I simply stated that they would have first option if they are qualified for the position.

One point that our detractors have failed to mention is that the Lifeboat will be carrying much more that a 5000 member crew. It will be carrying a Sperm and egg Bank that will be filled to the brim with samples from any individual who chooses to submit their specimen for the journey. Dwaine Franks will be tendering contracts for the construction of the first of these banks next week. We will of course be charging a nominal fee per deposit.

Mrs. Frederick, interrupted Conrad, there will be those you claim that charging even a nominal fee will exclude the very poor from being able to have their Genes included in the bank.

Thank you for bringing that up Mr. Chow, answered Virginia, There is no free ride on this voyage. Having said that I can assure you that there will be a way for even the poorest person to earn enough to pay for a deposit in the bank if they so choose. We will be sponsoring programs that will make this possible.

Our sole source of income will be from fees charged for services rendered. I would like to remind you that the monies to build the Sperm and Egg Banks is coming from the sale of the Survivors Certificates. These very "people of means" that there has been so much banter about are the people who will make it possible for the "people of lessor means" to also be included in this voyage to the stars. Most of these people of means are purchasing a Certificate as a statement of belief in the project rather than to garner any kind of favor. Your CEO, Gerald Tibatoe, is a perfect example of that. He and many others like him simply believe that our species is worth saving and that sending our DNA out into the cosmos is the most likely way to ensure that it is.

I would also like to suggest that every person who is running for an elected office would be well advised to have a lapel pin to display as well. It only makes sense that if you are asking the people to support you with their vote that you should be able to show them that you support the continuance of our species.

Thank you for a very concise answer Mrs. Frederick interrupted Conrad. Do you think that will be enough to satisfy your detractors? I am thinking specifically of The Workers Movement and their recent statements regarding the Lifeboat Project.

Thank you for asking that Mr. Chow, answered Virginia, I have been wanting to address that issue for some time. I have very little patience with naysayers and disablers and I'm sorry to say that this Workers Movement appears to have more than a fair share of these in their ranks. I would remind these people that the contracts we will be tendering starting with the construction of the Sperm and Egg Banks will be requiring workers. These workers will be paid fair wages from the funds we acquired by selling Survivors Certificates and these workers will very likely choose to take a small portion of the monies they receive to pay for a deposit in the Bank for themselves and/or their families. That, in turn, will generate more income that can be used to build more banks or to start work on the Starship.

Mrs. Frederick, interrupted Conrad, that begs the question? What will be the cost of a deposit in the Bank?

I'm sorry Mr. Chow, answered Virginia, we haven't settled on a price yet but I can assure you that it will within the means of anyone who is willing to work for it.

That's pretty vague, said Conrad, with the look of someone who had just found his opponents Achilles Heel, surely you have a figure in mind.

Mr. Chow, answered Virginia a little sharply, when we have accurate information we will release it. I can tell you that the hold back right now is not the amount of money we will need to complete the Starship. It is how we will be able to ensure that everybody is able to pay our price.

Mrs. Frederick, interrupted Conrad again.

Excuse me Mr. Chow, interrupted Virginia rather sharply, I wasn't finished. The most obvious way for people to afford our fee will be to set aside some of their wages for that purpose. I would like to suggest to the leadership of The Workers Movement that if they are looking for a cause to rally behind then they should consider scrutinizing the training programs in place for the workers they claim to represent. Our contracts alone will require thousands of qualified workers either working directly for us or for our suppliers both on and off Earth. People of foresight will beginning training these workers immediately.

I think that will be all for today Mr. Chow. Thank you for your time.

Conrad Chows mouth literally dropped open as Virginia got up and walked out of the studio.

We had certainly chosen our Communication Officer well and she was wrong. Her impromptu speaking skills were much better than she thought they were. Her inclusion of political aspirants in the pool of potential certificate clients resulted in a landslide of sales. Her disclosure that we would be sponsoring programs to enable people to earn enough to deposit their own Genes in the Bank caused quite a stir. It was the topic of every talk show of any importance for weeks to come as they tried to guess how we would accomplish that. Add to that her titrate against The Workers Movement and we scored a triple win with that interview. ILI was now instantly recognized worldwide.

The interview received worldwide distribution so The Workers Movement had no choice but to redirect their attention to examining the training programs available for their workers. It wasn't long before they were claiming that the lack of training programs available from both government and private business was actually a plot to keep the common people from benefiting from the Lifeboat Project. It was a wonderful day for us when their chief spokesperson called a news conference to decry this lack of training and she was proudly displaying her lapel pin that she had paid for personally.

The contract for the Sperm and Egg Bank was applied for by ten contractors, all of whom qualified to be considered. The contract was let and soon there was a crew preparing the foundation for the Bank in a sheltered crater not far from the

Moon Base. As soon as the media attention started to slack off we issued a news release that set the price for a single deposit in the bank at $50.00 global with a maximum number of 10 deposits per person. We explained that we had only enough room in the Banks for everyone on Earth to deposit 10 samples each and we didn't want to leave anyone out.

Chapter 39

We first realized that we had a serious problem when we tried to recruit workers to start on the Space Dock. Our contractor barely had enough men to be able to start on the Bank. There was a very limited work force on the Moon and most of them were already employed in the upgrades to the factories. We were going to need a lot more workers immediately and there just weren't enough workers available on the Moon to build the Space Dock or the Starship.

There were workers available on Earth but they were very reluctant to move to the Moon. The very low gravity of the Moon soon weakened their muscles to the point that they were virtually trapped on the Moon. They could not return to Earth without some very extensive physiotherapy. Even Dwaine had noticed the difference when he had returned to Mars after a one month stay on the Moon to help Kelly pack up the office for the move to the Moon. He said he was almost as tired after moving around for a day on Mars as he had been while they were on Earth after living on Mars. It was understandable that workers did not want to be forced to live on the Moon forever and for a short time we considered changing our main construction facilities to Earth. That would have worked well for the Sperm and Egg Bank but building the Space Dock and Starship on Earth was impossible because lifting the sections off the planet to even a near Earth orbit was out of the question. Even the cost of ferrying the workers and materials from Earth to build it in a low Earth orbit would have raised our costs astronomically because of Earths Gravity. The Moon was originally selected because it was the ideal location for the Starship to be built. When an extensive recruitment campaign failed to entice even one-quarter of the workers we would need, we knew we had to change our approach or everything would fall apart.

As is usually the case with us, the idea came from an off-hand remark made during one of our discussions. We were toying with the idea of housing our workers on a circular space habitant rather than on the Moon. That would have solved the weakening problem but it would have added a lot of costs in building the habitant in the first place and we would still have to find workers to build it in space. It was Kelly again who said, you know a circular habitant doesn't have to be built in space. I think she thinks more outside of the box than any of us.

We were in the middle of one of our morning conference calls and we all stopped talking as the reality of what she said sank in. Finally I said, alright Kelly, what did you mean by that?

I haven't thought it all the way through, she said, but it would be a lot cheaper and easier to build a habitant on the moon than in space.

Are you thinking of somehow lifting the entire thing out into orbit, I asked?

No, she answered hesitantly, I think it would be better to build one that stayed on the surface. As I said, I haven't thought it all the way through yet but I'm liking it more and more the longer I think about it.

I sort of like it myself, I said, but this sounds like something we should get together on. How about if Virginia and I come up for a visit.

How soon can you get here, asked Dwaine?

We'll need a day to get ready, answered Virginia, so we'll be there in two days.

We had kept more than the security team after the Military Police had left. The chef and nanny had freed Virginia from all her domestic duties and her duties as Communication Officer required that she be free to come and go as needed. She had also become an integral part of our planning discussions and had proven to an essential member of our team so we had no choice but to find our own chef and nanny. The kids were a little taken aback at first but when the news media started to refer to us as the last hope of humanity they realized the importance of the job we had taken on.

ILI headquarters is in an office tower in Calgary but our office at the ranch was our main working station. That allowed us to still have meals and most evenings with the kids and at the same time gave us the flexibility to leave on short notice for meetings either in Calgary or elsewhere. We even bought ourselves an aircar so we didn't have to fight traffic and our commute time was one hour instead of three.

Virginia was turning into a seasoned space traveller. The extra "G's" from the Executive Shuttle didn't bother her hardly at all now. We arrived right on schedule and went directly to the office. Dwaine and Kelly had waited for us before going to eat so we unpacked in the guest room at the office and went directly to the cafeteria. As soon as we had ordered, Kelly showed us a report she had found in the data base at the historical archives stored at the Moon Port.

It showed that this wasn't the first time that the problem of Moon Prisoners had been addressed. At one time there had been a proposal to try to create a gravity well on the Moon so that its gravity would be increased to equal Earths. The industrialists had vetoed this because the low gravity of the Moon has a lot of advantages for the factories and the cost of launching ships from the surface would have eliminated the competitive edge the Moon enjoyed over Earth.

Everyone had been able to work around the problem by an ongoing recruitment program that focused primarily on the poorer countries until then. We were going to need a large workforce of skilled workers and we didn't want to take the time or commit the resources to train them.

As soon as we got back to the office we did a detailed analysis of every contract we were going to let in the near future. You're not going to believe this, announced Kelly, we would need to triple the workforce on the Moon just to supply the workers we will need. Even if we can find the workers, there is no place to put them. The reason you guys are staying here in the office guest room is that there are absolutely no rooms available at the Housing Complex.

This could be a more serious problem than finding the manpower, added Dwaine. Even if we could find enough workers, we would still need a place to house them. It would take all the money we have raised to this point just to build the habitant for that many people and that would kill the momentum we have going for us. Our very lifeblood depends on a steady flow of dollars so if people lose the sense of urgency that we are trying so hard to create, then we might very well go the way of the Lifeboat Program.

Well, I said, let's tackle this one problem at a time the same as always. Do we need to build a habitant at all? Maybe we can get some enterprising developer to build a new housing complex for us.

Even if we could find a developer to build a new complex, added Virginia, I don't think they would go to the extra expense of building a rotating habitant just for us without a major injection of cash from us and that would leave us too cash poor to do anything else.

I agree, I said, and without the rotating habitant we almost certainly will not be able to find the skilled workers we need.

What if we offered anyone who stayed for a least five years a free Survivors Certificate, asked Virginia?

That might work, Kelly said, but that would be one less certificate we could sell and one for every worker would leave quite a hole in our financing plans. That number could get pretty big over the fifty years it's going to take to finish the Starship.

We went on like that for hours. Even Dad had joined us via video link but he wasn't able to add much of value because of the time lag. He had no way of knowing what was happening so when he started to say something we automatically yielded the floor to him. We had come to a standstill and were just sitting there in silence when Dad started to speak.

I hope I'm not interrupting anyone, he said, but I've just had an idea that may have some merit.

As always we settled back to listen as he continued. The way I understand the problem we have been trying to solve is that if we spend our money on a habitant then we won't need a habitant because we won't have any money to hire workers and if we can't find workers, we can't build the Starship. I know this isn't new to any of you, he continued, but I wanted to summarize the situation so you would understand where I'm coming from. I think Gem Space should consider building the habitant and rent out the rooms to the workers. If we do this right we could have our cake and eat it too. Gem Space would eventually get its money back and it shouldn't matter to the workers who they paid the rent to.

We just sat and looked at each other when Dad finished talking. Dwaine was the first to break the silence when he said, it was so obvious that we all overlooked it. We have enough money to build it because we have never had to touch our emergency fund and ILI is solvent enough now that it's not likely to need our help. It didn't take us long to flesh out the details since all the board members of Gem Space were present and Kelly put it to a vote. It was carried unanimously and Gem Space was in the space housing development business.

Next we moved on to where we were going to find the workers to build our habitant and where we were going to house them until it was ready.

Dad came to the rescue again. The upturn in business on the Moon created a downturn on Mars so there was a surplus of workers on Mars that we could tap into.

They may not be willing to move there permanently, he said, but they should be more than willing to come for at least one contract. All we need is a place for them to live.

I've been thinking, Kelly said, we are going to be a major customer for a lot of the businesses here so they should be willing to help us get started. I'm sure that they could talk a few of their single workers into doubling up during the construction of the habitant. That would be better for everyone than fighting over workers.

Chapter 40

Virginia and I were on the shuttle to Earth the next morning and things quickly returned to normal for us. Kelly on the other hand was quite busy.

Within a week Gem Space had incorporated Gem Housing as a wholly owned subsidiary of Gem Space. Dad had already recruited 200 workers who were anxious to start their new jobs and Kelly had negotiated a deal with the single people living in the Moon Housing Complex. Gem Housing would pay half their rental allowance directly to anyone who agreed to accept an extra roommate and the Housing Complex would not charge them for the extra occupant so they got to keep the money.

Dwaine took over from there and he soon had a crew working on the habitant and the Bank at the same time. Our habitant was going to be unique in the space community. The human body evolved over millions of years to work best at Earths gravity. If we were going to be able to find and keep a crew we needed to provide a place that will maintain their strength and bone density at Earths levels. That way, they can go home on leave and hopefully come back for another shift.

Artificial Gravity technology still eludes us so the only way we have to simulate it is with a rotating Habitant. That had worked good for years in space vehicles so there is no reason it won't work on the surface of the Moon. The low gravity of the

Moon presented a bit of a challenge but we believed we could compensate for it. In space we live inside the very outer rim of the wheel or portion of a wheel as is the case with the Spokes and Arcs. On the Moon we had to compensate for the presence of some gravity. We did that by building a compartment with the floor at a 58 degree angle to the ground. We created a computer simulation to get the perfect angle and it worked out great. Even the water in the drinking glasses looked level. Too little or too much angle would have meant that the people would feel like they were walking on a side hill.

When you stepped off the walkway onto your portal approach you had to walk up an incline until you reached your door. After you were inside the room and the door was closed so you couldn't see the approach ramp even though they were at the same angle as the ramp. After the door was closed, the floor, furniture, appliances and more importantly, you, looked and felt like you were in any room on Earth.

The beams to support the rails were offset by 58 degrees so the compartments could be made with a flat floor instead of the circular floors seen on some of the bigger wheeled habitants used for deep space travel. The compartment was supported by three rails to keep it steady and the front was arced so that it matched the walkway. Stepping off the walkway onto your portal felt like stepping onto an escalator on Earth except that it was moving twice as fast as a normal escalator. All three rails used frictionless electromagnetic bearings and linear electric motors and were independently powered. We had our own emergency back-up in the event of an interruption of power supplied by the Fusion Generators that supplied the power to the grid on the Moon.

There was a safety airlock half way up the portal even though the entire walkway was sealed and pressurized to one atmosphere. Each compartment contained the same safety features as the workplace. Enough water, food and oxygen to last two people for a week was stored in the compartment under the flooring as well as emergency space suits. Even if a freak meteorite strike (highly unlikely because anything even remotely dangerous to the colony had been removed by the miners years ago) or an explosion that damaged one or more of the compartments would not affect the safety of the remaining compartments.

The polymer dome that enclosed the entire walkway and compartment supporting structure was the first thing to be built. It was a radiation proof, tinted and transparent dome covering with inlaid solar panels. The habitant is 3 KM in diameter and the compartments are moving at a speed of 160 metres per minute to obtain the proper feel of Earths gravity.

The enclosure was agonizingly slow to be finished but the rail supports and rail bed went much faster because the workers didn't have to wear their space suits inside the enclosure. We contracted out the compartments to a business on the Moon because Dwaine wanted to keep a close eye on them to be sure they didn't take any short cuts. We paid top price and we insisted on top workmanship.

They had the first two compartments ready by the time we finished putting in the rails and their supports. We slipped them onto the rails and coupled them together with only one small modification to the coupling attachment. When they had finished coupling the first two together one of the workmen stood back and announced, we aren't building a habitant, we're building a bloody train. To this day our habitants are called Trains 1 through 4.

The rooms in the first one were all spoken for before we were half finished so we knew we had another winner on our hands. We quietly bought 3 more parcels of land on the outskirts of the Moon Base so we could encircle the Base with living quarters. We are profitable now and the largest landlord on the Moon.

Rent is usually provided to workers as part of their salary but we were charging 1/3 more to live on the Train. Even our workers had to pay the difference and they did so gladly so they could live comfortably and they would not lose their strength or bone density. A few of our newest workers balked at paying extra to live in the Train but they soon realized that comfort was more important than money. Gem Space and The Lifeboat Project workers had priority for renting in the Train but if a room did become available then it was quickly filled from the Complex and we would be getting full rent from their employer. As a matter of fact the only workers that we weren't getting full rent for were the people working for Gem Space. We received full price for everyone else including the construction workers for the Lifeboat Project.

As soon as Train 1 was finished, Dwaine filled it with the Gem Space people and our new workers he had hired to start on the Space Dock. Our recruitment advertisements on Earth made a big thing about not being Gravity Prisoners by agreeing to work in space so we were easily recruiting all the workers we needed. Our crew was so big now that we were actually having trouble getting enough material to keep up with construction.

The miners (including Gem Space under the firm guidance of Kelly) were going flat out to supply the factories and they in turn were hiring new people to increase their production. All this meant new accommodation was needed so Dwaine had started on Train 2 with the workers that became available when Train 1 was nearing completion. It could honestly be said that the Moon was humming with activity.

Most of this activity was being funded by the flow of money into the Lifeboat Project. That meant that Virginia was being hard pressed to keep that flow coming in.

The sales from the Sperm and Egg Bank were very constant and had offset the dwindling Survivor Certificate sales. Despite that, we needed more money now that we had started on both the Space Dock and the Starship. It was time for another interview with Conrad Chow of WNS.

That presented an unexpected problem. Conrad Chow had been quite offended when Virginia had walked away from his interview and he was quite vocal about it on succeeding interviews. That worked in our favor because we had received worldwide attention again as the talk show hosts debated the merits of her actions. In the end the consensus was that a host is the person who decides when the interview is over and the guest has an obligation to answer their questions.

Conrad Chow declined Virginias offer of another interview unless she promised to answer all his questions fully. Virginia was not about to do that because that could lead to a confrontation with Mr. Chow and some very bad press for us. Talk show hosts are notorious for eliciting guesses and conjecture from their guests if they are given a free hand and Virginia had proven to have a very short fuse when someone tried to manipulate her.

We needed to be seen as forthcoming and exact when we disclosed our plans even if that meant that we withheld information until all the details had been worked out. Leaving people guessing had also worked very much in our favor. We received a lot of extra attention in the media by the talking heads through their second guessing and conjecture and that kept our name in front of the public for much longer than the actual interview. It's a very firm credo in the business world, "the more exposure you get, the more customers you get", and that had certainly proven true in our case.

Virginia showed her mastery of media manipulation again when she contacted Global News Services (GNS) and made them an offer they couldn't refuse. She offered to grant them an exclusive interview and promised she would not walk out on them providing they would accept, "those plans have not yet been finalized", as her answer to a question. She then promised to issue a news release stating that WNS had not been granted the interview because they were more interested in badgering their guests than in providing accurate information to the public. That news release would finish with a statement that ILI would not be coerced or manipulated by anyone.

That was the carrot that GNS could not refuse. They were in second place to WNS in the rating wars and scooping this interview from WNS would change that. Our prior news release would ensure them almost universal coverage.

The main purpose of this interview would be to answer questions about our plans to create programs to enable anyone to be able to afford to send their genes out amidst the stars. Virginia made two additional requests of GNS which they granted.

She asked that the host be from India because that would be the focal point of our main Empowerment Operations and she asked to be able to make a statement at the beginning of the interview. They were a little reluctant to grant that request until she agreed to give them a copy of the statement 24 hrs. before airtime providing they guaranteed that there would be no advance leak of the contents.

GNS did more than provide an East Indian host for the interview. They flew Virginia to Bombay and put her up at the Hilton on their dime. The host for the interview was Jenhinder Singh and Virginia could not have been more pleased. Jenny, as she insisted on being called, was not your ordinary host. Although she was very striking in appearance, she avoided the glamorous look in favor of a much more relatable image of a down to earth advocate for the people. Virginia had provided her with a copy of her statement as promised and Jenny had some very detailed questions prepared by air time.

After the usual cordial greetings Jenny played the gracious host by inviting Virginia to read her statement. The show was being transmitted worldwide and translated with subtitles in the local language from every broadcasting station in their network. Virginia and Jenny were seated across from each other in the usual living room setting so Virginia stood and moved around in front of the coffee table to read from her tablet.

This will be posted on our website as soon as this interview is over, she began, we have finalized our agenda with regard to the carrying of our DNA out into the cosmos.

I'm sure that most of you are aware that we have finished the construction of the first Sperm and Egg Bank and that it is rapidly filling up. We have been very pleased with the quality of work done by Takiokko Contracting and as of today we have extended their contract so they can start building the first Embryo Bank. We are estimating that we may need up to ten of each Bank to be capable of carrying a deposit from everyone who wishes to contribute. There will be a maximum of 10 deposits per person in the Sperm and Egg Banks and 5 per couple in the Embryo Banks. As you know the fee for a deposit in the Sperm and Egg Bank has already been set at $50.00 Global and that will never be changed. The fee to store an Embryo in the bank has been set at $250.00 Global per individual because the procedure is much more complicated.

These banks will be built on the surface of the moon where they will stay until they are lifted up to the Starship as part of the final preparations for launching. We have made the decision to include Embryo Banks as well as the Sperm and Egg Banks because we realize that more than the DNA of an individual is unique. An Embryo created by two individuals is also unique. We are very conscious of the fact that this is a fifty year program so by providing an Embryo Bank at this time we will be able to offer the people alive today an opportunity to include their prodigy in the Bank.

With that she went back to her seat and thanked Jenny for the opportunity to read it.

Jenny started by saying, I am very impressed with the fore thought that has been put into your genetic programs but there are a few question that beg to be asked.

The inclusion of an Embryo Bank has never been mentioned before and I'm sure at least some people will be taken aback by the concept. There are a multitude of ethical questions that need to be addressed before people consign their prodigy to the care of an unknown entity. The most pressing of these will be, who will be responsible for the care and rearing of these babies? I can easily envision a bank of incubators producing genetically altered specimens that will be programmed to preform god knows what kinds of tasks at the whim of the scientists on board the Starship.

Wow, answered Virginia, you sure know how to ask a loaded question. We have given this a great deal of thought and I'm sorry to say there is no firm answer to that question. There will be a very specific clause in the Oath-of-Office of every member of the Leadership Team on board the Starship. This clause will strictly prohibit any alternation or interference with the natural development of an Embryo that has been deposited in the bank. Having said that, the evolution of the onboard culture will be completely beyond our control after the ship is underway. The screening of the Command Crew will probably ensure that the Oath will be honoured for at least one or two generations but that is the best we can do.

We can only predict a few of the problems that these voyagers will be faced with so we will have to trust in human ingenuity and their drive to survive to carry them through whatever they encounter. We have to keep in mind, she continued, that we have no idea what kind of a world they will have to adapt to when they do find a planet to call home. Ideally they will find a planet that we can populate with unchanged samples of humanity but it is much more likely that there will have to be some changes to our metabolic processes in order to survive in a different environment. It is quite conceivable that we may seed more than one planet from our Banks before the Starship becomes inoperable or it is destroyed. The question every person needs to ask themselves before they submit either an Embryo or their Sperm and Eggs is "Do you want your genes to die with the rest of the humans here on Earth or do you want them to venture out into the Cosmos to see what they can accomplish?

Wow, injected Jenny, you really know how to answer a question with a question. What do you have to say to the religious leaders who will accuse you of playing loose with Gods creation?

It could easily be argued that the changes to the humanoid species over the ages has been Gods way of adapting to a different environment. In any event, this is a completely voluntary program. Nobody will be required to submit a sample to either bank. As a matter of fact, there will be restrictions as to who may submit an Embryo because more than one individual is involved. We will require the permission of both individuals who created the Embryo.

I should mention that the same procedure will be followed as with the Sperm and Egg Bank. We will record the DNA of the contributing person or persons in the case of an Embryo. That information is solely for the purpose of identifying the contributing person or persons for our records only. We need to do that to be able to ensure they are within our contributing limits. After the specimen is deposited in the Bank it will be next to impossible to match it to the depositors. This is to ensure that there will be no favouritism to any economic class or ethnic group. To be clear, after the sample is stored in the Bank, there will be no way to trace the deposit back to the depositor. The DNA of the depositors will be recorded and stored so that nobody exceeds the limits and therefore dominates the bank. There will be no way of cross referencing the actual deposit to our records.

If I may, interrupted Jenny, are you saying that only married couples may deposit an Embryo in the Bank

An excellent question, commented Virginia. The short answer to that question is no. We do not presume to be the moral guardians of the human race. No deposit will be refused as long as neither creator has exceeded his/her deposit limit and they are both at least 18 years old.

Jenny couldn't help herself when she blurted out, are you saying anybody can deposit an Embryo even if they are not in a relationship?

Another excellent question Jenny. The short answer to that is yes. The reason we will be recording the DNA of each contributor will be to positively identify them for our records. It is possible that a person may choose to deposit an Embryo from a different partner and that will be recorded as part of their limit as long as both parties consent and they are of legal age.

Pardon me again, interrupted Jenny, but I'm having trouble with this concept. Are you saying that if a woman becomes pregnant by a different partner than her mate, you will accept the donation?

In that case, probably not unless she brings the real father in with her. We require the permission of both of the people who actually created the Embryo before we accept a deposit. If a woman tries to present someone else as the father we would discover that when we did the DNA comparison to confirm the parentage and we would be forced to deny the deposit.

That could create some very compromising situations for a woman don't you think, asked Jenny.

Absolutely, answered Virginia, so I suggest that people should be very sure of the parentage before they try to deposit an Embryo.

There was a long pause while Jenny considered her next question. I'm sorry if this puts you on the spot but what is your policy regarding sibling or incestuous parentage?

We are aware that in some parts of the world this is not an uncommon happening so as long as they are both of legal age and give their consent, we cannot refuse the deposit.

Jennies face lit up as she asked, what about clones? Will you also accept cloned Embryos?

For the time being, we will not be accepting cloned Embryos but we can see circumstances where that may be an appropriate option, answered Virginia.

What circumstances might that be, jumped in Jenny.

Virginia could tell that Jenny was smelling a hidden story here so she tried to change the subject.

I'm did want to talk about our Empowerment Programs if you don't mind Jenny.

Jenny caught the hint but her reporter instincts must have taken over because she jumped right back in on the morals issue.

As I understand your answers to the Embryo questions Virginia, you will accept Embryos from any source regardless of the moral implications as long as it doesn't come from a cloned donor. Is that accurate?

Virginia folded her arms across her chest as she answered, those plans have not yet been finalized.

It was clear to Jenny that she had crossed the line and she was not immune to the fact that if she expected another interview with Virginia she had better not pursue the point any further. She rightly guessed that Virginia had come to the end of her rope and was smart enough to take the easy way out.

Ladies and Gentlemen, I must apologise for this but we have overrun our time. I hope we will be able to explore the Empowerment Programs at a later date.

Virginia's temper had cooled enough for her and Jenny to shake hands and agree to talk about a future interview before they signed off.

As soon as they were off the air, Jenny tried to pin Virginia down to a definite time for the next interview. All Virginia said was "those plans have not yet been finalized" as she left for her car.

The issue of the cloned Embryos couldn't have worked better for us if we had planned it. The talk shows and media commenters were literally buzzing with activity. The talk shows were inundated with people who wanted a chance to express their opinions on the subject of not just cloned embryos but the concept of people donating their prodigy and basically abandoning it to the care and possibility the whim of scientists. We were called everything from the amoral agents of the devil to a righteous organization doing Gods work by helping him preserve souls that would otherwise be lost.

Chapter 41

The end result for us was a landslide of applications to have an Embryo deposited in the bank. We quite simply were overwhelmed. We had established a collection point for the Sperm and Egg Bank in every major city around the globe but they were not able to process Embryos. Embryo collection required very specialized equipment and was much more complicated than collecting Eggs or Sperm.

We were forced to start a registration list until we could get the equipment and personnel in place. We required a fifty per cent payment before a name could be added to the list. We integrated the Embryo collecting facilities with our Egg and Sperm collection depots and it was still a full two years before we had all the clinics operating.

The media frenzy tapered off after a week but there was always at least one talk show expounding on the merits or pitfalls of the Embryo Collection Program for at least a month. That kept our name in front of the public long enough for almost every person on earth to have heard of the program and to form an opinion about it.

In the meantime we were inundated with inquiries about our Empowerment Program and we were constantly pestered by the network moguls for an opportunity to host the next interview.

Just as the talk shows were starting to lose interest in the story completely, the ever present Workers Movement issued a press release that put us in the limelight again.

They were tooting the same old conspiracy theory about the working class being excluded from access to the Gene Banks because of our failure to announce our Empowerment Program. They hinted quite strongly that it didn't exist and never would. The media, always hungry for a negative story, gave it credibility by broadcasting their press release worldwide and referred to our apparent reluctance to release any details as proof that it may actually be a smokescreen to keep the poor at bay.

We received a request from GNS to do another interview with Jenny to answer these accusations. Virginia was a little reluctant to give Jenny another chance to put her on the hot seat but she agreed to the interview with three stipulations. The only topic of discussion would be the Empowerment Program, Jenny would not attempt to distort or sensualize any of the information we released and the interview would be held in our communication center. Jenny must have been under some pressure from GNS because she agreed without even suggesting a counter proposal.

Virginia also asked for and received permission to make a statement at the start of the interview. She of course gave Jenny a copy of the statement the day before the interview.

GNS got a lot of mileage out of being the exclusive outlet for information about our new programs. We agreed to do the interview the week following the Workers Movement announcement so they would have time to promote the interview properly. They were primarily interested in increasing their audience as were we. We wanted as much attention as possible because the Empowerment Program was intended to be our flowerchild to sway public favor permanently over to our side. If this turned out right, nobody would ever question our motives again.

The day of the interview came and our media room was transformed into a spider web of wires as the technicians connected it to the rest of the world. The living room setting in the center of the room was the only area that didn't have wires strung across it.

Jenny and Virginia were both dressed in smart business outfits and were seated in their chairs across from each other when the cameras started rolling.

Jenny started by saying, we are very pleased to have Virginia Frederick here with us today. We will be disclosing the details of the much awaited Empowerment Program and Mrs. Frederick will be making a statement to start things off.

With that Virginia stood and walked to the center of the floor. She started by saying, there has been some criticism of GNS for not providing enough time to discuss our Empowerment Program and some people have found fault with Jenny for spending so much time on the Embryo Bank during our last interview. I think this criticism has been undeserved. Both programs are critically important to the Lifeboat Project and both programs deserve to be fully explored in their own right. Jenny was quite right to cut the interview off when she did because there was clearly not enough time left to properly introduce this program.

As usual the following statement and other relevant information will be posted on our website immediately following this interview.

Ladies and Gentleman, she continued, we will be sponsoring make work programs in every country that will allow it. These programs will be designed to benefit the local populace as much as possible but they may be as simple as an earthmoving or road building project where all the work is done by human power. Garden farms, irrigation projects and educational programs are good examples of the types of projects we will be sponsoring. Our first efforts will be focused on education. A great many of our poorest populations are illiterate or have a substandard education. It is our intention to change that by offering credits to those individuals who complete various levels of their education. Please note that these will not be college level classes, we will be teaching basic knowledge skills such as reading, primary math and basic science knowledge as well as basic health and hygiene.

To start with we will hire teachers on short term contracts to teach others to teach so we can expand the programs until they are peopled by volunteers and therefore self-sustaining. We will establish benchmark levels that participants must complete in order to receive these credits. Please note that I said credits, not money. These credits will only be available to the individual who earned them and can only be redeemed by them to pay for depositing their specimen or that of one of their immediate family into one of the Gene Banks.

As always the people who do the most will receive the most credits. For example, the teachers will receive twice the credits as a student who completes a level. Teachers and students alike will be evaluated by their supervisors and those that fail to meet our standard will be asked to choose a different program. We believe that the education program has the most potential to benefit the general population so that is the reason we have chosen to start with it.

The education program will be followed very shortly by our work programs. It will not be necessary to be an intellectual to earn enough credits to deposit your genes in the bank. For every week spent on one of our make work programs that individual will receive the same credit as a student in the educational program. We will be sponsoring garden farms in every location we can gain access to. Underutilised park lands and floodplains as well as rooftop locations will all be utilized. We will even be sponsoring workers to existing farms that will volunteer part of their lands for garden farms. As always, these workers will have to meet the expectations of the farm supervisor to maintain their position and to receive credits for the time they spend on the farm.

There will be a maximum time that students and workers may stay registered with the program. To begin with that time limit will be enough to get the credits necessary to pay for one deposit in the Sperm and Egg Bank. Teachers will be allowed to stay long enough to get enough credits for an

Embryo deposit and if there is a need they may stay to earn more credits for additional deposits by becoming a supervisor or by continuing to teach. The credit schedule will be the same worldwide regardless of the local economic conditions. We have set that standard as one months involvement in any of our programs or the completion of a benchmark level whichever is shorter. At the end of that time the individual will be asked to leave the program to make room for the next person on the list. After the waiting list is exhausted, individuals will be allowed to re-enter one of the programs for additional credits. As well, two individuals will be allowed to pool their credits for the purpose of an Embryo deposit.

The educational programs will be supported by the revenue from the Garden Farms so that it is sustainable. The Garden Farm workers will also receive a midday snack and an evening meal made from the farm produce. It is our fervent desire that these programs be self-supporting but they will be subsidized if necessary to keep them operating. We will gladly accept donations from people or organizations that believe that these programs can be a benefit to our lessor privileged population. It will be a blessing if we can give a few of these individuals a helping hand up rather that the pitiful hand-outs they are used to.

As I have stated several times in the past, there is no free ride on the Starship. Every person and every gene sample must be paid for by someone that believes that they should be included in this sampling of humanity. To that end, we would like to take this opportunity to issue a challenge to the very vocal Workers Movement.

Up until now they have been playing the role of naysayer and profess to be the protector of the downtrodden workers of the world. This is an opportunity for then to do something positive for these people. There will be people who will not be able to take advantage of even these programs because of a physical or mental condition or because of the political situation in their countries.

Maybe The Workers Movement should rally behind these peoples by truly becoming their representative. They should be able to use their influence to pressure reluctant governments into participating in the Empowerment Programs and if that fails, they can establish charities that will fund these programs and those individuals that have no other way to submit their specimen. There may be further change to these programs as circumstances require so please check our website regularly for any changes that may apply to you.

At that point Virginia went back to her seat to allow Jenny to regain control of the interview.

I have to admit, began Jenny, that I was very impressed by your statement when I reviewed it last night. There are of course thousands of questions that need to be asked but I'll start with the most obvious. Almost every government on Earth has struggled to eliminate the poverty from their cultures and have failed. How do you expect to do it in such a short time?

I think you may have misunderstood the purpose of our programs, answered Virginia. It would be truly great if we were able to help some of these people improve their lifestyles but our goal is to provide them with an opportunity to earn enough credits so that they may make a deposit in the Gene Bank of their choice. Those people who chose not to make a deposit will probably not benefit from our programs. We will not be paying salaries or wages to anyone beyond the first couple of months it will take to find enough volunteers to replace our start-up staff. There will be a continual turnover of staff as soon as they have reached our benchmark levels.

That's a very commendable position, commented Jenny, but do you realize that you may very well be forcing people off your programs back into the abject poverty they want so desperately to leave?

Jenny, answered Virginia, I think you are confusing the issue again. We have promised and we will deliver programs that will allow anyone who is willing, the opportunity to earn the privilege of depositing a specimen in one of our banks.

Let me say one more time. We do not presume nor are we willing to accept responsibility for helping people rise above their circumstances. We will however offer these individuals an opportunity to be included in this sampling of humanity, regardless of their circumstances. I hope this clarifies that point for you.

This time Jenny took the hint and moved on to the next question. You mentioned that there would be revenue from your Garden Farms. Do you expect to make a profit from the volunteer workers who will be manning these farms?

The short answer to that question, answered Virginia, is yes. These programs are being instigated to fulfill our promise and objective of providing everyone an opportunity to have their genes included in the banks. We will be using funds that could be directed toward the completion of the Starship to fund and subsidise these programs if necessary. We will in turn try to reduce these subsidies by selling any excess produce from the Garden Farms and by charging local governments for work performed whenever possible.

Jenny immediately went to her list of questions as soon as Virginia paused. The Garden Farms sound like a good idea on the surface, she said, but I'm having trouble understanding how people from the inner cities will benefit from them. There isn't enough places available that is close enough for most of these people to get to so how is it possible for them to become part of the work force.

I'm glad you brought that up Jenny, answered Virginia. That very problem was the topic of several discussions for us and we can see no alternative other than to transport the workers to the farm sites. We are as committed to providing these programs as we are to completing the Starship so we will take whatever steps as are necessary to ensure that they serve the purpose that they are intended to perform. To be clear, these are make work programs that will provide individuals an opportunity to earn credits which they can then use to pay for a deposit in one of the Gene Banks. If necessary we will create programs that serve no real purpose other than to provide people with an opportunity to earn their credits. We will start with rooftop and park areas within easy reach of inner city residence and then we will start to transport people out of the inner city to the farms.

Each person will be expected to stay on site for one week at a time before they are transported back to where they were picked up. They may choose to stay for the full four weeks all at one time but after that they must leave the program to make room for someone else. After four weeks in the program they will be credited with enough credits to pay for one deposit in the Sperm and Egg Bank. They may rejoin the program to earn additional credits after the waiting list for first time users is depleted.

The transportation of the workers will take even more of our resources away from building the Starship because we will have to provide accommodation for them as well as meals. This is not a slave labour type of work but the individual must be able to perform at least one of the tasks requested of them or they will be asked to leave the program. We are going to need people to clean and cook as well as perform more vigorous physical labour.

How will you deal with people who refuse to leave, asked Jenny abruptly?

All of our sites will be owned or leased by us so they will be private property. If necessary people will be forcibly removed and bared from any further participation in the program, answered Virginia. I know that this may sounds harsh but the reality is that this is not a charity or a public works program and we will not allow it to be turned into one. There will be a continuous turnover of staff as people reach the first benchmark in their activity. After the waiting list for first time participants is depleted, people will be allowed to reenlist in the programs to earn more credits. I hope that clears up any confusion, finished Virginia.

When you say applicant, asked Jenny, does that mean people will be screened before they will be allowed into a program?

No, answered Virginia, anyone is qualified to enter any one of our programs as long as they are capable or are willing to learn how to perform the tasks we will be asking of them. The application process is simple a means of identifying them and to establish their position on the waiting lists.

When you mentioned the road building and irrigation dams built by human labour, I envisioned columns of workers moving dirt with wheelbarrows such as we've seen in prison or slave movies. Is that going to be part of your programs?

The short answer to that question is yes, if necessary, answered Virginia. There will be no whip snapping or armed guards but we will find some kind of a worthwhile job for every person to perform and if that means that they have to push an empty wheelbarrow around all day then that's what it will be. Let me restate our policy Jenny. Every person will have the opportunity to earn credits but if a person refuses to perform even a simple task to earn those credits then they are choosing not to have their genes included in the banks. There will be a sliding scale so the more worthwhile the service you perform the more credits you can earn in a given time. For example, a person who pushes an empty wheelbarrow around will receive less credits than someone who actually moves some material. That scale will be available on our website after this interview is completed. I think you will find the requirements very lenient.

If people aren't required to do any actual work then these projects may never get completed, mused Jenny.

That true, answered Virginia, but remember our goal is to have people perform a task to earn credits, not necessarily to build a dam or a road. Let me expand on that if I may. People pushing empty wheelbarrows around is a worst case scenario. We will be working very hard to find ways for these projects to provide a service to the general public and to become self-supporting at the same time.

Jenny had a smug look on her face as she asked, so when do you expect to start up these hard labour camps with a strong emphasis on the "hard labour".

Virginia paused and studied Jenny before she answered. Jenny, I think you might serve the public better by providing them with accurate information rather than trying to sensualizing an issue that has already been dealt with. Perhaps it would be best if we let your audience read the information from our website.

At that, Virginia stood up and walked to the center of the room and faced the cameras as she said. Thank you for listening ladies and gentlemen. Please send any inquires to our website. She then just turned and walked off the set without acknowledging Jenny in any way.

Virginia received a lot of criticism for walking off the set again but after the usual banter from the talk shows had subsided the consensus was that Jenny should have known better. We had proved in the past that we would not tolerate the usual tactics of talk show hosts so it was very predictable that we still would not.

Chapter 42

That was the last interview that Virginia or any of us, for that matter, did. We have chosen instead to make use of our website and news releases. We have been under continual pressure to explain our policies so every now and then we release a "state of the project" statement that invariably ends with the proclamation that everything is going according to plan and that the Starship will be finished on time.

The Embyro Bank became our best and most continuous source of funding. Unfortunately, we were having to divert a lot more money than we had anticipated to support the educational and make work programs. Those programs were starting to take a significant amount of money away from building the Starship and it didn't look like there was going to be any end to it. We had to do something or we would never be able to finish the Starship on time and maybe not at all.

The Garden Farms were self-sustaining but just barely. By the time we feed the workers and provided each of them with 5 packs of seeds when they were rotated out, there was very little left over to sell. We liked the idea that we were helping to feed people but we were fast becoming a social program and that would destroy us. It's a well-recognized fact that as far as social programs are concerned, the need will always exceed the funding. We were exploring every option we could think of when the idea of expanding the Garden Farms by reclaiming arid lands with irrigation systems came up. Finding the water to irrigate with was our biggest problem.

Eventually we began exploring the feasibility of using desalinated water for irrigation. It was obvious that it would solve our water supply problem but we still needed a cost effective energy supply. There were still lots of areas around the world that could benefit from this approach so we picked one that was close to Cairo, Egypt. We needed to be close to an ocean and we wanted to be as close as possible to a large worker pool and potential markets.

We still needed an energy supply and that discussion ignited a germ of an idea that had been floating around in my head for years. It has long been recognized that there is almost unlimited energy available from the wave action of the oceans. I have to admit that I got the idea for a wave powered water pump from the old hand pump that was in the barn on the Hathaway Ranch when we bought it. They had been using it to supply water to the animal pens and it was still operable even though it was over fifty years old. These water pumps were very simple in design yet extremely dependable. We wanted to keep the design as simple as possible because our pumps would be working in a very corrosive salt water environment. We used the hand pump as our model although we did change a few things to take advantage of new technology.

Simplicity of operation and construction was our overriding principle so our pumps do not include a seal or packing or a piston for that matter on the bottom of the connecting rod. The sealing packing is located on the top of the barrel for the pump where it is possible to repair or replace it without disassembling the pump. The pump piston rod is only one inch smaller than the bore in the barrel and it has two wear rings that are a loose fit in the barrel on the bottom of it. The wear rings act as a guide to keep the rod straight in the barrel and to allow it to move freely up and down in the barrel. The wear rings are a loose fit in the barrel and together with the porting built into the bottom of the rods, they allow the water above them to freely flow past on the upstroke. The collar at the top of the barrel also contains a guide bushing so that the two of them position the rod properly in the center of the barrel. The entire top collar is made in two halves and is clamped to the top of the barrel so both the upper guide and the piston rod sealing rings are easy to replace when necessary.

The barrel has an inlet port near the bottom and an outlet port included in the bottom housing for the barrel. The bottom housing and the barrel are welded together so that they are one piece. The inlet and outlet valve assemblies are bolted to the pump so they can be easily removed and replaced when necessary. A saucer shaped float chamber is attached solidly to the top of the piston rod by a bolted ring assemble.

The saucer shaped float is probably the most unique of any of the components. We refer to it as a saucer because the top of the float is shaped so it looks like a saucer from a cup and saucer set. The float is hollow with the bottom in the shape of a segment of a sphere so it displaces enough water to provide the lift for the rod.

Here again we have deviated from the hand pump because our pumping stroke is on the down-stroke rather than the up-stroke. The float has to be heavy enough to push the water in the pump up to the height of the reservoir and it has to float well enough to lift the rod up out of the barrel when a wave passes by it. It also has a safety feature in it that will allow it to sink much lower in the water during extreme wave action such as when a storm is passing through the area.

This feature is accomplished by a properly sized tube extending from the bottom of the indentation in the top plate to just below the water line at normal operating height. This will only allow any water that finds its way into the saucer to drain out at a controlled rate. During normal wave activity the saucer is empty and the float rides high in the water so it is very responsive to the wave action. As the size of the waves increases, some of the water will splash into the saucer indentation. The float will become gradually heavier and sink lower down in the water when the drain hole will not allow this water to drain out as fast as it is coming in. In very heavy seas the float will be almost completely submerged and therefore not as exposed to the fury of the waves. The float will still be buoyant and ride up and down with the waves but the force transmitted to the pump structure is much lessened by the weighted and low riding float. As the wave action returns to normal again the volume of water splashed into the reservoir will lessen and eventually the float will drain itself and float high in the water again.

In this application it is the wave action on the surface that lifts the float and pulls the rod out of the barrel. This allows seawater to be drawn in past the inlet valve to fill the cavity left in the barrel by the raising rod. After the wave has pasted under the float, its weight causes it to push the rod back into the barrel and this forces the water out the outlet port and into the collecting infrastructure.

This design has resulted in a pump that is beautiful in its simplicity, yet very durable and dependable. Each pump connected to the system adds more volume so a staggered pump configuration will supply a continuous supply of water to the system as a wave traverses the floats. Several pumps that are interconnected via a crisscrossing of strong support pipes are able to withstand the forces from heavy seas far better than one rigid structure. The number of pumps connected to the system is the only limiting factors for the volume of water delivered to the reservoirs.

In order to be cost effective the main pump components are all the same size. The length of the piston rods and the weight of the float is different for most locations because they must be matched to the depth of the water and the height of the reservoir. The float and the piston rod combined must be heavy enough to produce sufficient pressure to pump the water up to the height of the reservoir.

The reservoir can be an earth filled dam across the mouth of a mountain gorge or a collection of elevated chambers that are connected together so that they become the reservoir. In either event there is a continuous flow of water to supply the turbine located down at beach level as the saltwater is returned to the sea. Most of our systems are built with double generating capability so we can chaptalize on the high water volume during periods of strong wave activity.

The collection chambers are just that, they are square chambers that can be coupled together to form a reservoir without the need of a dam. They can be used in areas where the ground is very porous and will not hold water or they can be elevated on platforms in areas where there is no high ground. They work best if they are placed all on the same level but they may be terraced with the use of the proper valves.

The use of chambers afforded us an opportunity to make further use of the system. They are ideal for fish farming because of the continuous supply of cool nutrient rich water pumped up from the bottom of the bay. The only serious problem we had with them is the contamination of the penned fish by resident species that had been drawn in through a damaged screen on the pumps. We solved that by installing grinders on the input stream to the tanks. Anything that managed to get through the screens was ground to a fine meal and became food for the penned fish. The on land fish farms also solved the major problems that had plagued the fish farming industry almost from its infancy. The contamination of the resident species was virtually eliminated because anything that did manage to escape into the feed stream for the generators was killed as it passed through the turbines.

The chamber system also allowed us to drain and clean individual chambers after the fish had been harvested from them. This system has worked so well and has generated so much capital that we even installed chambers around our earth filled dams.

The food from the fish farm and the electricity from the generators turned things around for us. We now had a reliable income stream to support our Empowerment Programs. We were able to transport the workers we needed to the worksite to construct the fish farms and generating plants. We established factories on the outskirts of the poor ghettos in most major cities. These factories built the fiberglass chambers and the piping for the water collection systems and to deliver the desalinated water to the farms. We even made the scaffolding and support structures for the elevation platforms. This gave us the means to cycle thousands of workers through the factories and reservoir building projects so they could earn their credits and deposit their specimens in the banks.

We have been able to work with The Workers Movement to bring in long term workers from remote areas and the dictatorships that would not allow us to operate in their countries. We have created a special credit program for these workers because they will not be able to return for additional credits. They are required to stay for at least one month but they may extend that to six months to get enough credits for an Embryo deposit if they so choose.

We have been able to reclaim thousands of acres of arid lands around the planet by using the energy from our generating plants to desalinate water so we could pipe it to our farms for irrigation. We have built dams along the mountainous coastlines of every continent that are supplying energy to the respective national grids. At last estimate we have displaced over 200 coal fired and hydrocarbon fueled generating plants. Several of the worlds remote islands now generate their power from a wave-powered saltwater generating system.

It has been a gargantuan job but I'm very pleased to be able to say that every person who was willing to do the work has had the opportunity to earn at least enough to deposit one specimen in the banks. I think I should give The Workers Movement credit here. They have done a fantastic job of raising funds and supporting those people who were unable to participate in any of our programs.

An unforeseen benefit from all this effort has been the creating of thousands of jobs that were filled from the workers we trained through these programs. It took twenty-five years for us to deplete the first time worker pool and by that time our Farms and Generating plants were contributing so much of our cash flow that we couldn't afford to shut them down. There was still a steady flow of first time users as the adolescents in the populations came of age but we needed to have a permanent staff to manage the facilities so we turned those positions into full time paid jobs with priority given to people who had gone through our programs.

The break over point came for the Lifeboat Project when the Starship and Space Dock were big enough to be seen from Earth with the naked eye. Shortly after they became visible, GNS did a documentary on the evolution of the Lifeboat Project. There had been several attempts over the years to find a suitable name for the Starship and we decided that this was an ideal time to announce our decision. We had decided that Starship 1 was the most appropriate because it carried with it the implication that there would be more to follow.

Our cash flow skyrocketed after people could see something concrete being built, I guess that made it easier to believe in the project. There was still lots of space on the walls for names and it was a bragging point when someone became affluent enough to afford to buy a Survivors Certificate.

As I look back, the day that we realized that, was one of our most gratifying moments because for us, it justified the work we were putting into this project and the sacrifices we had made in our personal lives.

From that point on things just seemed to fall into place and with the huge injection of money into our system we were able to accomplish things that even we had once thought of as impossible.

As we approached the final stages of construction of Starship 1 we were able to move the extra workers over to start on Starship 2. The support infrastructure for both the workers and the physical construction of a starship were already in place so the cost to build the second Starship will be much less. The transition to start the second ship was almost seamless. Our income flow was still constant thanks to our Garden Farms and the Wave-Powered Generating Plants as well as the new generation of buyers for the Survivor Certificates. The income from the Embryo Program and the Sperm and Egg Banks had never tapered off. We had immediately started on the Banks for Starship 2 after the Banks for Starship 1 were filled. That ensured a steady flow of money coming in from them as well so we were looking really good as far as cash flow was concerned.

We had struggled with a format to replace Dad on the Board of Directors when his health forced him to retire for good. There were lots of people who wanted the job but we needed someone who was willing to put their own interests aside and who was capable of working with the rest of us.

Thankfully we didn't have to endure the politics and the selection processes that accompany appointments to political posts. We did however have to be very selective in the candidates that we did interview. To begin with we were looking at people who could bring Dads type of experience to the Board until Dad pointed out that we were now the old and experienced hands so we should be looking at much younger candidates who could evolve into the core of the new leadership team. With that in mind our list of potential directors was much lessened. We also preferred someone who was self-sufficient so they would not need to be compensated. The fact that none of us were accepting any salaries or compensation package had been one of our best defences over the years when one group or another tried to accuse us of corruption or somehow seeking personal gain from our position of leadership.

What we were looking for most was someone who was passionate about the project and strong enough to resist the temptations of leadership. They also had to be used to dealing with the power brokers in the world.

Just because Dad had retired from the Board didn't mean that he didn't have anything to contribute to it. We still valued his opinion and when we had narrowed our list down to a member of the British Royal family or a son of one of the internet moguls from the Silicon Valley days, he suggested a surprise candidate.

She was Rebecca Cruise, the granddaughter of the Chairman of the Board of Stellar Steel who was fast becoming a leader in her own right. She was quite surprised when we invited her to meet with us and she admitted to being thrilled at the prospect of being involved with the Lifeboat Project. We knew after that first meeting that we had found our replacement.

There is no doubt at all that she has more than lived up to our expectations and that her contributions to the Board have been very significant. What you probably don't know is that we got a lot of mileage out of ribbing Dad over the fact that he was easily replaced by a mere woman. Unlike today, that was a bit of a putdown in his generation. He took it in good spirits and his dying thoughts were filled with the promise of the future because of what he had helped create. Nobody knows what the future holds but at least now there's a good chance our species will survive to be part of it.

As you can see it has all been worth it. We have finished Starship 1 five years ahead of schedule and Starship 2 is starting to take shape. We have made a few changes to the original design but it is still built on the same basic design as the old asteroid mining ships.

Ring 2, or the low gravity ring as it is commonly called, of the center ring is twice the size of the outer rings so it can house all the Gene Banks and it rotates in the opposite direction so it negates the gyroscope effect of the other rings. That, plus the fact that even ring three is one third bigger in diameter than the other outer rings makes it the stabilizing section for the Starship. We had to make it larger so it could house the live animal and fish biospheres.

The inner ring is usually referred to as the hub because it so closely resembles the hub on a wheeled vehicle. It also houses the loading dock and outer race for the rotation bearings.

The center housing is stationary with all three rings rotating around it similar to the Spokes. It contains the docking ports, primary thruster and rocket packages as well as the connection passageways to all of the ships rings. The center tube also supports the inner race of the rotation bearings that secures the different wheels in their relative positions.

Virginia and I decided not to become involved with the selection of our replacements. We continued in our roles until the Starship launched and then left Kelly, Dwaine and Rebecca with that responsibility. They all three have deposited their Embryos and specimens in the Sperm and Egg Banks so they are well represented on this voyage.

Virginia and I called a family meeting exactly one year before the scheduled launch of Starship 1. The kids weren't really surprised when we told them we were considering leaving on the ship. The only thing holding us back was the reality that we would have to leave them behind so we asked them to consider coming with us. I assured then that I could find a place on the ship for any or all of them. The thought that we would have to leave our grandkids behind weighted really heavy on us so we were hoping that at least Ruth and Peter would come. We wouldn't have been too surprised if they chose to stay because they had lived in our shadow most of their lives and it would be understandable if they wanted a chance to stand alone in the sun. Ruth and Daniel had both married good people and they would have to leave their families behind if they came with us so it wasn't an easy decision to make.

Luckily for us, Peters parents had several other grandkids so they weren't completely devastated when Peter broached the subject with them. They weren't exactly pleased either but after they had time to think about it they realized that this wasn't a great deal different from when the pioneers left the old world for a new life in the Americas. In many cases, back then, the families never saw or heard from each other again. In todays world with our video communications systems they could see and talk to each other every day if necessary. They gradually began referring to their grandkids as the new pioneers and the Starship as a covered wagon.

Daniel on the other hand caused quite an upheaval when he mentioned it to Olivias parents. Olivia was an only child and they still didn't have any grandkids so they were very upset over the prospect of never seeing their grandkids. Olivia finally consoled them with the fact that they had been trying unsuccessfully to conceive. They were quite confident that the best genetists in the world were on board the Starship and if a grandchild were going to happen it would happen on board. That plus the fact that we would be in easy communication range for at least the next 30 years turned the tide for them and they reluctantly gave their blessing.

We understood their anguish but we couldn't help but be pleased with their decision to come with us. Virginia and I consider the fact that our entire family chose to accompany us on this journey as a marvellous affirmation of the life choices we have made.

The only preferential treatment I have ever requested was when I asked to be named the Commander of Starship 1. Captain Der Groot was actually pleased to have someone to help with overseeing the human population. As Commander, I will have final authority on matters of policy affecting the human population, including the Gene Banks. The Captain will have final authority over the operation and safety of the Starship.

I am extremely pleased with this arrangement because it will allow me to help shape our moral and cultural evolution for at least the beginning of the voyage. Our detractors are right when they point out that if our Gene Banks were misused, the species that finally reached the new world or worlds may have very little resemblance to those who began the journey. I am very aware and accept that a new world and a new environment may require some adaptation. My goal is to help instill a culture on board that will treat our genetic heritage as sacred and resist any effort to bury it in an unrecognizable body under the guise of expedience. I have often wished for an extra hand to help me hold things, but that doesn't mean that we should create a three or four armed human body just because we can.

Writing this has caused me to look back and even though it seems like we have come a long way in the last few years, it pales in comparison to where we are going.

We are underway and about to enter the Asteroid Belt as I finish this and I have a feeling of intense excitement because we are embarking on a fantastic journey into an unknown future. At the same time I am at ease and very pleased because regardless of what happens in the future, we will survive to be a part of it.

Wade Frederick